'Everything you love about romantic comedy – hilarious,
sharply observed, smart, and sexy as hell'
Rachel Hawkins

'A must read for fans of Nora Ephron rom-coms!'
Denise Williams

'Smart, sexy, and feminist Elizabeth Davis just became
an auto-buy author for me'
Annette Christie

'Compulsively readable!'
Alicia Thompson

Elizabeth Davis is a full-time nerd whose interests include cold weather, rainy days, coffee, Minnesota Public Radio, and rom-coms where characters' homes vastly outstrip the income they would get from their jobs. Born and raised in suburban Milwaukee, she now lives in Minneapolis with her husband and two children.

To learn more, follow Elizabeth on Bluesky: **@elizabethdavis.bsky.social**, and on Instagram: **@elizabethdavisromance**.

Also by Elizabeth Davis
I Love You, I Hate You
The Player Next Door

Never Fake Date Your Roommate

Elizabeth Davis

HEADLINE
ETERNAL

Copyright © Elizabeth Davis 2025

The right of Elizabeth Davis to be identified as the Author of
the Work has been asserted by her in accordance with the
Copyright, Designs and Patents Act 1988.

First published in 2025 by Headline Eternal
An imprint of Headline Publishing Group Limited

This paperback edition published in 2025

1

Apart from any use permitted under UK copyright law, this publication may
only be reproduced, stored, or transmitted, in any form, or by any means,
with prior permission in writing of the publishers or, in the case of
reprographic production, in accordance with the terms of licences
issued by the Copyright Licensing Agency.

All characters in this publication are fictitious
and any resemblance to real persons, living
or dead, is purely coincidental.

Cataloguing in Publication Data is available from the British Library

Paperback ISBN 978 1 0354 1051 4

Typeset in 11/14pt Minion Pro by Jouve (UK), Milton Keynes

Headline's policy is to use papers that are natural, renewable and recyclable
products and made from wood grown in well-managed forests and other
controlled sources. The logging and manufacturing processes are expected
to conform to the environmental regulations of the country of origin.

Headline Publishing Group Limited
An Hachette UK Company
Carmelite House
50 Victoria Embankment
London EC4Y 0DZ

The authorised representative in the EEA is Hachette Ireland,
8 Castlecourt Centre, Dublin 15, D15 XTP3, Ireland (email: info@hbgi.ie)

www.headline.co.uk
www.hachette.co.uk

For Jess, a wonderful agent and an even better friend.

Chapter One

A stack of books dropped onto the desk in front of Nick, an assortment of middle-grade chapter books and half a dozen comics, plus one non-fiction about volcanoes. Nick gave his usual polite half-smile to the kid across the desk, Henry, one of the library's summer regulars. Henry's mom, Jenny, was lingering a few feet back, typing something on her phone while he checked out. 'This one's my favorite,' Nick said as he scanned a chapter book about a boy and his pet dragon. 'Have you read this series before?' Mary tended to do most of the purchasing for the children's section, but Nick did his best to keep up with the more popular series, at least.

Henry was grinning up at him in an odd way, like he was waiting for something. 'Nope,' he said, eyes gleaming behind his glasses.

'Well, it's funny, especially the third one,' Nick replied. 'We've got the whole set, when you're ready.' He kept scanning the stack, working hard to keep running through his public-librarian script. Usually, kids were easier for him to interact with, but Henry was being . . . odd. Nick glanced up, but Jenny was still busy with whatever it was on her phone. He let the receipt print out and tucked it into the *Volcano Fact Book*, sliding the stack back to Henry. 'Have a good –'

'BUT WHAT ABOUT JAKEY?' Henry practically shouted, and Nick's smile froze on his face. He loathed that catchphrase for about a hundred reasons, primarily because he had spent most of his childhood either saying it on camera or to overly enthusiastic strangers who stopped him on the street. His twin brother, Josh, had thrived on the attention – and still did, in fact – but it always made Nick want to shrivel up.

'Henry,' his mom scolded, tucking her phone into her purse. 'I told you not to do that.' She looked up at Nick, grimacing. 'He was sick last week and was binging a lot of TV, and he stumbled on *Just Us Girls*. But I promise, I told him we should leave you alone.'

Nick hadn't dealt with a reminder from his past like that in years, and he couldn't say it didn't throw him a little, even though Henry was now looking sheepish. 'It's fine,' he said awkwardly, although it sort of wasn't – Henry was a kid, so he wasn't angry or anything, but Nick wasn't known for his improv skills or adaptability. 'Glad he's, um, enjoying my previous work.'

Jenny shot Henry a look, and he flushed. 'I'm sorry,' he said, and then Nick felt worse, because he'd made a kid feel ashamed for normal kid behavior.

'Thank you. And it's okay, really,' he said as genuinely as he could, but he was relieved when they finally trooped out of the doors.

'Have you got it from here, Mary?' Nick asked, picking up his cardigan from where he'd draped it over his desk chair. After that last interaction, he was desperate to be done.

Mary swept her gaze around the Swede River library, taking in the dad with his two toddlers in the children's section,

Margie Schumacher hunting and pecking at the keyboard on one of the public computers, and the three old men tucked in the corner with their newspapers, which they did every Thursday afternoon. She gave him an eloquent look over her bifocals. 'Oh, I don't know, I might need reinforcements.'

He knew she was teasing, and honestly, Mary was one of the few people who could get away with it. She was the one who had advocated hiring him in the first place, when the library board wasn't sure he was the 'sort of librarian they were looking for' and that he might 'bring too much Hollywood attention to town.' But Mary had believed in him, and her steady mentorship over the past few years had helped him adjust and even set down roots. Nick felt more at home in Swede River than he had anywhere else; certainly more than he ever had in Los Angeles, and he owed a big part of that to Mary. If it wasn't for her, he'd probably be dealing with 'But what about Jakey?' several times a month at least. His phone rang and he silenced it the second he saw who was calling. Nothing good came from talking to Candace Ford.

'It's a lovely day out there,' Mary observed. 'Are you walking?'

'I was planning on it,' Nick replied. The sweater he had on now would probably be too warm, he realized, since the September sun had a tendency to start out weak in the mornings only to decide somewhere around lunchtime that it was actually still summer. He took it off again, and Mary thoughtfully turned her attention to her computer. She knew he hated being watched, which yes, was ironic considering his prior career. But in his defense, his mom had picked that life, as not many four-year-olds had jobs.

Speaking of mothers, his called again, and he hit ignore, wishing that was an option in real life, too.

'How's Val?' Mary asked without looking up.

Nick shrugged and decided to just abandon his cardigan in the work room. He'd be back again tomorrow, and it wasn't like Mary, with her petite frame and love of bright, vivid colors, was going to do anything with a camel-colored cardigan made for a man nearly a foot taller than her. 'She's, um, fine.'

Nick didn't like talking about his roommate, largely because, well, he didn't much like his roommate. Not that he knew her very well or anything, but what he did know really irritated him. Renting out a room hadn't been part of the plan, but then Josh had to go and be Josh, and Val had arrived in Swede River like a desperate, marginally employed tornado barely a week later. It had seemed like an easy enough solution at the time, but Nick had come to regret his impulse on a near daily basis. Selling a kidney to finance his twin's stupid vanity projects would probably have been less painful than living with someone who loved loud music and had a chronic aversion to doing her goddamn dishes.

'I see,' Mary said with barely concealed amusement. 'Have a good evening, Nicholas.'

'You too, Mary,' he replied, and headed out the main doors, past the columns holding up the portico and down the grand steps to the sidewalk.

The Swede River public library had been built at the turn of the century by a robber baron when Swede River was little more than a collection of farms that had the good fortune to be on a direct train line to Minneapolis. Now it was mostly just antique stores and a couple of B&Bs off of a state highway, with the train route long abandoned. Every so often local politicians would bring up the idea of revitalization and setting up a commuter rail to Minneapolis and St Paul, but the state government didn't really seem too excited about investing that much money for a town with barely four thousand people.

A text rolled in on his phone, which meant Candy was desperate. *Nicky, call me.* She knew he wouldn't, at least not until the situation was completely untenable, but Candy was not known for quitting.

Unlike Nick.

Nick turned left and decided to stop by Pete's Coffee for a cup of tea before walking home. Main Street was only three blocks long, lined by brick buildings with old-fashioned streetlights studding the curb. Pete's Coffee had a tiny sidewalk patio of three tables, and two doors down The Happy Pig had set out a chalkboard stand with their evening specials listed. The Swede River was roaring dully in the background – they'd gotten more rain than usual that summer – and one story up, the servers at Happy Pig were busy setting up their rooftop patio.

Swede River High had already let out, so most of the tables in Pete's were full of teenagers killing time, crowded around laptops and hunched over their phones. Pete himself was behind the counter, his infant son strapped into a baby carrier on his chest.

'Nick! How's it going? What's the roommate up to?' Pete asked, Felix's hand curled tightly around his thumb.

One of the curses of a small town was anyone new drew a disproportionate amount of attention, and obviously Val fit the bill. 'Editing today, probably,' Nick said, scanning the menu like he was trying to decide what to get.

But Pete knew him too well, and was already pouring boiling water over an Earl Grey teabag. 'You said she does weddings, right?'

As far as Nick knew, that had been Val's main source of income in her photography business, pre-catastrophe. She still had a few to finish editing, she claimed, but he wasn't sure how she was going to pay rent beyond that without any new clients.

Getting himself a roommate who might not be able to contribute to the mortgage when his only reason *for* getting a roommate was to have someone help with the mortgage was clearly one of his worst ideas, but then again Nick wasn't Josh Ford's twin brother for nothing. One of Hollywood's beloved minor catastrophes, Josh veered from box-office bomb to critically-panned-but-made-almost-enough-money-to-break-even vanity projects, coasting almost entirely on charm and long-banked goodwill, so obviously 'making stupid choices' was genetic. Nick just thought he'd left that all behind him, was all.

'Mostly weddings, yeah.'

'Does she do families? Aaron and I want to do some photos with Felix for our Chanukah cards this year.'

'I could ask,' Nick said, accepting the to-go cup and handing over his credit card. Honestly, Val didn't seem like the cutesy-family-photo type since her surly disposition would probably scare children. But Nick liked Pete, so he agreed to ask. It meant talking to Val, which was painful all on its own, but it was in his best interests that she have money, so he'd suck it up.

'Thanks, man,' Pete said, and kissed Felix's head absently. 'See you tomorrow?'

'We don't open until noon tomorrow,' Nick replied. 'So yeah, just before lunch.'

'I'll make sure to save you a blueberry scone,' Pete said, and waved to him as he left.

Nick's house was three blocks from the library, four from Pete's Coffee. He only ever bothered to drive when he had to run to get groceries from the EconoFoods out near the highway, and while sometimes – like when it was blizzarding – it could be unpleasant, days like today reminded him of why he moved to Swede River in the first place. The leaves were just starting to change, and it wasn't cold yet, but the breeze was just brisk enough to remind him it was fall. There were other people walking toward downtown; families with kids in strollers and elderly couples who were wandering hand in hand, looking in the store windows and bickering about whether or not they needed another sideboard.

Nick's phone pinged with a voicemail. He wanted to delete it without listening, but ignoring Candace was about as far as his rebellion stretched. *Hi sweetie, it's Mom. I can't imagine what you're doing that would keep you too busy to answer my calls, but I'm working on something big big big over here, and I think it's just the thing we need. Give me a call ASAP so we can figure out the details.* Nick had no idea what she was talking about, and Josh hadn't mentioned working with her on anything. Whatever it was, he wasn't interested, but he was also hoping to avoid having to directly tell her that.

He turned off Maple Avenue onto Vine Street, his two-story Victorian house standing proudly halfway down the block, right at the top of the hill. Compared to LA prices it was dirt cheap – he was reasonably sure he could get a studio in Burbank for the cost of his mortgage on the 2,000-square-foot, three-bedroom, two-bath house – but that didn't mean it was *cheap* cheap, especially on a public librarian's salary. And after Josh's third self-funded vanity project tanked and failed to find a distributor, Nick had had to step in to save his twin from filing for bankruptcy. Of course, that meant he had to find a roommate to save *himself* from needing to declare bankruptcy, but that was how Nick and Josh operated.

Josh screwed up. Nick stepped in to fix it. Repeat, ad nauseam. Some people might think being aware of the problem would be enough to stop the cycle, but those people didn't really understand what it was like to be Nick and Josh Ford. The Ford brothers stuck together through hell and high water, even if both of those were usually triggered by Josh's enthusiasm and poor judge of character.

Nick could hear Val's music before he even put his key in the door. It was seeping out through the walls, the bass thumping like a racing heartbeat. He unlocked the door and immediately tripped over her combat boots. The shoe rack was right there, but no, his roommate was apparently completely incapable of putting things away where they belonged.

Nick tucked his shoes neatly onto the shoe rack and placed his keys and wallet in the bowl he left on the stand near the door for that exact purpose. He couldn't hear himself think all the way out into the living room, and her room was not just upstairs, but at the other end of the house. She'd said she liked to have music playing as loud as humanly possible while editing photos, claiming it helped her 'concentrate.' She did usually wear headphones when she knew he was home, and he reminded himself she probably thought he was still at work, so he couldn't fault her for this.

Didn't mean he liked it, though. Nick knocked on the door of his former guest room. He waited, smothered a sigh, and knocked again, louder this time.

That one did the trick, and he heard her stumble over at least two things before she opened the door. His roommate was, much to his chagrin, incredibly pretty. Her long, dark hair was somewhere between curly and straight, giving her a perpetually disheveled appearance, especially when she was in a threadbare hoodie and joggers. It was a look that shouldn't work for him, but it did, and it always took him a second when he saw her before his brain could click back over into annoyed roommate.

'What are you doing here?' she said, her words barely audible over the din of her music.

'I live here.'

'What?' she yelled, and then, 'hang on, lemme –' as she stumbled back through her room – the only light was coming from her computer screen and honestly, how did anyone live like this? – and hit a button on her keyboard to silence the music entirely.

His ears were ringing faintly, and Nick briefly wondered if Val would have permanent hearing damage from this little ritual of hers. 'Sorry,' she said, picking her way back through the maze of clothes on the floor. 'When did you get home?' She shoved her hair out of her face, sighed when it fell back over her eyes, and pulled a scrunchie out of her pocket.

Nick made himself look away from the curve of her neck as she wrangled her hair into a messy bun. 'Just now,' he said. 'And –'

'And you want me to keep my music down, I know,' she finished, and while she didn't roll her eyes when she said it, it certainly felt like she did. 'Sorry, I thought you worked until five tonight.'

'Mary came in a little early in exchange for me taking the afternoon shift tomorrow. Eng has a doctor's appointment in the Twin Cities in the morning.'

'Oh, uh – oh,' Val said awkwardly. Nick reminded himself that she probably didn't care about *why* Mary came in early; she wasn't used to the rhythm of small towns like Swede River, where people didn't just say what had happened, they explained why and threw in about five extra details for good measure. It could be exhausting, but it also felt good to him. Like a home he'd never quite had. Nick had never loved the spotlight, but in a town like this one, after the first initial surprise of finding a former child star as their librarian, most people got over it quickly. Hardly any permanent resident had asked him anything about Hollywood in the last five years, and while there had been that incident with Henry earlier, he was definitely the exception. Outsiders and tourists occasionally gave him odd looks and every so often someone would lose their cool, but the fact that no one expected to see anyone famous in Minnesota now that Prince was gone meant very few people put together that Nick, Swede River librarian, was also Nick Ford, one half of the breakout duo from *Just Us Girls*. It made having to talk to people at least slightly more tolerable.

Val watched him quietly, her hazel eyes wary. 'Right, well – like I said, I thought you were working until five. I'll put the headphones on now.'

He didn't like how she was looking at him, like he was scolding her. That wasn't what he meant to do, no matter how much he hated the volume of her music. He had just been trying to let her know he was back. Nick wasn't great with people; he liked silence and knowing he would be able to find a colander exactly where he'd left it in the kitchen. His bookshelves were alphabetized, and he rarely left anything out of its assigned place for more than a couple of hours.

In contrast, Val had turned his formerly-bright-and-crisp guest room into what could only be described as a den. Or maybe a cave. A nest? She had all the shades drawn against the late afternoon light, and her dresser looked like it had exploded. Arms of shirts and sweaters reached out of the drawers like they were searching for rescue, and he was reasonably sure those were bras draped over the back of her desk chair, although it was hard to tell through the gloom. Clothing, several bags, and what he assumed were camera parts littered the floor, while the image of a blonde bride smiling sweetly on Val's computer screen cast an eerie blue light over everything.

Nick thought about protesting, maybe explaining that he wasn't mad at her for not knowing he was home from work, but he just wasn't good at this sort of interaction. He needed to know someone and trust them before he could make chit-chat, and Val's icy demeanor and messy habits – not to mention her inconveniently pretty face – put him at a major disadvantage.

But he wasn't sure how to say that without sounding accusatory, or like he was assuming something about her that wasn't true. Maybe Val just didn't like him. He'd never had his brother's easy way with people, and at some point, he'd completely stopped trying. People could either like him, like Mary and Pete, or not. Like Val.

So instead, he just nodded tightly and let her close the door in his face.

Chapter Two

Val had been editing photos for her last remaining client for almost an hour when she pulled her headphones off and listened to the sounds of Nick cooking downstairs, trying in vain to remember if she'd thrown out the remains of her burger from last week. It very well might still be molding in the fridge, slowly driving him up the wall. He would probably have that muscle jumping in his jaw whenever he saw it. It was already bad enough that Nick had come home early to her editing routine, which involved blasting EDM loud enough the International Space Station could probably hear it.

Okay, so Val was a shitty roommate. She wondered sometimes why Nick even agreed to let her move in, seeing as he clearly disdained almost everything about her. But moving to Swede River hadn't been in her plan that day six weeks ago when she threw everything she owned in her car and drove until she had to pee so badly, she was forced to stop at a public library. By the time she left the restroom, her earlier panic had bled away, replaced by bone-deep exhaustion.

Because as usual, Val had royally fucked up. She normally double-checked every photo she uploaded to the public album for her bridal clients. And for the Herman wedding, she had done the same, or at least thought she had. But apparently, the bride's plunging neckline had shifted ever so slightly during a dance at the reception, baring her breast and nipple. It was the sort of thing that Val normally would have caught, but she'd seen Caleb earlier that day – from a distance, entering a coffee shop, and at least he hadn't seen her – and the sight of her sort-of-ex always threw her off her game. She'd been jittery while scanning the photos one last time, and she should have stopped herself and posted them the next morning.

But she didn't, and the bride's extremely conservative family had had an epic meltdown. Val's online reviews went from a respectable 4.3 out of 5 stars to 1.7 in one morning, thanks to a series of angry posts by the bride's very large and apparently Very Online family. What should have been an embarrassing-but-recoverable professional error turned into a Full-Blown Valerie Costa Catastrophe in under twenty-four hours. No fewer than three couples canceled on her that next day, two who had already put down deposits and one who had been almost a sure thing. How the bride's family had found her prospective clients was beyond her, but clearly, she'd pissed off the wrong people.

Obviously, Val had decided to fight back. She had a minor reputation as a bitch, and honestly, it was well-earned. She had a sharp tongue and a short temper, and when the bride called to ream her out, Val had just read the eighth – eighth!! – shitty review from the bride's aunt, who claimed this was some sort of malicious plot to destroy the bride's happiness. So instead of the apology she had been rehearsing initially, Val refused to apologize. It was stupid and she never should have doubled down, but being called a *conniving, talentless piece of shit* had set her off. Val told the bride in no uncertain terms that she wasn't sorry, which wasn't quite true but *felt* true in the moment, and hung up.

More negative reviews rolled in, followed by the cancellations, and then the worst thing of all happened: her father called. In his endless quest to convince her that photography was *just a fun hobby* and not something a real career could be made of, Anthony Costa had set up a Google alert for her name. That meant when the bride posted a ten-tweet rant about the worst photographer in the Twin Cities, her dad knew immediately. Anthony never let a good crisis go to waste. He called, told her he'd seen what had happened and said the sensible thing to do would be to shut her entire business down and move back to St Cloud to work for his car dealership. He also helpfully informed her that he and her mother were done with emergency financial bailouts, which meant the money she had in her tiny savings account was all there would be for the near future.

So, Val did what she always did when faced with adversity: she ran. Her shitty apartment was on a month-to-month lease anyway, ever since Linds had moved to California for med school, and Val hadn't been able to bring herself to find a real place to live. She packed her crap into her shitty Honda Civic that Dad was always on her to trade in for a nicer model and left.

She drove blindly, taking random turns and exits until she had no idea where she was. Val stopped to use the bathroom at a public library in a town called Swede River, sat down to try and figure out what to do next, and promptly gave up. Literally. For close to two hours, she just sat at a table, alternately staring off into space and reading the next wave of shitty reviews that rolled in on her phone. If it hadn't been for the librarian approaching her to softly announce the library would be closing soon, Val didn't know what she would have done. But the librarian's kind smile was probably the first nice thing she'd seen all day, and so when she asked if Val needed anything, Val blurted out that she needed a place to stay.

The librarian, Mary, gave off that air of quiet competence that women seemed to acquire in their fifties. 'I think I have an idea,' she'd said, and guided Val to a tiny coffee shop a few blocks away. The inside of the café was much hipper than Val would have thought in such a tiny town, with an almost industrial feel warmed up by touches of blond wood. The coffee was good too, her blended iced mocha not nearly as saccharine as some chains. There they waited together, Val in her ratty flannel and Mary in a crisp yellow blazer that set off her dark brown skin perfectly, until the tallest, broadest, handsomest man Val had ever seen walked in.

It was like a cartoon lumberjack come to life, if that guy also barely spoke, didn't seem all that pleased with her, and apparently needed a roommate. At first Val didn't think he'd bite, given that she was currently unemployed, but it seemed that the opportunities for roommates were thin in Swede River, and he was desperate. And his place was beautiful – way nicer than anywhere else she'd lived, and with a lot more character than the cookie-cutter McMansion she'd grown up in – so she would just grit her teeth and deal with him. It was that or sleeping in Christine's guest room, and Val would literally rather do anything than subject herself to her perfect, overachieving sister's flawless life.

That was how Val had ended up moving to Swede River: a too-full bladder, a kind stranger, and a grumpy man who needed a roommate.

A notification flashed on her desktop, jerking her back to the present. Val skimmed the email, sent from her website with the auto-generated title BOOKING. Her stomach jolted, because – new business? Just an hour ago she had been debating canceling her Netflix account and begging Nick to let her use his, but new business might forestall the humiliation of him seeing just how often she had rewatched *Bridgerton*.

Valerie,

I thought about DMing you on IG, but it looks like your last post was a few weeks ago and I didn't want to miss out on the chance to book you. I just got engaged (fiancé is a bit camera shy, hence no big reveal yet so please keep this quiet) and I'm looking for someone who would be available for multiple events. I recently parted ways with a photographer who didn't quite vibe with my vision, so you should know up-front I have some very specific ideas and I want a photog who would complement my aesthetic without directly replicating it.

Right now, I need someone to shoot the engagement photos (I would credit you on my posts, don't worry about that!), engagement party, wedding shower, bachelorette party, and bachelor party, in addition to the wedding itself (obviously, lol). I've looked through your feed and I think you've got the eye I'm looking for, so would you be available for a consultation?

Warmly,
Autumn

Val was only on social media enough to promote her photography business, and hardly at all since the Nipple Incident, but the name at the bottom of the email had given her a jolt. Even she knew who Autumn Kirchner was. @AutumnKay was an up-and-coming influencer, who leaned hard into her name and the fall aesthetic (sometimes a little too hard, in Val's opinion). Autumn was known for photos of herself looking perfectly snug and cozy on rainy days, buried under very expensive blankets with expertly done makeup and a blowout to die for. She had made a niche for herself as a sort of thinking-girl's influencer, largely because she liked to have a large stack of books near her in the pictures and sometimes posted book reviews. She also had a series of tutorials explaining how to get the perfect no-makeup look, which several of Val's previous clients had cited as inspiration.

Her general style was a bit gauzier than Val's, who tended toward sharper contrasts since she liked playing with shadows and vibrant colors. She re-read the line *I want a photog who would complement my aesthetic without directly replicating it* and frowned. There were some ways her style would complement Autumn's, but in general it was fairly different – and if she had already parted ways with someone for not being able to match her vision, that meant she would be either a tricky or discerning client. The first was tough, but the second could be an interesting challenge. She did some mental calculations for her rates, estimating how much this would bring in. Val had never been hired to take photos of a bachelor party, but she wasn't about to look a gift horse in the mouth. Besides, if Autumn liked her, there was always the possibility of working with her on some of her more formal shoots for her Instagram. This was a lifeline at the exact moment she needed it most, and it wasn't like she could afford to be picky. Her bank account was circling the drain, and if she ran out of money she would have to move out of Cranky Lumberjack's house and then – well, she had no idea what she would do, so she was just going to have to do whatever it took to land this job.

Val replied, offering to meet Autumn at a coffee shop up in the Twin Cities and then started browsing Autumn's page to get a deeper sense of her style. She needed to be perfectly prepared; ready to suggest things that would please her but also stand out. Val had to show her that she could pull this off while still making it worth the money to hire her, which was easier said than done.

Six weeks deep into Autumn's Instagram feed, Val took a deep breath and rubbed her eyes. The glare of the computer screen was getting to her, and whatever Nick was cooking – stir-fried veggies, if she had to guess – smelled incredible. Her stomach grumbled loudly, and she decided it was time to dig out something marginally edible from her stash for dinner.

Val understood her habits put her somewhere between 'goblin' and 'raccoon' on the spectrum of 'functional adult human behaviors.' But cooking for just herself seemed like a complete waste of time, when frozen dinners and reheated takeout sufficed. Was it as good as the meals Nick made for himself every night? Definitely not, and her stomach gave another loud growl just to emphasize that point. But it was serviceable, in that it kept her from starving and let her keep working as long as she needed to.

She closed out of Autumn's Instagram and double-checked to make sure her edits were saved and nipple-less. Val didn't have any more clients lined up for weddings, obviously, but maybe the guy at the coffee shop with the cute little baby would want her to do some family photos. Val wasn't a huge fan of working with kids, so she didn't do many of those, but desperate times called for desperate measures. Caleb had always wanted her to branch out into newborn photos too, saying she was leaving money on the table by not offering that as a service. Val had countered that working with kids – especially babies – took special skills (and patience) that she lacked, but of course Caleb had just pointed out that maybe that meant she needed to work on developing those skills, too. Caleb had always made her feel like she was failing to live up to his standards, but fortunately, Val was incredibly familiar with the feeling of being a disappointment. That was probably why they lasted so long, even if it was never really a relationship the way most people would define it.

Val walked into the spotless kitchen, greeted by complete silence even though Nick was standing at the counter. Keeping up with his cleanliness standards in common rooms was hard, which was why Val spent most of her time hiding in her room. Nick didn't turn around as she started rummaging through the fridge – the burger was nowhere to be seen, so she must have tossed it, thank god – and emerged with the remains of a flatbread pizza she'd picked up several days ago. Val grabbed a water glass from an upper cabinet and Nick threw her an inscrutable look.

Nick wasn't a bad guy, to be fair. Maybe not the most suited to having a roommate, but at least he wasn't a serial killer. He could be annoyingly particular and weirdly introverted for someone who used to make his living in front of cameras, but he wasn't mean or anything.

Val hadn't recognized him at first. He had that vaguely familiar look of someone who loaned her a pencil during a college lecture or something, although Val personally thought she would remember someone that handsome. Men who were six-foot-two and built like Superman tended to stick out in her mind.

It wasn't until she was carrying trash bags of clothes into his spare room and she saw a photo in the living room of him and his twin that she put it together – he wasn't Nick, possible college classmate, he was *Jakey*.

Jakey had started out as the precocious youngest boy in a family of all girls in the most popular family sitcom at the turn of the millennium. But Jakey – and the twins who played him – quickly became tween heartthrobs as the show (and Jakey's main fans) approached puberty. Val had never been one of those girls with Tiger Beat posters and fansites dedicated to Josh and Nick Ford, but her best friend Lindsey had been and as a result Val had accumulated plenty of second-hand information about them. She knew that Josh was supposed to be a 'fun-loving prankster,' while Nick was the 'bookish' twin. That much, obviously, was true. She was reasonably sure they were Leos – Linds had created a whole astrology chart and accompanying PowerPoint explaining why she was destined to marry Josh Ford when they were twelve, although Josh coming out as gay at nineteen had likely put a crimp in that plan – and that Nick had somewhat abruptly given up stardom somewhere around the time she was in college.

Apparently, he gave up acting for college. At least, she was pretty sure being a librarian required a college degree. She had no idea *where* he had gone to school, because that would involve small talk, and small talk with Nick was like trying to make conversation with a very handsome but cranky rock. Nick stepped out of her way as she reached for a fork, and then frowned down at her open takeout box. There was a grand total of three restaurants in Swede River, five if you counted the two fast-food places out on the highway, and she was essentially rotating through them.

'That's it?' he asked. 'That's your dinner?'

Val shrugged. 'What else would it be?'

He looked desperately uncomfortable. 'No, I just – do you want some of mine?'

She looked at the bowl of rice and veggies he had steaming

on the counter, and her traitorous stomach rumbled. This was also the most overtly nice thing he had said to her in days, but Val always struggled with people being nice to her. It felt like a trap, somehow. 'Really?' she said, barely keeping the suspicion out of her tone.

'I have extra.'

'Sure,' she said after a painfully long pause, and let him spoon some onto the empty space in her compostable takeout container.

It looked like he was about to say something, and Val wondered if maybe she should risk eating in the kitchen. After all, he'd just made an effort with sharing some of his dinner, so maybe she could repay the favor.

'Make sure you bring the glass and utensils back to the sink, otherwise we'll get ants,' Nick said, and Val decided that no, eating in her room was definitely the better choice.

Chapter Three

Josh knew very well that Nick loathed surprise FaceTime calls, but rarely let that stop him. So, when Nick's phone lit up with an incoming FaceTime at 10:30 p.m., he let it ring out. Then it immediately began again, and his stomach sank.

What did you do now? he thought, picking his glasses up off the nightstand and accepting the call.

His brother materialized onscreen, and Nick didn't recognize the background behind him. He was either at a new 'friend's' place, or he'd moved. Again.

'Don't be mad,' Josh started before Nick could even say hello, which was never a good sign. 'But there's something you need to know.'

'What now?' Nick groaned, resigned. 'I can't afford to bail you out again, you know that.' He'd already had to get a roommate to help cover the second mortgage he took out after Josh's last catastrophe, and he wasn't sure he could handle yet another Josh Crisis.

Nick glanced around for his earbuds, but they weren't in his bedroom, which meant they were in the entryway near his keys. He normally loathed people who carried on conversations in a way they could be easily overheard, but Val was constantly having long, involved conversations with someone named Linds over speakerphone while she wandered through the house eating crackers and leaving a trail of crumbs behind her, so turnabout was fair play. She could deal with listening to one measly phone call with his brother.

Josh glanced off-camera, his nervous energy seeping into Nick's chest cavity. 'I might have, um, fucked up a little,' Josh said, and yeah, that was not helping Nick's anxiety at all. 'I had lunch with Mom, and –'

'Is that why she keeps calling me?' Nick interrupted.

'I'm trying to explain that,' Josh said, more exasperated than was warranted, in Nick's opinion. 'I agreed to have lunch with her, and I thought it would be just with her, you know? I should have suspected something because it was at this fancy place, like, way fancier than she can afford. I was even like "whoa, are you sure?" when she said she would make reservations there, but she just blew me off and was like –'

'Josh,' Nick interrupted again. He could hear Val moving around in the room next door, either getting ready for bed or organizing an obstacle course out of the junk on her floor. For someone whose entire livelihood depended on cameras, she sure was careless with them. 'What happened?'

'I got there and there was this suit with her from Universal Streaming, and I guess she's been having talks with them for months about a reality dating show.'

'She wants to have her own dating show? What's she going to call it, *Date a Stage Mom*?'

'It's supposed to be for us, actually. So more like *Date a Has-Been*. Except I'm about to sign on to something. It's really big, Nick. There's still a lot of details for Jan to work out, but basically, Netflix wants to do a reboot of *Just Us Girls* and I'm in talks with them to lead. Obviously, I wouldn't be able to do both.'

'A reboot?'

'Sort of, also sort of a spin-off,' Josh explained. 'Jakey would inherit a group of siblings, mostly boys but one girl, from a cousin no one has ever mentioned before.'

'Good for you,' Nick said sincerely. It sounded big, and a lot more reliable than Josh's usual attempts. 'But how did Mom take that?'

'I mean, on the one hand she was pissed, because I guess she pitched it as, like, a double header – me and a bunch of thirsty dudes, and you and a bunch of ladies. But it's Candace, so she shifted quickly to it just being a dating show with you.'

Nick could not think of anything he'd want to do less than be on television again, this time with cameras covering his every waking moment, surrounded by fame-hungry social climbers. 'Absolutely not,' Nick said. 'No way.'

'I know, I said that, but she wouldn't take no for an answer, and the guy from Universal Streaming was there, pushing hard, so I said you're seeing someone.'

Nick closed his eyes and pinched the bridge of his nose. 'But I'm not.'

'I know, I just thought –'

'I know what you thought,' Nick said, trying to keep his voice soothing. Josh really was looking out for him. He just had a habit of doing so in the worst way possible, like the time he told craft services Nick would break out into hives if he so much as saw a slice of roast beef when, in fact, Nick was simply a vegetarian.

'I'm really sorry,' Josh said sincerely.

'I know.' He understood why Josh had gone that route, but it also meant that now Nick would have to lie to Candy the next time they talked, and Nick was *terrible* at improv. He had been dodging her all day but wouldn't be able to do that forever. Candace Ford was a relentless force, which was how Nick and Josh had gotten on to *Just Us Girls* in the first place. Nick had never figured out the trick to saying no to her, and neither had Josh.

Nick walked away from Hollywood a decade ago, but that remained his one big rebellion. Avoiding Candy and giving vague, non-committal answers when he couldn't, was the best he had been able to do ever since. After all, Nick leaving Hollywood had been the trigger for the disintegration of the entire Ford family, and his guilt over that was still as strong as ever. But if she had a firm plan – and worse, the backing of a studio – it would be a lot harder for him to get out of it. Candy had never once listened to him, and there was no reason to think she'd start now. She only ever saw his 'no' as a starting point for negotiations, rather than the end of them. Theoretically a girlfriend might solve it, but Candy didn't roll over easily when there was money on the line. He could hear her already – *I gave up my career for you boys, and this is how you repay me?* He would have to convince her and Universal Streaming it was a relationship serious enough to keep him off a dating show, which would require acting skills that were at best rusty. Further complicated by the fact that there were about four thousand Swede River residents who knew it was a lie, which meant even the slightest investigation would collapse this house of cards.

'I can try and walk it back,' Josh offered.

'Don't,' Nick said loudly. 'Best to just – stick with it, hope she buys it.'

'You really think she will?'

'No, but what choice do we have?'

'I could always say your girlfriend lives in Canada.'

Nick snorted. 'Wasn't that what you told Stacy when she guest-starred and tried to ask you out?'

'No, I told her my girlfriend lived in Utah.'

'Why Utah?'

'I didn't think Utah had the internet. Look, it made sense at the time.' Josh laughed, and Nick found himself smiling back. His brother was a first-class train wreck, but he was the only family Nick had. Or more accurately, the only family Nick had that he liked. Dad was somewhere in Hawaii now, doing god knows what, and Mom was apparently still shopping them around like Nick hadn't abandoned Hollywood a decade ago.

Their parents being the definition of *Terrible Stage Family* made him that much more protective of Josh. Nick was all of three minutes older, but he took his responsibility to Josh seriously. That was why as much as he hated the idea of having to figure out how to keep this charade going, he couldn't let himself be too mad at his brother. The Ford twins stuck together.

'It's fine,' Nick said, even though it wasn't, not really. But if the shit hit the fan, he would deal with it. He always did.

Chapter Four

Val checked the time, relieved to see she still had twenty minutes to spare before she had to leave for the meeting with Autumn. Val tended to be chronically late for almost everything, and generally only managed to be on time for client meetings by putting them in her calendar for a half-hour before the meeting was scheduled to begin. That meant she was already ten minutes late by her calendar but would probably be on time for the actual meeting.

It wasn't a great system, but it was at least *a* system. Christine liked to point out she could just be on time, but Val's relationship with time didn't work that way. She slid her tablet into her purse and walked out into the hall, proud of herself for being nearly early to a meeting.

But down in the living room, Nick was having an unusually angry-sounding conversation. Val paused at the top of the stairs. She didn't mean to eavesdrop, but she also didn't want to interrupt. Nick liked his privacy, and probably would get annoyed with her for walking through the living room while he was on the phone, even if it was technically *her* living room too, but he was almost always annoyed with her anyway.

Okay, fine, she was a little nosy too. His brother had called last night, the wall between her bedroom and Nick's not enough to muffle their conversation. Val hadn't caught all of it, but it seemed like Josh had done something Nick was pissed about. And Val was dying to know what.

'Mom, I get it, I really do,' Nick was saying, although in Val's opinion, he really didn't sound like he got it. Also, *Mom* was not Josh, so maybe this was a separate thing Nick was mad about. 'But I'm not –' He paused, and she could practically feel his annoyance vibrating up the stairs. 'I know Josh said –' he started, but clearly his mom didn't like to let him finish a sentence. Val looked at her phone. She had just fifteen minutes to spare, so either Nick had to wrap this conversation up in the next two minutes, or she would have to risk his irritation. 'Yeah, I know. But I've got a girlfriend. I can't.'

Val's curiosity stayed her footsteps. That was what he'd been arguing about with Josh, she was almost positive. Nick listened to whatever his mom had to say next. 'Like I said, I'm seeing someone, and it's getting serious.'

I'm seeing someone, and it's getting serious. As far as Val knew, Nick had no partner of any gender, but then again, she didn't pay that much attention to his personal life. Except if it was serious, why hadn't his girlfriend moved in instead? And if he didn't have a girlfriend – and she was almost positive he didn't – why was he telling his mother he had one? *What sort of uptight dork has to invent a girlfriend?* she thought to herself.

Nick sighed again. 'Fine,' he said, sounding resigned. 'No promises though, okay?'

She made a mental note to do some internet stalking to see if she could locate this mysterious girlfriend who never visited her boyfriend's house – Val also mentally added 'nosy bitch' to her list of terrible qualities – and decided she couldn't wait any longer. She had an influencer to charm.

'Oh my god, I am so sorry I'm late!' Autumn said, collapsing into the chair across from Val with a dramatic flourish. 'I did that thing where you plan to leave on time, but then you're scrolling on your phone or whatever and then all of a sudden, you're late.'

Despite her frazzled words, Autumn looked perfectly put together in a very Nineties-Mall-Babe sort of way. Her hair was a deep auburn – natural, as far as Val could tell – and while a tangerine blouse was a risky choice on someone with her complexion, Autumn was fully pulling it off. Whether that was innate charisma, flawless skin, or just her perfectly symmetrical face, Val couldn't tell.

In contrast, Val looked like someone who hung out behind the school smoking, or whatever burnouts did in the nineties while Mall Babes were shopping – oversized flannel, leather jacket, and combat boots included. 'Don't worry about it,' Val said. She herself had only sat down about five minutes ago, at the exact moment they were supposed to meet, so it wasn't like she'd been waiting long. 'I do that all the time. In fact, I've started lying to myself about when things start, in hopes that gets my ass out the door at the right time.' She was usually a lot less interested in small talk and putting a client at ease, but it was not an exaggeration to say her entire career hinged on Autumn.

'Does it work?' Autumn asked, glancing quickly at her phone and wrinkling her nose. 'Sorry, fiancé got held up at work and is also running late.' She redirected her attention to Val. 'The lying to yourself thing, is that something I should try?'

'It depends. The problem is, I know I'm lying to myself, so sometimes I just ignore it and I'm late anyway.'

'And here I thought you'd cracked it,' Autumn said, laughing, and Val grinned back.

'Did you want to get started?' Val said, motioning to her tablet. 'Or should we wait for your fiancé?'

'Cal might not be here for a bit so we might as well,' Autumn said, and Val's stomach jolted uncomfortably at the first syllable. But Val's Caleb had been very vocal about how much he hated the nickname Cal, in large part because he loathed how 'Cal and Val' rhymed. 'Anyway, Cal has absolutely no eye for photography, so this is going to be my call no matter what,' Autumn continued.

Val really didn't want to do this next part, but she couldn't risk booking Autumn and then losing her. 'You should know that I have, um, a rather upset former client who –'

'Oh, I know,' Autumn said breezily. 'I kind of know her. She's incredibly vindictive, usually when something else in her life is going wrong, so the second I saw she was launching a campaign against you I knew you probably didn't deserve it. I checked out your stuff and liked your style, so don't worry about it, okay?'

Val swallowed hard. She wasn't used to that sort of trust, especially from a stranger, but she wasn't about to complain. 'Well, thank you,' she said and flipped open the cover of her tablet, calling up the folder dedicated to Autumn. 'I looked through your feed – I hope you don't mind – and here's what I've come up with,' she started.

'Of course I don't mind,' Autumn said cheerfully. 'That's what it's for; for people to look at.' Val found herself smiling back again, and while Val certainly wasn't as dour as, say, Nick, she didn't usually smile this much, either. Autumn was just so *nice*. It was like sitting across the table from a Disney Princess, if said princess also had a fierce business sense. Val walked

Autumn through some engagement photos she'd taken of couples in casual settings, as well as more formal, posed wedding photos. Val had some of her best candids from several receptions as well, to show she would be capable of capturing the spur-of-the-moment fun of bachelor and bachelorette parties. There was also a vision board, showing various places throughout the Twin Cities that Val thought would be good backdrops for photos that would work well with Autumn's established style. Obviously, she left off the nipple pic.

'Are you thinking of shifting your style at all once you're married?' Val asked. 'Going for a different angle, maybe?' A lot of influencers went from 'cool single girls' to 'perfect homemaker wives' seamlessly, Val had noticed. She wasn't sure why getting married meant their interests had to change from fashion to home design, but it was a pattern a lot seemed to follow. 'Because if you are, we could always start weaving it in with these photos; prep the audience for a change.'

'Not yet, no,' Autumn said. 'I haven't told fans I'm engaged yet, and I want to see how that plays out first. If it seems like I'm losing my target audience, I might have to rebrand and reach into different sectors, but for now I want to stay with my established aesthetic.'

'Got it,' Val said and swiped past a few photos she had done for a local magazine shoot two years ago. Autumn looked at all her examples carefully and had a few suggestions of locations of her own. One was good in theory if not in practice (Val had tried to take engagement photos there once, but being so close to an off-leash dog park space meant a lot of unscheduled four-legged guest stars who were cute but not terribly well behaved), but the other wasn't one she'd considered. When Autumn showed her some images from the area, Val was immediately sold.

'You live nearby, right?' Autumn asked, studying a photo Val had taken two years ago at a Cambodian wedding ceremony held in a local Chinese restaurant-slash-event center.

'Not too far. I used to be based in Minneapolis, but I live out in Swede River now,' Val said as matter-of-factly as possible.

'By yourself?'

'No, no, I'm living with someone,' Val explained.

'What's his name?' Autumn asked.

'Nick,' Val said, not quite sure how that was relevant, but then Autumn asked another question about possible locations and the conversation slowly shifted.

It was so easy to talk to Autumn about shoots and lighting and filters that Val forgot all about her fiancé coming to join them. She had the job, that much was clear, and what Autumn was willing to pay would be enough to cover rent and Val's half of the utilities for at least six months, which was more job security than she'd ever had before. Val was feeling good – confident, even – for the first time in months, so of course it couldn't last. She and Autumn were laughing about an incident Autumn had that involved a selfie, a moped, and a precariously balanced iced coffee when a familiar voice broke in. 'Val?'

All the joy drained out of her immediately. She looked up and there he was, looking as blond, handsome, and bland as ever: Caleb Dupont, in the flesh.

Her ex.

No, scratch that: her toxic, sort-of ex, because Caleb had been very adamant that they weren't ever officially dating. They were hooking up, nothing more, even if it lasted for almost two years, on and off, because he had a very specific vision of the woman he was going to settle down with, and 'fuck-up photographer with approximately four outfits, three of which involved flannel and the other one was a hoodie' didn't fit. Autumn clearly met his requirements: she was pretty in a seemingly effortless way that could only be achieved by at least an hour of work, she had a clear sense of style that was both classy and chic, and she probably was the sort of woman who ate salads regularly, rather than being unable to remember the last time she had eaten a vegetable.

Val had gone out of her way to learn absolutely nothing about Caleb since their last, permanent breakup eighteen months ago, but maybe she should have kept slightly closer tabs on him, because *fuck*.

'Cal!' Autumn said, jumping up and kissing him on the cheek. 'You know each other?' she asked, seemingly oblivious to the sudden tension.

'Val's an old college friend,' Caleb said, and while it wasn't technically a lie, it wasn't the whole truth, either. He never was very good with confrontation, preferring instead to list out the reasons he was upset and then announce he was ready to move on, without ever letting Val address or fix what she'd screwed up. Val, on the other hand, tended to be a walking confrontation, something that had irritated him to no end.

'Oh, awesome!' Autumn said. 'That will make things so much easier.' She paused, her eyes lighting up. 'Wait, what's his name again?'

'Who's?' Val asked, bewildered.

'Your boyfriend. Would it be weird if we double-dated?'

Val blinked. Autumn started chattering so quickly Val couldn't get a word in edgewise, much less figure out how to explain that Nick – starchy, boring Nick – was definitely not her boyfriend. 'Oh my god, I'm sorry, that was so weird. It's just that you said you were living with someone and I thought – I mean, you're just so cool, and I thought if you guys were already friends then we could all hang out, and oh my god I have just made this so uncomfortable,' Autumn babbled, adorably awkward. Val could never pull that sort of regret off; she always came off vaguely hostile and accusatory. 'Ignore me, it's fine if you and your boyfriend don't want to double-date.'

Val was trying to figure out a not-awkward way to set the record straight when Autumn stood up. 'Now that I've thoroughly embarrassed myself I'll go to the restroom and let you guys catch up, and then when I get back, we can just pretend this never happened, okay?' She headed toward the back of the coffee shop, and Caleb sat down in the chair next to Autumn's, apparently unfazed by her enthusiasm for Val.

'Cal, huh?' Val said acidly. 'I thought you hated that nickname.'

Caleb shrugged. 'Autumn likes it.'

Val had half a mind to get up and leave, but then she remembered how much money was on the line. 'How long have you known her?' Val forced herself to say. She could make small talk with Caleb if it killed her. She had to.

'About a year,' Caleb said. 'I swear, I didn't know it was going to be you; Autumn has been handling all the wedding stuff. But how are you?'

'Fine,' Val replied, channeling Nick's terseness and clenched jaw. 'What was that *old friend* business?'

'Autumn is really sensitive,' Caleb said quietly. He threw a nervous look over his shoulder. 'Before she comes back, though, are you sure this is a good idea? Given our history?'

Val leaned back in her chair. 'What would be the problem?' She knew him well enough to know what his deal was, but she was going to make him say it anyway.

'You know – things with us were always so . . . complicated.'

Complicated was understating it by a mile. Val and Caleb

had never really worked, but they had also never really managed to make their many breakups stick. Caleb was, to use Lindsey's phrasing, *perpetually afraid of being the bad guy*. On the surface, it would seem like that would make him a perfect match for Val, who really had no problem being a bitch. But Caleb also wasn't nearly as nice as he wanted to be, and way more of their time together than she cared to admit had just been him pointing out her many, many flaws, and wishing she would be a totally different person – maybe then he'd actually date her, not just sleep with her and occasionally order takeout. It had worked for Val at the start – it meant she didn't have to pretend to care about his feelings – but had worn her down the longer things dragged on. She was embarrassed by how long it took for her to completely break the cycle, but whenever she had tried to end things, he would get so *sad*. He would start talking about how much he *felt* for her, even if it couldn't ever be something more, and how much he needed her in his life. Even worse, a part of her had started to care about him, so when he was sad, she would feel bad and decide to give it yet another try, until her patience finally ran out.

She'd be damned if she let him screw her out of this. 'Sure, things were complicated,' she admitted. 'But it's over.' An idea occurred to her and suddenly, she had a lot of sympathy for Nick having to invent a girlfriend to get out of a conversation. 'Besides, like Autumn said, I have a boyfriend.'

'I was wondering about that,' Caleb said with mild surprise. 'I thought commitment wasn't your thing.'

Again, not quite how I remember it. 'People change,' she said, waving her hand. 'And whatever you want to tell Autumn about us is your business, not mine. I'm just here to take the pictures.' Caleb opened his mouth to protest, but Val kept going. 'And besides, if we do go our separate ways – well, then maybe it might be harder for me to keep the truth from Autumn. Probably best to be honest about why we aren't working together.' Val flashed him a fake-ass smile and waited for her threat to sink in.

Autumn was winding her way back through the tables, stopping to talk to someone at a two-seater near the window. Val tipped her head toward her in acknowledgment. It was a risk, blackmailing Caleb like this, but she needed this job even if it meant dealing with his faux-considerate face every day, and he was the one who started off with a lie in the first place. The seconds ticked down as Autumn glanced over, as if she was getting ready to return to the table. Val's palms were sweaty, her heart racing.

'I'll pay extra if you don't tell her,' he blurted, which wasn't what she was angling for, but she wasn't about to turn extra money down.

'How much?'

Autumn was clearly saying goodbye, and Caleb's panic grew more evident. 'An extra third. Whatever your fee is, add thirty percent.'

'Thirty-five percent. Call it a tip.'

Autumn started walking toward them. Caleb nodded to her in surrender, and Val's grin grew a touch more genuine.

Now all she had to do was keep Caleb and Autumn from figuring out she lied about having a boyfriend. Specifically, a boyfriend she lived with, when in fact she lived with a man who clearly wished he never met her. That wouldn't be too hard.

Right?

Chapter Five

Nick clicked his phone off and sighed, sinking back into the porch swing tucked against the north corner of the backyard. It was a mild fall evening, the sort that had hints of woodsmoke in the air and dried leaves skittering across the pavement. Darkness had fallen at some point while he texted with Jan, and he should go back inside, but for now, he was enjoying the peace and quiet.

Josh had roped Jan, his current (and Nick's former) agent, into trying to figure out how to sell the lie to Candace. Jan had just sent over her 'solution' – a client of one of her friends had a big movie coming out next summer and could use some low-key press before the full court blitz started in spring. The idea was to plant a few stories with friendly outlets about them, and maybe send her up to Swede River for a few days as a cover. She was originally from Iowa, so Jan thought they could make it seem like they ran into each other while she was home visiting family and things progressed from there.

Nick wondered if it was worth explaining to Jan again that Des Moines was not, in fact, 'just down the road' from Swede River and instead a solid four hours away, but he also knew that living in California for too long really warped people's sense of relative distances. The actress herself looked nice enough, although Nick personally felt she was a little young for him – she had just turned twenty-one and even though there wasn't anything *wrong* with an eight-year age gap, he was already hesitant and that didn't help. Aside from being on the young side, the photo Jan sent was of her walking past a wall of paparazzi with practiced ease, which made him wonder if she'd called them herself. Plenty of actors did that, especially people who were on the rise and wanted to make sure they were noticed, but *will call the paps on herself* was at the bottom of the list when it came to qualities Nick wanted in a girlfriend, something Candace would notice immediately.

Then there was the fact that practically everyone in Swede River would know if someone new was in town, especially someone who wore a bikini top and cut-off shorts so tiny the pockets hung out the bottom to go to the grocery store. No judgment on her clothes, but that sort of thing would get noticed, so even the slightest scrutiny of that story would fall apart if even one reporter or fan asked around. Besides, was she going to come visit him more than once? Or was he going to have to visit her? There were too many variables and honestly, too much effort involved, to sell the lie convincingly.

Besides, Nick didn't think Candace would buy it, anyway. She didn't know her sons very well, but she knew Nick hated the entire Hollywood scene, which made an actress girlfriend wildly implausible. And if she figured out the woman in question wanted a little more press, Nick wouldn't put it past Candy to try and convince her that the drama of being dumped so Nick could go on a dating show would be better than just having a nerdy, long-distance, former-child-star boyfriend. He was going to have to tell Jan and Josh no, and then muddle through on his own.

The seal to the sliding glass door cracked and Val's shadowy form stepped out onto his small back deck. She was backlit against the bright kitchen, and when she turned to close the door a slice of light landed on her face, and Nick's breath caught in his chest.

Sometimes, he wished he hadn't listened to Mary, because if he hadn't, maybe his life would be a little simpler. Mary wasn't usually a meddler, but she had texted that she'd found him the perfect roommate. All he needed to do was walk on over to Pete's. Mary had been right, if by 'perfect' she just meant 'able to move in immediately and can cover her share of rent this month, at least,' and Nick had to admit he had been struck by how lost Val looked that evening. There had been a softness to her, a vulnerability that kicked his protective instincts into gear, only to realize far too late that had been an aberration. She didn't need him to take care of her, she needed to learn that eating outside the kitchen was asking for a mice infestation.

Val turned toward the yard, head falling back to look at the sky. She took a deep breath, shoulders releasing slightly. She twisted the top off a beer bottle that was in her right hand and sank into a chair just a few feet away from him, sighing loudly to herself.

Belatedly, Nick realized she probably didn't know he was out there too. He hadn't turned on any of the outdoor lights, and his bedroom door was probably locked, the way he left it whenever he wasn't in there.

It wasn't that he thought she was going to steal from him. He wouldn't have agreed to let her move in if he was worried about that. But Nick had a lot of irrational anxiety and sometimes, it was just easier to do things that seemed a little asshole-ish to quiet those nagging feelings in his chest.

Val sighed to herself again and Nick cleared his throat awkwardly. She jumped about a mile, sloshing her beer over her hand, and pressing her other palm to her chest. 'God, you scared me,' she said, although she sounded more surprised than pissed. Val unwound her legs and put them on the ground. She never sat normally; her legs were either pretzeled or draped over the arm or folded under her. He wondered if that was because she had an aversion to having her feet on the floor, or if this was just how people who didn't have constant anxiety sat.

'Sorry,' he said, his voice gruffer than he intended. It always came out like that with her, like he was trying to make *sure* she didn't like him. He cleared his throat again and composed himself. 'I mean – it's your yard too.' He added an almost smile, but they were a solid five feet apart, and Nick wasn't sure if she could see him very well. He was tucked under the walnut tree on the porch swing, and the kitchen lights didn't reach very far.

The silence between them stretched on, and Nick remembered Josh's admonishment from his most recent text: *If you keep being a silent grouch all the time your roommate is going to think you're a silent grouch.* 'So, uh, what's new with you?' he asked, wishing he could read Val's face. He couldn't tell if she was glad he was breaking the silence or annoyed that he spoke at all.

Probably annoyed. That would make the most sense.

'You know, finally landed a huge client and her fiancé is my ex, so yeah, everything's great,' she said drily. 'Oh, and I lied and said I have a boyfriend to keep my ex from firing me, so now there's that.'

He could tell she was trying to make it sound like a joke, but there was an undercurrent of real despair to her tone. 'Your ex was going to fire you?' he asked, trying to sound less stiff.

It must have worked because after a brief hesitation, she nodded. 'It's a long story, but the point is, I don't have a boyfriend, and now I have to get a lot better at lying, fast.'

'Convince yourself it's real,' Nick offered. 'That was always how I handled acting. I just . . . made myself believe I was Jakey. Or at least that whatever Jakey was facing was real.'

'Isn't that just acting? Like literally what acting is,' she said, and her tone was one that would usually make him clam up.

But for some reason, it didn't bother him this time. He could tell she wasn't being mean, just deadpan. 'For some people. Other people are better at separating themselves from it, but for those of us who aren't as good – yeah, that's what works.'

Val huffed out a breath. 'I wish I could act,' she said. 'But Caleb knows me. He knows my tells, and he just – he gets under my skin. I'll get flustered and screw up.' She shifted in her chair and took a sip of beer. 'It's fine, it's – it's whatever. Not your problem.'

Nick looked at his phone, where the photo of his Agent Approved Solution was lurking. 'I'm in a similar situation, actually,' he said, not quite believing that he was admitting this to a woman who didn't seem to like him all that much. Maybe it was just that Val didn't strike him as the gossipy type. She had a lot of faults, but he instinctively knew he could trust her. 'My mom thinks I have a girlfriend.'

'But you don't. I mean, I'm assuming, because of how you just worded that and because no one's come over in the whole time I've been here. I haven't been stalking you, I swear,' Val added quickly. It had never occurred to Nick that she might be worried about seeming too interested in him. If anything, he was way too interested in her.

'I don't. And now I need to make it sound like less of a lie.'

'Does it matter?' Val asked. 'I know all about having a crappy family, but when it comes to the list of things I feel bad about, lying to them isn't usually one.'

'It's not just Mom. She's got this – plan. She pitched a dating show to Universal Streaming, and it was supposed to be me and Josh, but he's already booked. Which leaves just me, and with things already in motion at the streamer, just saying I don't want to wouldn't cut it. She's relentless, and I wouldn't put it past her to claim I've verbally accepted to try and force me into it. Hence Josh claiming I have a serious girlfriend.'

'You really can't just lie your way out of it?'

Nick's acting was rusty, but it was more than that. He wouldn't put it past Candace to come out to meet the girlfriend herself or send someone to do it for her. Besides, the most Nick had ever managed to do was ignore her; saying no to her face was a lot harder. 'It's complicated,' he admitted. 'But honestly, I think it would be easier if it seemed true, at least for a while.' He chuckled to himself, and then said the dumbest thing he had ever said aloud. 'Too bad we can't just date each other; that would solve everything.'

The words were out of Nick's mouth before he even consciously realized what he was saying, and he immediately wanted to take them back, but it was too late.

Dammit. Now he was going to have to find a new roommate.

Chapter Six

Too bad we can't just date each other. The words hung in the air and Val could *feel* Nick mentally backpedalling, but her brain was already churning. She didn't want to *date him* <u>date him</u> – she already had enough experience being with someone who thought she was an incompetent fuck-up, thank you very much – but maybe she wouldn't need to. Aside from his brother he didn't seem to have much of a connection to Hollywood, and it wasn't like Val was going to be hanging out all the time with Caleb and Autumn. All she needed to do was show some sort of subtle proof she wasn't lying, and then she would be in the clear.

Of course, she *was* lying, but she didn't care too much about that. 'We could though,' Val said before Nick said anything else. 'Not literally date, obviously, but we could pretend.'

Nick was silent for long enough that she started having doubts. It was a stupid, impulsive idea, and Christine was always telling her she needed to think things through before jumping into them. Maybe she shouldn't have suggested it, and maybe he was about to ask her to move out instead. That would suck, because she didn't have enough for a deposit on a new place, and with Linds out in San Francisco she really didn't have anywhere else to go.

'My mom is – a lot,' he said cautiously. 'She's got a reputation for a reason.'

Okay, that wasn't a *no*. Besides, his mom lived several states away; how hard could it be to convince her they were dating? Nick seemed like the type to overreact to stuff anyway. 'It'll be fine,' she said. 'And it'll be easy, since we already live together.'

'And there's no way we'd develop feelings for each other,' he added. 'No offense, but you're the opposite of my type.'

Val couldn't say why that stung so badly, but she made herself shrug it off. They had a problem to solve, and she wasn't about to let the solution slip away just because he hurt her feelings by saying out loud what she was already thinking. 'Honestly, I have never been one for commitment, so yeah, we're safe,' she said as airily as possible. 'And do you have any social media accounts?'

'Jan is sitting on them,' he said. 'She always claims our legal names any time a new social media site pops up, but I've never touched any of mine.'

'I'm guessing your mom is on social media?'

'If it gets people to pay attention to her, she's on it.'

'That makes this easier then,' Val said, moving her legs to sit pretzel style. 'We could just take a few photos together and upload some of them to your Instagram and some to mine. Caleb doesn't follow me anymore, but obviously Autumn does, and it would seem more legit if I didn't go out of my way to prove it to him, you know?'

'Sorry, Caleb and Autumn?'

'My ex and my client, who happens to be his fiancée.'

'What about everyone else?' he asked. At her blank look, he went on. 'Everyone else in Swede River. We'd be lying to them, too. And we'd need them to believe us, just in case my mom starts asking around.'

Val paused. She hadn't really considered that angle, since she wasn't used to having anyone other than Linds who cared that much about what she did, unless you counted her family. And since they mostly just cared if they could judge her for it, she didn't. 'Does that bother you?'

'I don't know,' he said, sighing. 'Kind of, yeah.'

'Okay, but – you know Mary wants us to date, right? That's totally why she convinced you to let me move in,' Val said, first on impulse and then, after a second thought, deciding she was right. It made sense, anyway.

Nick frowned. 'Is that it? Mary's never been much of a meddler, but –' He paused, seemingly lost in thought. 'You might be right,' he conceded. 'But still, we'd be lying to them.'

'I don't want to discount that, but how is it different from acting?' she asked, honestly a little surprised at the arguments she was managing to pull out of her ass on the fly. 'Besides, how hard can it be? We already live in the same house so like, who's to say we're not sleeping together all the time in here and just not into PDAs? We could do like, one coffee run to Pete's holding hands, and I bet the entire town will believe it by the end of business that day.'

Nick looked at her for a long moment. Val held her breath – which was dumb, why did she care if he shot her down? – and let it out slowly when he nodded. 'Then I'm in.'

It was stupid to get nervous about walking into a coffee shop. Val had to remind herself of that because her heart was racing as Nick opened the door to Pete's. It was a busy Saturday morning, with people jostling for tables and awkwardly apologizing for bumping into each other in line. She spotted a table being vacated by two women she vaguely recognized from around town and swooped in, earning herself at least two reproachful looks from those around her. She wanted to stare back at them, but she had a mission today that didn't involve making new enemies, so she made herself look rueful and apologetic.

'You got this quickly,' Nick said when he arrived with their drinks. 'Did you –'

'No, I did not run over any grandmas to get it,' she sighed. 'Possibly annoyed some townspeople, but you win some, you lose some. I ran into some dude the other day, and he was really cranky about it, even though he definitely was the one who should have moved. Anyway, who was that you were talking to?'

Nick, a mug in each hand, had spent a few minutes chatting with an Asian woman who looked to be about the same age as her parents, before walking over to her. 'That's Mrs Lim – she wanted to know what I was doing here with you.'

'And you said?'

'That we were getting coffee,' he replied. 'But I said it in a way she'd know it was also a date.'

'How do you even do that?'

'Subtext,' he said drily.

'Think she'll tell anyone?'

'The real question is who won't she tell,' Nick said, nodding toward where Mrs Lim now stood near a small crowd of people at the door, clearly passing along some juicy gossip.

Nick sat down and slid a mug over to her. Every mug at Pete's was different, she had learned, and sometimes people got competitive over which one they had. Today she had gotten the Pig Mug, a bright pink one with a snout on one side and a handle that was twisted like a pig's tail.

'How high does this one rank?' she asked Nick, not sure if it was a good thing or a bad thing if she got a Highly Coveted

Mug – on the one hand, it could be a sign that Pete liked her, which she was reasonably sure was true, but on the other hand, if it looked like she was getting a Good Mug and hogging tables she might look greedy, all porcine-related puns aside.

'Not as high as the corncob one, but not as low as this one,' he said, lifting up a purple mug that just said *I Heart Minnesota* in yellow block letters. 'Pete always swears it has nothing to do with how he feels about us customers, but I've always suspected he's lying.'

It took her a second to realize he was making a joke, because he did that so infrequently. Or at least, he rarely did it with *her*. 'What'd you do to get on his shit list?'

'There was a dispute over a television show, and that's all I'm at liberty to say,' he said, and this time, she caught the twinkle in his eye.

Val laughed and noted at least one person standing in line glanced their way. 'This is good,' she said. 'Keep being funny.'

'It's a truth universally acknowledged that demanding someone be funny immediately makes them unable to be funny at all,' he said with an eyeroll.

Val narrowed her eyes. 'Wait, did you just make a Jane Austen joke about not being able to make a joke?'

Nick chuckled and to her surprise he held out his hand on top of the table, palm up, like he wanted her to hold his hand. 'Is this okay?' he asked quietly.

She loosely tangled their fingers together and leaned forward like she was excited to be near him. His fingertips brushed the skin of her palm and a pleasant tingle spiraled up her arm. 'Keep this up and I'll start to think you don't hate me,' she said, mostly to keep herself from thinking about how nice it felt.

Nick frowned. 'I've never hated you,' he replied. 'What have I done that –'

'It was a joke,' she interrupted, because now she'd gone and hurt his feelings, and she didn't want to do that. And that sort of caring wasn't her usual impulse, but she wasn't going to examine that. 'But now that we've officially debuted as a couple, what's next?'

He let her faux pas go and shrugged. 'I was thinking of this as more of a soft launch, I guess.'

'I thought you didn't follow stuff on social media? How the hell do you know what a soft launch is?'

'I have the internet on my phone, same as you,' he said primly. 'But I did have something else in mind, if you're up for it. It would involve being a little more – public.'

'You are aware we're in public right now?' Val replied. 'Like, we are in a public space, hopefully triggering a massive wave of rumors?'

Nick pursed his lips, clearly a little annoyed, but not as annoyed as he would have been a few days ago when she was just his roommate and not his roommate-and-also-fake-girlfriend. 'Do you want to hear my idea, or tease me a little more?'

'Can't it be both?' she asked, earning herself a tiny, genuine-seeming grin from him.

'There's a town dance coming up.'

'I'm sorry, you guys have a town prom?'

'Prom is in the spring,' he said in a put-upon tone. 'And this is unrelated to high school, just a community event. But it would be a good chance for us to build on what this started; make it seem more definitive.'

A dance meant – dancing. That involved a lot more touching, and she was already acting like a complete weirdo just from half-holding his hand. Val pulled her hand away and rubbed it surreptitiously on her jeans. It was sweaty, which was... weird, considering it wasn't particularly warm in the coffee shop. 'Is it a hoedown?'

'What even would that be?'

'I don't know, but I would imagine it involves cowboy boots and weird frilly dresses.'

Nick's lips quirked up, amused. 'No, it's not a hoedown.'

'Are you sure about this?'

'Trust me, it'll work,' Nick assured her.

Val leaned forward, peering out the windshield of his car. Nick's car was so clean it looked like he'd just left the dealership. Hers, by comparison, was basically a trash can. 'It looks... like a dance hosted by a senior center at an old movie theater,' she said, wrinkling her nose. 'Is this really what you do for fun out here?'

He rolled his eyes grumpily, which she was beginning to realize was a defense mechanism for him. 'It's a town tradition. There's a whole story that goes along with it.' She waited expectantly, and he sighed. 'There was a couple in the 1800s whose families didn't want them to be together. They would stand on either side of the river just to be able to see each other, and then one day they disappeared.'

'Let me guess, they disappeared in mid-September.'

'They did. Some people think they drowned, but others think they just ran away to be together. Either way, it started small, just people exchanging tokens of affection, and then sometime after World War Two the town started holding the Swedehearts' Dance in their honor. It's the closest thing we have to a town holiday.'

'What do you think happened to them?'

Nick leaned back, his face half illuminated by the streetlight nearby. 'I'm a romantic. I like to think they ran away,' he said with a soft smile.

Val looked away abruptly. She wasn't sure why it was suddenly so difficult to look at him, but it was. 'I bet they ran away together and a week later he realized the magic was in the sneaking around, so he left her,' she said, more to shock him out of that gentle smile than anything. 'Anyway, let's get this over with.'

She wiped her once again oddly sweaty palms on her dress. It was not quite knee-length with long sleeves and a tiny blue floral print on cream, and probably the closest she had to something that could be called 'delicate.' It also happened to be the only dress she owned that wasn't black and super short, which she suspected wouldn't go over well at a small-town dance. 'And you're *sure* it's not a hoedown?'

'It's not a hoedown,' Nick confirmed with great patience. She'd probably asked him that half a dozen times over the past week, partially because she really thought it might be a hoedown, and partially just to see how annoyed with her he would get. To his credit, he'd kept his irritation in check.

Maybe he wasn't so bad, this Nick. 'Then Swede River Swedehearts' Dance, here we come.'

There was a scrum at the door to get in, which should have been her first clue that this wasn't just some rinky-dink dance attended by ten senior citizens and one sullen teenage grandchild. But Val wasn't quite prepared to walk into a baroque theater, complete with a stage. Instead of seats it had a two-tiered dance floor, and it was *packed*. Val spotted the only two people she recognized, Mary and Pete, right away, along with two men who must be their husbands, but the four of them were deep in conversation.

And maybe it was her imagination, but it seemed like everyone else was staring at her. Literally. Everyone.

She sent a dark glare at a young white woman with blonde hair, who turned away quickly. 'What is going on? Is this town not big enough for the both of us?' she hissed under her breath to Nick.

His brow furrowed just slightly. He surreptitiously took her hand in his, and despite the current chill in the air her cheeks started to heat. His fingers were strong, his palm dry and warm, and her heartbeat abruptly picked up. It was like every single nerve ending in her hand had woken up at the same time, sending tingles up and down her arm. Apparently, that moment in Pete's wasn't a one-off, which was honestly not great for her. If they were going to do more of this fake dating thing, her body was going to have to stop overreacting to every single touch. 'People are probably just surprised,' he said, leaning down to whisper in her ear.

That sent pleasant shivers along her spine, but Val was good at multitasking and managed to send a dirty look at the boy in his late teens who was gaping at them. He paled and swallowed hard, which coincidentally Val was having to do too. 'Not getting a surprised vibe,' she replied out of the corner of her mouth. 'More "burn the witch."'

'Don't worry, we haven't burned a witch in Swede River in years.'

She snorted, which only succeeded in drawing another round of glares. Going to Pete's together had been intended to spark the rumor mill, but she hadn't expected to make people angry. She was debating whether or not dancing would make things better or worse – she was thinking worse – when Nick leaned down to murmur in her ear. 'We should dance,' he said. 'Dance first, circulate later.'

Fortunately, or unfortunately for Val – she couldn't decide – the DJ chose that moment to switch from Prince to a slow, crooning country song. It was good, in that she was pretty sure rubbing her ass against Nick's groin, which was really her only go-to dance move, would not win her any favors with the clearly seething townspeople. But it was bad because it meant slow dancing, which meant being face to face with him.

Or face to chest, which she realized once he had towed her out to the dance floor. Intellectually, she had known she was living with and now fake dating a giant, since it was hard not to notice when someone was six foot two with shoulders like a lumberjack. But knowing something and *knowing it* were two different things, and when he placed his hand on her lower back and tugged her close, the tip of her nose was right at the base of his throat.

Val hated feeling small and delicate, because both of those feelings were far too close to vulnerable for her to be comfortable, and Nick was making her feel all three things at once. She set her jaw, refusing to let those feelings show, and let him start leading.

Unsurprisingly, because he seemed to be annoyingly good at everything, Nick was a pretty good dancer. 'You must have taken lessons,' she said, fixing her gaze on the top of his shoulder. That was a nice, neutral spot; no risk of blushing or anything embarrassing like that.

'In what, witch-burning?' he asked, a bare hint of a smile playing around the corner of his lips.

'Dancing,' she clarified, a little chagrined to realize she'd been having a whole series of thoughts about him, and then asked a question like it had been a conversation and not a one-person rumination.

His jaw tightened, and she wondered if she'd ever stop stepping in it with him. Everything she said, did, or wore was wrong. But then he spoke, and he sounded perfectly even and conversational. 'I did, yeah. Just long enough for my mom to realize that managing a boyband was not in her future.'

'You sing?'

'Josh can,' he said. 'Me . . . not so much. Or at least not at the level she wanted.'

'Ah, so you know what it's like to be the family disappointment too?'

There was that almost smile again. 'I do, actually.'

That was the most Val had learned about Nick's life from him directly. It felt strangely good to know that he wasn't as perfect as she'd assumed. 'I wouldn't think "not wanting to be a Jonas Brothers clone" is a major crime,' she said, her stomach doing a little swoop thing when his hand flexed against the curve of her waist.

'It is when your mother is Candace Ford.' He fell silent for a moment, leading her nearly effortlessly through the waltz steps. Around them everyone was still staring, and it took everything in Val's power not to flip them off.

The music stopped and so did Val, her desire for him to keep holding her close warring with the itchy feeling of people watching her. She wanted to throw up walls around them, build a fortress that was just her and Nick, and let the rest of the seemingly angry townspeople go fuck themselves. She let go of him and stepped back, more to get a grip on herself than anything else.

Nick opened his mouth to say something, but before he could speak an elbow dug sharply into Val's back, shoving her forward.

Right into his chest.

Chapter Seven

Nick caught Val automatically as she lurched into his chest out of nowhere. 'Careful,' he said, grasping her by her elbows and putting her back on her feet. That was better than having her cheek pressed against his chest – she'd be able to hear his heart‑beat if she stayed that way too long. He had been momentarily caught between the desire to hold her there longer and risk her hearing it racing, and the need to put approximately three meters of space between them.

As always, his desire for space won out. Val frowned at him and then looked behind her, scanning the crowd. 'Did you see who it was?'

'Who what was?'

'Who pushed me,' she grumbled, rubbing her forearm. He must have gripped her too tightly, and he wanted to apologize, but then again, he probably needed to apologize for a lot of things, like holding her waist and touching her without per‑mission and –

His brain finally caught up with what she had said. 'Wait, someone pushed you?'

'Did you think I tripped while standing still?'

Honestly, he'd been far too preoccupied with the feel of her against him to notice anyone else. But now he felt the hostility in the room again, all directed at them.

It was baffling. They hadn't done anything other than arrive and dance, and Nick couldn't for the life of him figure out why there were so many wary looks their way. He had expected gossip, but he hadn't expected this level of suspicion.

Across the room, Mary waved urgently at him. 'Mary wants to say hi,' he said, pulling Val out of her glaring contest with the entire town. Nick started guiding her with his hand on her lower back but quickly dropped it – he hadn't asked her if that was okay, and he was rapidly realizing his restraint was somewhat thin when it came to Val.

She made him hungry. Hungry for touch, for connection. *I am too touch-starved to handle this*, he thought, but knew better than to say that out loud. It would make it sound like he wanted to ignore her boundaries, which was the last thing he wanted. He just wanted her *close*, and there was no way for him to say that without sounding like a creep.

'No offense, Mary, but what the hell is wrong with this town?' Val said without preamble. She nodded to Mary's husband, Eng. 'I'm Val, the town pariah,' she deadpanned, holding out her hand for him to shake.

Eng was a short man a few years younger than Mary with a mustache that hid his cheerful grin, which in turn hid his sarcastic wit. 'I'll be careful not to be seen with you,' he replied in the same wry tone.

Mary turned to Nick. 'This is . . . new,' she said carefully. He wondered if rumors of their date at Pete's had gotten to her, or if this was the first she was hearing of them. Pete would have seen them, obviously, but while he could gossip with the best of them, Pete also knew how much Nick valued his privacy.

Nick took a deep breath. This was the part he had been dreading – lying to people he cared about. But it was necessary if they were going to pull this off. 'Very new,' he said, and glanced down at Val. It was easier if he was looking at her, he realized. 'Didn't think it would cause this much of a stir.'

Eng and Mary exchanged a look.

'Yeah, is there a reason everyone's so pissed at me?' Val asked with her typical bluntness.

'Well, there was, um, an incident shortly after you arrived,' Mary said.

'What incident?'

'You were hurrying out of Pete's one morning, and you ran straight into Charles Poulson.'

Val looked blankly at Mary. 'Who?'

'Charles is a bit of an institution. He's lived here forever, and his wife passed away last year.'

'And am I somehow responsible for that?'

'People tend to be protective of our own,' Nick explained. It was part of what had drawn him to Swede River.

'Exactly. You ran into Charles, spilled his coffee, and then kept on going, without even saying you were sorry.'

Val's eyebrows hit her hairline. 'Probably because if it's the incident I'm thinking of, he actually ran into *me*.'

'Be that as it may, between that and, well, you two, it's safe to say that people are concerned. Probably more about Nick, but the Charles incident didn't help.'

'Concerned? That I'm taking advantage of her?' Nick asked.

Val snorted. 'No, that I'm taking advantage of *you*.'

'That's about the sum of it, yes,' Mary said diplomatically.

Nick's stomach plummeted. The last thing he wanted to do was make Val's life harder. 'Taking advantage of me?' Nick echoed. 'How? I'm your landlord. If anything, the power dynamic is more messed up because of that in my direction.'

Now it was Mary and Val who exchanged a knowing look. 'I'm an outsider,' Val explained. 'I blew into town like a fucked-up hurricane – pardon my language, Mary.'

'I am a whole adult,' Mary replied, hiding a smile. 'I've heard the f-word before.'

'And she's even said it once,' Eng chimed in. 'Maybe even twice.'

'Anyway,' Val said, with more good humor than he'd maybe ever seen on her face. 'I blew into town, a complete mess, and now I'm dating the town's beloved golden boy, who, and correct me if I'm wrong, hasn't dated much before now. I'm an outsider, so they're worried about my motives.'

'They think you're a gold digger?'

'They think I'm going to break your heart,' she said bluntly.

'More or less,' Mary agreed.

Just then Pete and Aaron appeared at Nick's elbow. 'Are you guys discussing the current ice-cold reaction to Val?' Pete said, eyebrows raised. 'Because yikes.'

'Double yikes,' Aaron said sagely. 'Charles definitely ran into you that day, but he's a bit of a gossip and it looks like it's gotten around.'

'Should I apologize?' Val asked.

'If you want it to go away, yeah. But also, congrats. Pete said he saw you guys together last weekend, but we didn't want to assume anything.'

Nick looked at Val again, taking in the way her light-colored dress set off her dark hair and hazel eyes. It was a fascinating contradiction; her iron personality and firmly set, angular jaw, coupled with the soft waves of her hair and dainty dress. It was a combination that shouldn't work, which was why it did.

'Like I was telling Mary and Eng, it's new,' he said, and when he tore his eyes from Val, he noticed his friends were all trying to smother their smiles. That meant they were believable, at least, but that didn't make him feel any better, for some reason. Instead, he just felt more exposed.

Fortunately, Aaron took control of the conversation, leaving Nick to his pained ruminations. 'By the way, we were wondering if you did family photo shoots?' he asked Val.

'If I do, will you testify at my trial that I'm not, in fact, a witch?'

Pete and Aaron pretended to consider her question. 'Depends. Will we get thirty percent off?'

'Twenty. And I'll even do a solo shoot for Felix, which I never do because honestly, I'm a little scared of children,' Val said without missing a beat.

'It's the creepy, sticky little hands, isn't it?' Aaron said.

'Exactly,' Val replied, and Nick couldn't help it – it was nice to see his fake girlfriend get along so well with his real friends. It made it feel a little less underhanded. He tried to remind himself that it was just acting, but that worked better when the audience were faceless strangers on the other side of a TV screen. It was harder when the target audience was 'Mary and Pete and their husbands.'

'Nick!' He turned to see Jenny walking over with Henry, otherwise known as Jakey's newest fan, in tow. 'I wanted to say thanks for suggesting those books. Henry won't put them down, and we haven't had to deal with –' she broke off, clearly searching for a word, '– let's say, "catchphrases," for a while,' she finished. Henry grinned up at him, clearly unperturbed by having annoyed his mom and favorite librarian with Jakey's best-known phrase.

'Yeah, sorry about that,' Henry said cheerfully. 'But my

mom checked, and the library runs out of the series after book five. I looked it up, and there's like, eight?'

'You want us to order the rest?' Nick offered.

'Yeah!' Henry exclaimed. 'Can I come get them tomorrow?'

'Tomorrow is Sunday, buddy,' Jenny said patiently. 'And it will take more than a day to get them.'

'It will, but I will let you know as soon as they come in, deal?' Nick told Henry. The entire time, Val had been watching him with an odd, almost soft look on her face. 'Oh, and Jenny, Henry – this is Val.'

'Your . . . roommate?' Jenny said.

'Roommate originally, now girlfriend, too,' Val supplied with a quick glance his way.

'Ah,' Jenny said, while Henry appeared desperately uninterested in the news. 'Welcome to Swede River.' While it wasn't exactly a parade in Val's honor, it was at least one person who wasn't mad at her.

But that left the rest of the town, and the rest of the town was still throwing surprisingly hostile looks at Val. Nick waited until Jenny and Henry walked toward the refreshments table to place his hand lightly between her shoulder blades. 'I did want to say hi to Margie,' he reminded her.

Coming to the Swedehearts' Dance was only part of the plan; they needed to sell their relationship to a couple of key Swede River gossips, so on the off chance his mother flew out to make sure this was real, the story would hold up. Mrs Lim had already been checked off the list, but she was only one woman. And if the gossips confirmed they were dating while openly disliking Val, that would just give Candy an excuse to try to pressure him into the dating show. They also needed to get into at least a few photos that the senior center would post on their

Facebook page, to bolster their case once Val went 'public' and posted a photo of him on her Instagram account.

Val had tensed ever so slightly at his touch, but the smile she sent him appeared genuine. She was much better at acting than she gave herself credit for, that much was for sure. 'On a scale of one to ten, how likely is it that Margie already hates me?' she asked after they said their goodbyes to Mary, Eng, Pete, and Aaron.

'Uh, five?'

'Which means you have no idea if she does or doesn't. Great,' Val groused.

'Honestly, I don't even know if she likes *me*,' Nick countered. 'Margie is . . . a little hard to read.'

The woman in question was sitting in a metal folding chair next to a table covered in an autumn-leaf-themed tablecloth, cane in hand. She looked at them imperiously as they approached, and Nick automatically reached for Val's hand – not to comfort her, but to comfort himself.

Margie Schumacher could be incredibly terrifying. She was the closest thing Swede River had to an unofficial mayor. There was an actual mayor, of course, but everyone knew that the real power in town belonged to one cranky woman in her eighties who knew every skeleton in every closet. She was the keeper of the story behind every feud, every scandal, and she more or less controlled the way people felt about newcomers. Nick hadn't bothered to introduce Val before this, since it didn't seem like it would matter to her whether the town liked her. Now, though, it did, and Margie was the biggest hurdle to that.

'I see,' Margie said, not quite under her breath.

'How are you?' Nick asked, deciding to avoid the bait as long as he could.

'Hi there, Mrs Schumacher,' Val said in an unconvincingly cheery voice. 'Nice to finally meet you.'

'You two are already dating,' Margie said without preamble. 'That was fast.'

Val narrowed her eyes and Nick sucked in a breath. 'Wouldn't you be fast?' Val said and waved her hand up and down his torso. 'I mean, look at this.'

For a beat Margie said nothing, and Nick wondered if they were *both* going to have to move. And then Margie did the unthinkable: she laughed. Cackled, even. She threw her head back and laughed loud enough that more people turned to watch. A triumphant grin spread across Val's face. 'He's a nice hunk of meat, that's for sure,' Margie said, and now it was Val's turn to cackle.

'Meat?' Nick asked, and usually, this sort of attention – especially when it came to his looks – made him desperately uncomfortable. But he knew Margie well enough to know she sent an email to her granddaughter every week, even though she loathed using the internet. He knew the name of three of her deceased cats, dating back to the 1980s, and that despite her hard outer shell, she wasn't unkind. So, when Margie abruptly joined up with Val to catcall him, it didn't make him feel self-conscious; it made him laugh. It reminded him of Beth, the woman who played the matriarch of the Kramer family on *Just Us Girls*.

By now, Val had pulled up a chair and had said something else that made Margie snort, and truly, Nick had never seen someone charm Margie so fast. She had regarded him with icy suspicion for nearly a year before warming up to him, and it had taken probably another year before she made a crude joke in his presence. Watching Val and Margie laugh like old friends sent an odd feeling through his chest, something like – pride?

No, not quite that. Admiration, maybe. Margie was a tough nut, but Val had cracked her immediately. He wouldn't have characterized Val as charming, but then again, he'd been surly to her until recently. Maybe she was better with people who weren't him. That thought sat uneasily in his chest – that he was the problem, and that he maybe wanted her to see him differently than she did right now.

'Oh yes, the incident with Chuckie,' Margie was saying. 'I'm sure he was in your way – that man has never known how to get out of the way, it's unbelievable how many times I've had to ask him to move – but with him losing Sheila, people are probably feeling a bit defensive about him.'

'How do I fix it?'

'You'll have to apologize,' Margie sighed. 'He can be a bit of a crank, but he doesn't bite.'

Val rolled her eyes. 'I'll see what I can do.'

'Mind if I grab a picture?' Livvy, the afternoons-and-Saturday-mornings barista at Pete's Coffee, was standing next to him with her phone. She had a shaved head, a pierced septum, and just about the sunniest disposition a high schooler could possibly have. 'Senior Center said they'd pay me a hundred bucks if I handled their Facebook posts for tonight.'

'Do kids your age even know how to use Facebook?' Nick asked.

'I can handle the basics,' Livvy replied with a grin. 'It's not like it's hard or anything.'

'Probably harder than getting into Harvard Law,' Val chimed in, and at Livvy's blank look she sighed. '*Legally Blonde* joke. And now I feel old.'

'Picture?' Livvy asked again, and then stopped. 'Wait, aren't you like, a real photographer?'

'I am. But don't let that stop you,' Val said. Nick draped his arm over her shoulder and Livvy took a quick photo. She held up the phone for them to look at, and then focused on Val. 'How is it?'

'It's great,' Val said warmly, but Livvy wasn't done.

'Are you sure? I never know if I'm framing things right.'

'Are you interested in photography?'

'Just a perfectionist,' Livvy replied.

Val nodded and started explaining what she called *the basics*, while Margie watched interestedly from her table. 'She's a good one, this girl of yours,' Margie said.

It wasn't winning over the whole town, but it was a start. It felt good, her starting to fit in like this, but the moment his brain asked *Why do you care, this isn't real* he immediately shoved that thought away. No good could come of that.

Nick almost reflexively said *She's not mine*, but remembered at the last second that they were pretending she was. Instead he just nodded and smiled in a way that he hoped didn't look too awkward.

The rest of the night went a little better – Charles Poulson arrived, and despite an epic eyeroll in Nick's direction, Val tracked him down to apologize. Nick hung back for that too, not wanting to seem too involved, but whatever she said did seem to brighten the otherwise dull look in Charles's eyes. Margie had watched the interaction with great interest, and after a short conversation with Charles, she started waving over a few of the other biggest busybodies in town.

After that, the hostility seemed to lessen. No more shoves, at least. And Nick would have to work to show that he wasn't being taken advantage of, but the first steps had been taken. Val stuck close to his side for most of the night, something that probably had more to do with their cover story than an actual desire for closeness, but he had to admit it felt good.

'You know, that wasn't as bad as I thought it would be,' Val admitted later that night, as they walked upstairs toward their bedrooms in what he hoped was companionable silence. 'Kind of dorky, but also kind of fun.'

'Dorky but fun is our town motto,' Nick replied with a sidelong glance her way.

Val drew to a stop in front of her bedroom door, looking awkward. 'I'm afraid if I open the door, you'll make that face.'

'What face?'

'You know, this one,' she said, and pursed her lips in a very prim-and-a-little-disgusted sort of way.

'I do not do that.'

'Do too,' she argued.

Nick chuckled. 'It's not my fault your room is a Federally Designated Disaster Area.'

'Don't drag FEMA into this,' she protested with a grin.

'I'm surprised they haven't arrived with tents,' Nick replied. At her glare, he chuckled again. 'Fine, I'll go to my room and let you open your door in peace.'

He had just reached his door when Val spoke again. 'Hey, Nick? I had a lot of fun tonight.'

'Me too,' he said, and waited until she was safely inside her room to let a smile spread across his face.

Chapter Eight

'I was thinking here would be a good place, especially around this time of day,' Autumn said, sweeping her hand toward the small outcropping of boulders just above Minnehaha Creek. 'And if we can get it done next week, we'd catch the end of peak fall color.'

Val nodded and scanned the park, taking a few more mental notes. She'd done quite a few engagement shoots here so she was already familiar with the layout, but she didn't want to leave anything to chance, and Autumn needed more than just the bog-standard engagement shoot. She contemplated the bridge above the creek but ruled it out immediately – too shady – and then did her best to envision Autumn and Caleb sitting at one of the picnic tables on the nearby restaurant's terrace, wondering if that would be too casual or just the right amount of low-key.

'Val?' Autumn asked, and Val snapped out of her shoot-planning reverie. 'I said, how are you handling everything? Your follower count has ballooned, and I know that can be kind of intimidating.'

Val was strangely touched that Autumn was monitoring her

Instagram follower count and worried about her newfound semi-fame. All it took was one public post of the photo Livvy took, plus one comment by Josh, and Val went from a respectable-but-not-impressive follower count to something much, much larger. It wasn't anything approaching Autumn's level – she had something like over two-hundred thousand – but Val's count had tripled in the past two weeks. Nick knew his mom had seen the post – she had sent him an annoyed text about it – but now there were people with names like Jakeymyman and Idriveafordbrother going through photos Val had posted two years ago leaving comments like *What's he like in bed*, which: gross.

Not that the idea of sleeping with Nick was gross. He was hot and a decent human, and unfortunately Val had already slept with men a lot worse than that. It was more the invasiveness of saying it to a total stranger that grossed her out, and she understood why he had run as far away as he could from that.

'It's fine,' Val said, stuffing her hands into the pockets of her motorcycle jacket. There was a hole in the lining, and she rubbed the frayed edge between her thumb and forefinger absently. 'A weird number of people think I'm a studio plant? He told me to expect that, but I really didn't think *that many* people would think I've got secret Hollywood connections.'

Autumn gave her a knowing smile. 'Have they started trying to track down your family members to prove it?'

Val was doing her best to stay out of it, but late last night she had fallen down a rabbit hole, jumping from commenter to commenter. She'd somehow ended up on 'Stan Twitter' which was, quite frankly, a terrifying place to be. People had incredibly, incredibly strong opinions about the stars of a show that had been off the air for a decade, and even stronger opinions about her. Val had learned a surprising amount about herself, ninety percent of it completely made up. They had, of course, discovered BridalNippleGate and the subsequent trashing by the bride's family, which some of them seemed to have taken as an indication she wasn't really a photographer, but a studio employee pretending to be a photographer, because no *real* photographer would have made that mistake. If one of them figured out their relationship was fake, Nick's mom and Universal Streaming would know within twenty-four hours, she was sure of it.

'I have a step-cousin who works for a catering company in LA that sometimes works events held by the studio that produced *Just Us Girls* a million years ago, so naturally she's part of that diabolical plan,' Val said. 'Given that I met her once at her mom's wedding to my uncle, she'd probably be pretty surprised to find that out.'

Autumn touched her arm briefly. 'You can turn off the comments on your posts if they get too invasive or weird.'

Val did know that, but turning off the comments would make it harder to monitor how believable their relationship seemed. Obviously, she couldn't tell Autumn that. 'It's fine,' she said again. 'Honestly, most of them are positive.'

That was true, at least. The number of fans who were convinced this was part of some conspiracy was limited and they seemed to exist in their own incredibly intense echo chamber. And to be fair, Val and Nick dating *was* part of a conspiracy, just a much smaller, much stupider one than they thought.

'Okay, good,' Autumn said, and then grinned. 'Because when we first met and you said you had a boyfriend, I had no idea you were dating *Nick Ford*. I spent like, *so* much of my childhood in love with him and Josh. Locker shrine, a Tumblr dedicated entirely to them and *Just Us Girls*, all of it. I don't want to be creepy, but – what's he like?'

'He's fine.' She shrugged. 'That came out weird,' she amended, because *he's fine* sounded like something she would say about a random guy she met at a party, not a boyfriend. 'I'm not great at sentimental stuff, but he's thoughtful, you know? He notices stuff about me, stuff no one else does.'

The lie came out more easily than she thought it would, and then she realized it wasn't really a lie. Nick did notice things about her, like that morning when he had handed her a cup of coffee after she stumbled into the kitchen. It was stronger than he usually made it, and when she commented on that he'd simply shrugged. 'You like it better that way,' he had replied shyly, which had done something absurd to her stomach.

No. She was *not* thinking about that right now. She had to keep her shit together.

Autumn made a high-pitched squealing noise that reached a register only dogs could hear. 'I always thought he'd be a good boyfriend! I always knew he was a sweetie, but I mean – that's just so adorable and awesome! That I was right; he's a darling.'

Val smiled hesitantly, because that was – a lot. Genuine, but a lot. 'He really is kind.'

Autumn clapped her hands excitedly. 'We should double-date some time, like I awkwardly tried to set up before! You and Cal are already friends. You can tell Nick I promise not to go all fangirl on him.'

Val's stomach jolted like she'd missed a stair. 'Oh, um, I'd have to talk to Nick about that. He's, uh, not great with new people.'

'I promise not to be weird, okay? I won't even bring up how heartbroken I was when Crystal moved to Florida and broke up with Jakey.'

Val snorted. 'Trust me, it's not you. He's just shy.'

'That is incredibly cute. And I love how protective you are of him,' Autumn said, leading Val toward the small stone bridge over the creek. 'I'm sorry fans are being weird. Some are just – I don't know, they just don't get boundaries. It's like we're not real people, just paper dolls for them to fight over, you know? And it sucks. And yes, I hear the irony of me saying that when I was just flailing about Nick Ford, but in my defense, my intense fan stage was mostly limited to a really cringe Tumblr.'

Val chuckled, but Autumn's sympathy made her feel terrible. She was such a sweet person, even just in their few interactions. Always willing to laugh at herself and thinking about how Val – a person who was only her photographer, and who she hadn't even officially worked with yet – felt about internet drama. Lying to her was crappy, but then again it wasn't about her, it was about Caleb. If Caleb hadn't lied about how he knew Val, she wouldn't be in this mess.

Really, it was all his fault. She needed to remember that. Everything was Caleb's fault.

'Thanks. And you know what, I'll talk to Nick,' she said impulsively, and then wanted to kick herself. 'See if we can make that double-date happen.'

'Oh yay, really?' Autumn squealed. 'Oh my god, this is going to be so much fun.'

Val wished she could believe her.

Chapter Nine

'Uh, Nick?' Val's slightly muffled voice followed two short, soft knocks on his door. 'There's something I need to talk to you about.'

Nick's heart jumped and he dropped the T-shirt he was about to pull on, swinging the door open as fast as he could. 'What's wrong?' he said, anxiety clawing at his ribcage. 'If I did something to make you uncomfortable –' He stopped at the look on her face, which didn't look upset so much as shocked. 'Val?'

She jerked her eyes from his chest to his face, and Nick belatedly realized that he still hadn't put his shirt on. 'Um, are you going to get dressed? Or are we doing it like this? Because I can take mine off too, if that's the vibe we're going with,' she said, snapping back to attention.

Nick snorted and snatched the white undershirt from the edge of his bed. 'It's not my fault. You said we needed to talk, which is universally agreed to be the worst way to start a conversation.'

Val stepped past him and settled cross-legged on his bed, like that was a normal thing they did and not the first time she'd ever been in his room. Even on her brief tour the day she moved in she hadn't done more than glance in from the hallway. 'It's true, though. There's something I need to talk to you about.'

Nick finished pulling the shirt down and Val swallowed hard, looking away. 'What's wrong?'

'Nothing's wrong, it's just – Autumn wants to go on a double-date.'

'With us?'

'No, with Mulder and Scully. Yes, of course with us.'

'Never pegged you for an *X-Files* fan,' Nick said, smothering a grin. He sat down in his desk chair, a distant part of his brain wondering why this interaction felt so much less fraught than their previous ones. Maybe the dance had unlocked something in him; or maybe he was just finally getting used to her. His anxiety usually calmed down a bit around people he'd known for a while.

'My sister is like six years older than me and would take a bullet for Dana Scully. Everything I know about *X-Files* I learned through osmosis.' She tilted her head to the side and her hair fell down over her shoulder like a waterfall. 'And am I imagining things, or are you trying to distract me from my original question?'

'Technically, you never asked a question.'

She rolled her eyes, but she was grinning. 'Fine. Would you go on a double-date with me and Autumn and Caleb?'

'A double-date with your client and your ex, who we are currently lying to?'

'Well, when you put it that way, it sounds bad.'

'Yeah, the fault is definitely in the phrasing. Why did you and Caleb break up?'

'Does it matter?'

'If I have to drive all the way to Minneapolis and eat a whole meal with him, yeah.'

'Autumn wants to come here, as a matter of fact.'

'Fine, if I have to eat a whole meal with him, I'd still like to know why you broke up.'

She shrugged, picking at her cuticle. 'We were just on and off a lot. Eventually I got tired of it, and then we were off for good. I don't really do relationships, basically. I tend to run, rather than stick around.'

'You dumped him?' Nick wasn't sure why that mattered but suddenly, it did. He didn't like the idea of Val pining over someone else.

'It was messy,' was all she said. 'But you'll do it?'

There were a dozen things Nick wanted to say, and probably a dozen more that they should discuss. Stuff like *What are your expectations for me on this date, do you want to be very couple-y, we should really lay some ground rules for this, do you expect me to kiss you or anything, not that that would be bad but I should really know upfront, maybe that would be weird to kiss in front of other people never mind*; but instead he just nodded.

Val tugged her jacket closed against the brisk wind, and Nick fought the urge to offer her his scarf. The morning sun hadn't quite started warming things up yet as they walked toward the park. Being friends with a married couple with a kid meant opportunities to hang out were pretty much limited to 'go to the park with them in the morning,' so here they were, going to the park in the morning to hang out with Aaron, Pete, and Felix. Pete had texted yesterday to ask if they wanted to hang out, and Val had declared it the perfect opportunity to practice for the double-date.

Nick cleared his throat, deciding that now was as good of a

time as any. 'I've been thinking – between this and the double-date coming up, we should probably have a more thorough cover story about how we got together.'

'I started as your roommate, and then we started hooking up. Simplest explanation, hardest to disprove.'

'And so romantic,' he deadpanned. 'But we should probably also, you know – know things about each other.'

'You alphabetize your books, what more is there to know?'

'They're alphabetized by genre, thank you very much.'

'That's worse,' Val said, fighting a grin.

Nick ducked his head and looked away, to keep her from seeing him smile back. It was better if he kept up his grumpy front with her, to keep the distance safe between them, but that was getting harder by the day. 'I think the big thing is – how much is okay with you? I know we held hands, and it's not like there's going to be much call for PDA at the park with Felix, but when we're on a double-date – I just don't want to cross any lines.'

Val shrugged, her hands jammed into the pockets of her leather jacket. 'I guess I don't really mind? You're not a creep, and you're better at acting than I am, anyway, so I can just follow your lead.' She paused and looked up at him thoughtfully. 'What about you?'

Nick turned the corner and she followed suit. 'Honestly, I got used to people touching me on set. It doesn't bother me.'

'Really? I'd think it would bother you more,' Val said shrewdly.

'The people who had to touch me were always just doing their job. Hair, makeup, other actors, that sort of thing, and I was lucky – we had a good set with decent people, so I never really felt uncomfortable when it came to that. I felt uncomfortable about everything else, but that's one thing that I never really minded.'

'So, what I'm getting here is neither of us have boundaries, but we probably should figure out what level we want to go with,' Val said, nodding ahead toward the playground, still about half a block away. Pete was holding Felix up at the top of a slide, while Aaron sat off to the side on a bench, a tray of coffees waiting.

'I'm okay with handholding,' Nick said. 'And like – arms around each other.'

'Same. But I'm not a good enough actress to handle kissing.'

Nick had been about to suggest the same thing, but it stung nonetheless. But if it stung, that meant – no, he wasn't going to let himself go there. It only hurt because he was doing his old acting trick and lying to himself, to make it feel less like he was lying to the people he cared about. That was all, because that was all it *could* be.

'What made you leave Hollywood?' Caleb asked, and look, he was pleasant enough. He seemed like your average white guy real estate agent; outgoing and charming enough, if a little bland. Nick couldn't see him being with Val, though. She was all sharp corners and snarls and claws, and Caleb was... cardboard.

Soggy cardboard, even.

'Honestly, I just didn't like acting,' Nick said, and decided to mimic Caleb's posture. He had one arm slung casually behind Autumn – she was busy taking a photo of the milkshake she'd ordered for dessert while Val held up a menu to 'get the lighting right' – so Nick did the same, resting his arm on the back of the booth. A real boyfriend would probably show some casual, limited affection. 'Being a librarian suits me a lot better.'

'You didn't want to direct, or anything like that?' Caleb

asked. He struck Nick as the sort of man who was always striving, wanting something better than he had and looking down on those with the nerve to simply be content.

'Never really got the appeal.' In theory he did understand it, of course, because being an actor meant having your literal every move directed by someone else, and when actors *wanted to get into directing* that usually meant they were craving more control over their lives. It was understandable, but Nick had never wanted that sort of responsibility. He preferred dealing with cranky patrons over entitled actors any day, because usually the cranky patrons could be placated and there weren't millions of dollars riding on his ability to calm them down.

Autumn nodded to Val, seemingly satisfied with her picture. Autumn was outgoing and cheerful, although she had that look in her eye that fans sometimes got when they were working overtime to restrain themselves. Val had warned him that Autumn had been a huge *Just Us Girls* fan. 'I told her if she said "But what about Jakey?" at this dinner you would probably have a rage stroke, so she's promised to be cool,' Val had explained on their way over, much to his relief. Nick was coming to realize that Val could be fiercely protective of people, and he appreciated that more than he probably should.

They were out on the Happy Pig's rooftop deck, taking in what was probably the last pleasant fall evening before it got too cold. Above them a string of old-fashioned lightbulbs looped along the slats of the pergola, while a breeze off the river ruffled Val's hair. The door to the deck opened and the vague sounds of a couple being led to their table punctuated the brief silence. 'This place is adorable,' Autumn said. 'In fact, the whole town is. And what about that coffee shop we passed on the way in? I love it and I haven't even been inside yet.'

'Next time you're here, coffee's on the house,' Aaron said

from the table directly behind Nick. 'Sorry, didn't mean to interrupt, but that's my husband's shop.'

Pete blushed and shook his head fondly. 'Leave them alone, Aaron,' he chided.

'I did love the look of it, though,' Autumn said, craning her neck to talk to them over Nick's shoulder. Meanwhile, Caleb pushed sulkily at the remains of his steak with a fork. 'Next time I'm here, I'll definitely swing by.'

'Please do,' Pete said.

The server arrived to take Pete and Aaron's drink order, and Autumn turned her attention to Nick. 'You never told me how you two met,' she said, flipping her phone face down on the table.

Val leaned back, glancing sideways at Nick when she realized where his arm was. 'I needed a place to live, and he needed a roommate,' she said.

'In Swede River?' Caleb asked.

Val shifted. 'I also wanted to get away from the Cities for a while,' she said in a sugary tone that to Nick, sounded dangerous.

Caleb must have picked up on it because he turned to interrogating Nick instead. 'Don't you have a lot of money? Like, from working your entire childhood?'

Next to him Val tensed. She curled her hand into a fist, but Nick kept his face neutral while Autumn elbowed Caleb. 'That's rude,' she said playfully. 'Sorry about that. Sometimes Cal's just a little blunt about money.'

'Nick lost it all playing poker with me,' Aaron called. Pete raised his eyebrows at his husband, who shrugged sheepishly. 'I wasn't eavesdropping. It's a small space and we're the only ones here.'

'I lost ten dollars to you three years ago and you're never

going to let me forget it, are you?' Nick replied, twisting slightly to look at his friends.

'It was fifteen dollars, thank you very much.' At another look from Pete, Aaron sighed. 'Sorry, sorry, butting out now.'

Autumn giggled and waved to Pete and Aaron. 'They're fun,' she observed.

'More fun when they're not taking your money,' Nick muttered. He didn't gamble often – it reminded him too much of his dad – but every now and then Pete and Aaron hosted a game night in their small apartment above the café. The arrival of Felix had put a pause on those indefinitely, but Nick was just now realizing how much he missed those evenings. The morning at the park had been fun and easier than he thought it would be, which just made him feel lonelier. Val was starting to fit into his life, he realized, and that made it easier to keep pretending, but it also made it a little harder for him to remember it was all just pretend.

Despite the levity, Val's hand was fisted under the table so tightly her knuckles were turning white. He rested his hand over hers, silently willing her to understand that he wasn't *that* bothered by Caleb. He'd met way worse people in LA. Hell, his *mother* was worse people. Caleb was a run-of-the-mill asshole; Candace Ford would eat him for breakfast and pick her teeth with his bones.

'To answer your question, the show is exclusively streaming now, instead of in broadcast syndication, and residuals are a lot lower from streaming than broadcast,' he said with an easy shrug. *And my asshole parents took most of what we made originally and then wasted it all divorcing each other.* The trusts he and Josh had been left at the end of the run were decent, but nowhere near enough to cover college, grad school, and Josh's repeated catastrophes. Those had been long depleted for both of them.

'And I'm glad to see you getting your business back on its feet, Valerie,' Caleb said, shifting his ice blue eyes to her. 'You always were a very talented photographer.'

On the surface, it was a perfectly polite thing to say to an ex or an old college acquaintance, depending on what version of Caleb and Val's past someone knew. But Val was still strung as tightly as a bowstring. Nick gently loosened her fingers and wove his in-between. It felt good to touch her, probably better than he was even willing to admit to himself.

'Thanks,' she said tightly, but her shoulders relaxed infinitesimally. 'Stupid question,' she said, turning to Autumn with a fairly forced laugh. 'Is there a reason you're not posting that milkshake picture? Because we don't mind if you need to get it up now.'

Autumn noisily slurped the last of her milkshake. 'I never post anything when I'm out,' she said cheerfully. 'People can get a little invasive, and if they know where I am they try to like, come say hi. You probably know about that,' she added, looking at Nick. She looked cozy leaning against Caleb's side and again, on the surface it made sense, why she was with him. But Caleb would have set Nick's antennae prickling even if it weren't for the fact that he clearly stressed Val out beyond belief. Autumn seemed genuine, while Caleb didn't have any depth. They looked good together, but that was about it.

'Social media wasn't really a huge thing for most of my time in Hollywood,' Nick said. 'But yeah, Josh has had a few close encounters. For a few years there our agent kept control of the passwords to keep him from saying anything too dumb or accidentally starting a commotion at the Grove.' Val let out a quiet, slow breath, and Nick realized he had been drawing circles on her palm with his thumb. She relaxed against him, and across the table Autumn made that frown-pout people tended to make when they saw kittens.

'Awww, look at you two,' she said. 'You're so cute. Aren't they cute, Cal?'

'So cute,' Aaron agreed.

'Oh my god, I cannot take you anywhere, can I?' Pete interjected. 'Once again, sorry about that.'

Caleb looked irritated, which in turn irritated Nick. Sure, Aaron was being nosy, but that was part of the territory with a small town. Everyone was all up in each other's business, which stressed Nick out at first, but now he had come to appreciate it. Just about everyone in Swede River knew who he was, but they were also fiercely protective of his privacy. He'd once seen Pete claim he didn't have a TV and had never seen a single television show to a tourist who was asking about him, when he knew for a fact Pete's main hobby was 'watching TV and arguing about it on the internet.'

Caleb cleared his throat and gazed at Val and Nick for a long moment, and Nick could have sworn there was a flash of jealousy in his eyes. 'It's just wild to see, is all. Valerie Costa, settled down. Never thought we'd see the day.'

'Really?' Nick asked. He didn't bother to hide the ice in his tone. 'Why's that?'

'Oh, just – she's Val, that's all. She was always . . .' Caleb seemed to realize he was treading on dangerous territory and stammered for a minute. 'Just not that into commitment.'

'Maybe she just needed to find the right person,' Nick replied, and looked down at Val with as much fondness as he could muster. Which as it turned out, was an awful lot.

'I got really lucky, finding Nick when I did,' she said, and the way she was gazing into his eyes, her smile soft and clear, Nick almost thought she meant it.

Chapter Ten

Linds
Okay where are we meeting again?

Val
The cider stand

Linds
No, what's the name of the orchard? I know you sent it to me in our other chat but like hell I'm searching back through that mess

And don't say Apples Cider Cheese Fudge, ALL apple orchards have the same damn sign

Val
Apples Cider Pie Fudge

Linds
VALERIE NICOLA COSTA, STOP IT

Val
It's off State Highway 59, just past the sign for Kildahl College

Also I thought you were the responsible one? How can you not remember this?

Linds
My brain is full
If you'd like some organic chem downloaded into your brain then maybe I'll have space for dumb stuff like 'the name of the apple orchard'

Val reread her texts with Lindsey for the fifteenth time, realizing belatedly that she hadn't actually given her friend the name of the orchard, just the general location. Now she was going to have to hope there was only one apple orchard just outside Swede River, or else she was going to have to have a supremely awkward conversation with Nick – or at least a conversation that was even more awkward than their usual ones.

Because their brilliant plan was only half working. Sure, the town believed them, and Autumn and Caleb seemed to buy it, although Caleb had looked at her a little too suspiciously during their double-date for her to be completely comfortable there. But Nick's mom was another story. She was texting him constantly, reminding him that there was *a lot on the line* if he refused to do the dating show, and arguing that Nick couldn't possibly be that serious about a woman he'd known for not even three months. *You could always explain the situation to her and tell her you need to take a break. No reason you couldn't get back together after shooting wraps up, and if you meet someone better it's a win–win. And think of how much money is on the line*, one of Candace Ford's texts to her own son had read. Val's family wasn't the best – there was a reason she only saw them a handful of times per year – but at least they wouldn't try and convince her to break up with someone for their own financial gain. The bar could not be lower, but still.

Candy wasn't their only issue, however. Nick had a small but dedicated remaining fanbase, and someone had gone so far as to submit a 'tip' that they weren't really dating to Ohyesss, a fan-sourced gossip Instagram that published both utterly bogus and completely legit rumors and sightings. It was just a place where fans and disgruntled and/or gossipy crew members could send random rumors and candids of celebrities they'd taken on the streets.

Now rumors were everywhere, including one that Val had an OnlyFans (she didn't, but it seemed 'dark haired white woman' was the only criteria that fan was using) and thus must have been hired to play his girlfriend. She had no objections to people thinking she was a sex-worker, but the fact that the internet still wasn't buying the relationship was a problem. And of course, Candy had immediately sent a link to the Ohyesss story to Nick, apparently under the impression that if fans thought he had a studio-plant girlfriend it would look 'better' if he ended that relationship and did what she wanted. Nick had gotten an email from a producer attached to the show shortly after that post, urging him to *consider his options*, which Nick took as proof that they were also monitoring his relationship with Val. She personally thought that was a little far-fetched and the timing was a coincidence, but either way, Nick felt like they needed to step it up.

Josh had been the one to suggest using Ohyesss in return. Since Ohyesss had several million followers and didn't bother to vet any of their stories, it was the easiest place to plant a story and let it catch fire. If Nick was right and it wasn't just his mother monitoring the rumors about them but the studio, too, one persuasive submission to Ohyesss could go a long way toward convincing everyone they needed to convince.

Thus the apple orchard.

Or more specifically, meeting Linds at the orchard and having her take what would hopefully look like candid photos of them acting like a couple and then submitting them to Ohyesss. It was more aggressive and involved than she'd initially planned, but the last thing she wanted to do was make *more* problems for Nick.

It was weird, that impulse. Not one of her usual ones. Val made messes. She didn't clean them up, and she certainly didn't clean them up for other people, literally or metaphorically. But Nick brought out a protective side of her that she never realized she had. When he had shown her the texts from Candy, Val had had to remind herself that stealing Nick's phone and texting *What is wrong with you?* to his mom would just stress him out more and wouldn't fix anything. Then again, Val didn't need Candy to like her, she just needed Candy to believe they were together, and an angry text from Val might help sell that. Val filed that thought away for future reference.

Next to her, Nick had his hands in his pockets as he rocked back and forth on the balls of his feet. 'It's not like her to be late,' Val said, scanning the crowd.

So far it was mostly young families and groups of women in their early twenties in flannel shirts, giant scarves, and knee-high boots. There was one woman about their age who seemed to be eyeing them, but when Val looked back at her she'd melted into the crowd. Autumn had done a shoot here last fall, which was where Val got the idea – it was busy enough that someone might feasibly see them and take a few stalker photos, but also low-key enough that it would be more plausible they were just hanging out there with her friend. It also attracted a fair number of tourists from the Twin Cities, which increased the likelihood of someone who didn't feel overly protective of Nick's privacy noticing them.

Nick shrugged and looked at his feet. Val decided to give up trying to make stilted conversation and just wait until Linds got there – at least Lindsey didn't think she was a constant fuck-up. Fortunately, Val spotted Linds's light brown hair and the pressure in her chest eased slightly.

Linds was here. Things were about to get easier.

Val waved and Lindsey waved back, waiting politely for a family with three identical blonde girls to go past her before charging over to them. 'Oh my god, hi,' Linds said, gathering her into a familiar hug. 'I've missed you so much,' she added into Val's hair. 'Whose stupid idea was it for me to go to med school in California?'

'Yours,' Val deadpanned, pulling back and wiping away an errant tear. She never cried, but Lindsey always brought out her soft side. 'We have a perfectly good med school right here, you know.'

'I know, but Minnesota also has *winter*.' Linds made a face and turned to Nick, holding out her hand. 'Lindsey Strachowski,' she said brightly. 'You must be Nick.'

Nick hesitated for the barest of seconds, and Val knew he was trying to make it fit. Linds was the stereotypical image of a nerd: plain brown hair in a ponytail, sensible glasses, sensible shoes, and a sweater. Val hadn't told him much about her, but given their sharp differences in style it wasn't surprising that he needed a moment. Linds always looked like she should be carrying a heavy stack of books and lecturing someone about proper grammar, and meanwhile Val looked like someone who had almost failed sixth grade English, because she was.

Linds and Val had been friends since then, when Lindsey had offered to tutor her in exchange for Val's help in Ceramics. (Val still had Linds's lone solo attempt at a mug in her bedroom; it was hideously ugly and also her favorite piece of art, ever.) Her laugh and easy acceptance of all of Val's flaws had quickly earned her a place in Val's heart, even if Linds's grades were far too reminiscent of Christine's overachieving ass for comfort.

Lindsey moving to San Francisco had been incredibly painful, although Val wasn't about to tell her that. Val had briefly thought about joining her, but the idea of having to pay rent in the Bay Area on her freelance photographer barely-a-salary had quashed that idea before it was fully formed. Besides, Linds had been so excited about her chance to start over in a place where she was completely anonymous that Val didn't want to ruin that by being codependent.

Nick finally shook her hand and Linds flashed him a mile-wide smile. 'Let's pick some apples and take some stalker photos, yeah?' She was doing an excellent job of hiding the fact that at one point she knew Nick's entire astrological chart, as well as his brother's favorite color, food, and movie.

Nick smiled shyly, and obligingly fell into step beside Linds. She had her arm threaded through Val's, giving her yet another quick cuddle as they walked. 'Val said you're in ... med school?' Nick asked, and Val wondered if he thought she had been lying to him or something.

'At UCSF,' Lindsey confirmed, picking up a basket and striding toward the row of trees. 'And I hear you're pretending to date my best friend?'

To her surprise, Nick took Linds's bluntness in his stride. 'That's the idea, anyway,' he said, taking the basket from her hand and letting them both go in front of him. There was an unconscious chivalry to his actions that made Val's chest tighten, so of course it also annoyed her. It wasn't fair. Men shouldn't be that good. Most weren't, granted, but it irritated her when Nick was better than the rest.

It also sort of bothered her that he was getting along easily with Linds, because it just underscored that the problem was, as always, her. He'd gotten all weird after their double date ended, refusing to come within two feet of her – doing stupid things like 'waiting in his doorway for her to walk past' when there was plenty of space in the hallway. Then they'd gone on that date, and he'd been good – great, even – at pretending to adore her, but as soon as they got home, he went back to his usual stiff, stick-up-his-ass grumpy self, and the message was very clear: whatever she had felt between them was completely in her head, and he didn't want a repeat.

Which was fine with her, because she had far too much experience of being with a seemingly perfect guy who was terminally conflict-avoidant. Nick was twice the man Caleb was, but Val didn't want to risk becoming Nick's bad idea he just couldn't quit. It hurt badly enough when it was Caleb, and Val was already sure her heart couldn't take history repeating itself with Nick.

Lindsey stopped at a tree and pulled down a few apples, tossing them carelessly into Nick's basket. 'Wait, we're doing this, right? Actually picking apples? Or is this just a photo op?'

'We're doing both,' Val assured her, and plucked one that had a misshapen growth around the stem. *Of course I would pick the fucked-up apple*, she thought bitterly, and placed it gently in the basket. It wasn't the apple's fault it was messed up, after all. Both Nick and Linds seemed to be looking to her for instructions, since she was the one involved with the most experience setting up photoshoots. She stopped ruminating on the apples and cleared her throat. 'I was thinking we take a few of the three of us just hanging out – get someone to take one, then maybe a few of each of us in various combinations. Then we can do the paparazzi-ish stuff in the corn maze. It'd make more sense for us to be, um, a little more affectionate there.' Val had been hesitant to broach the idea with Nick, but he had been more receptive than she would have assumed.

'Then let's get to it,' Lindsey declared and immediately grabbed Nick's arm and tugged him against her with an exaggerated, open-mouth smile and her free arm thrown into the air.

To Val's everlasting shock, Nick tossed his arm around Linds's back and grinned without a second thought. She took a few more pictures of them, and then Linds swapped and took a few simple shots of Val and Nick – talking with their heads close together, Val reaching for an apple on her tiptoes and Nick getting it for her, and then one staged one where their arms were around each other's backs, smiling at the camera like it was just a quick snapshot documenting their adorable, couple-y trip to the orchard. Val was going to upload those to her Instagram to bolster what would go to Ohyesss, but the real purpose was in the corn maze.

First, though, they needed to make this look like a real trip a couple and their friend took to an apple orchard. There was a hay bale with several pumpkins set up on either side of it, clearly a ready-made family photo set-up, so Val led her group that way. She flagged down a passing dad and held up her phone. 'Mind taking a picture for us?' she asked, and as expected, he readily nodded. Val positioned herself to Nick's left, with Linds already on his right, and Nick draped his arms around them both. It felt very natural, which was *unnatural*, in her opinion.

The man lowered her phone and peered at the pictures.

'I think I got some good ones,' he said, handing it back over. He was about to go and join his wife and daughter when he paused, looking at Nick with a puzzled frown. 'Wait, did we go to high school together? You look familiar.'

Nick shook his head. 'I grew up in California. Just one of those faces; I get it a lot,' he said.

It took longer than expected to find a section of the corn maze that was suitably deserted. The shots had to seem secretive, like neither Val nor Nick knew someone was there. Nick was notoriously private, after all – this had to look like an unexpected coup for a fan, catching a glimpse of him with Val when they thought they were alone.

It had all been Val's idea, so it made no sense that once they were in the maze, her courage failed her. One of the few things she had going for her was that she had generally perfected the art of seeming to not give a damn when she, in fact, gave several. But when Nick turned to her and asked if she was ready, suddenly she wasn't.

'Sure,' she lied, carefully avoiding Linds's razor-sharp gaze.

'Are you sure? Because we don't have to go through with this,' Nick said, his brown eyes unexpectedly soft. Somehow, that made her nerves worse.

'It's fine, let's just do this,' she said, tossing her hair over her shoulder. She wished it was a little colder so she could have worn her favorite motorcycle jacket. She always felt a little better in that, like it was armor against the world. As it stood, she was going to have to make do in her thin crewneck sweatshirt.

Val stalked to their chosen corner and lifted her chin, defiant. What she was defying, she couldn't say, but it helped. Nick stood in front of her, shielding her from Lindsey. 'Seriously, we can just bail,' he offered.

Of course he's trying to get out of kissing me. 'Like I said, it's fine,' Val said. 'But you should move, you're blocking her angle.'

'I know,' he said firmly. 'Because you're clearly freaking out, and I want to be sure you're okay first.'

'I'm *fine*,' she insisted, but when he went to put his hand on her waist, she flinched.

'Easy,' Nick said lowly, removing his hand. 'I'm just going to move you so she can see you better, okay?'

She didn't need him to stage the shoot – that was literally her job – but she let him guide her a few steps to her left anyway. Her back was up against the hay bales that lined this section of the maze, Nick directly in front of her. 'Put your arms around my neck,' Nick said in that same soft, soothing tone. She did as she was told, her heart pounding so loudly they could probably hear it back in the orchard. 'Now I'm going to put my hands on your waist, okay?'

Val nodded and sucked in a sharp breath when his hands went around the dip of her waist, his large hands spanning from the top of her hip up to the bottom of her ribcage. 'Easy, girl,' he said again.

'I'm not a horse,' she said with a weird, breathless laugh that sounded nothing like her.

'You aren't?' he said, and his gentle teasing coaxed another strained laugh out of her.

'How is this so easy for you?' she asked.

He shrugged and threw a tiny nod to Linds, who had been watching all of this with keen interest. There was no doubt that Val was going to get the third degree from her tonight. But that wasn't her problem right now. Her problem was a man with impossibly broad shoulders looming over her, looking down very intently. 'I've done this before,' he said vaguely.

'You've fake dated before?'

'I've kissed people I barely knew,' he said, moving a little closer. 'It's not that hard. Just – make yourself believe it.'

'Believe it,' she echoed, now trapped in that warm, brown gaze. She was drowning, or maybe breathing properly for the first time.

'Are you sure?' he asked quietly. 'You said before that kissing would be too much.'

'And I changed my mind,' she insisted, although *too much* was probably exactly what this was right now.

He leaned closer, just far enough that the tip of his nose brushed hers. She was breathing his air and the maze felt hot and claustrophobic, but instead of the urge to run she had the urge to burrow in, make this exact spot her home. 'That's all acting is; it's pretend,' he said, and just when she thought she might combust, he put his hand on her jaw, tilting her face up to his. 'I promise, it's nothing,' he said, and then he kissed her.

Oh god, did he *kiss* her. Val had been vaguely prepared for the sort of stage kiss they teach in freshman drama class, but maybe she should have specified what sort of kiss she was envisioning when she floated this stupid idea to Nick.

Because this wasn't a stage kiss; it was a real kiss. A kiss she felt down to her toes and up to her scalp, where his hand was now gently sliding into her hair. He nibbled softly at her lower lip, coaxing her mouth to open for him, something she gladly – and idiotically – did without a second thought. Her own hands were moving of their own accord, one tangling in his soft brown hair. Nick surged forward, holding her more tightly, and she let out a quiet, needy sound.

He chuckled against her lips and kissed her harder, both of his hands now holding her face, his tongue brushing hers. Val's limbs went liquid, her stomach reduced to a pack of shivery butterflies. Nick pulled back by barely a centimeter, and she chased him, not willing for this moment to end. Maybe she would get lucky, and the world would end right that very second, and then she'd never have to consciously stop kissing him.

From five feet away, Linds cleared her throat. 'Okay, um, I think we've got what we need, team,' she said.

Nick came to his senses first and jumped away from her, his hands fisting straight back into his pockets. Val licked her lips, not quite able to stop herself, and brushed her hair back from her face. Her breathing was all kinds of weird, and when she turned to face Linds, she knew she was in for it tonight.

Chapter Eleven

Nick waited until he could see Val and Lindsey climbing into Lindsey's black sedan with rental plates before he rested his forehead against the steering wheel, letting out a long, slow breath.

Because that – whatever the hell that had been – was not the plan. Not at *all*. Nick hadn't had as many onscreen kisses as Josh, but he'd had a few, and absolutely nothing compared to *that*.

He wasn't even sure what had come over him; he couldn't remember the last time he had felt that calm and confident, and he certainly couldn't remember the last time he'd flirted that easily with a woman he was about to kiss. But Val's nerves had flipped a switch inside of him. He didn't like seeing her like that; Val was brash and confident, not skittish and jittery.

It reminded him of why he had decided, against his better judgment and literally all possible evidence, to agree to have her become his roommate. Her employment history was checkered, her income was barely sufficient and frequently irregular, and she freely admitted she struggled with clutter and keeping her space clean. But within five minutes of meeting her, he had the sinking feeling that despite all of it, he was going to offer her the room. It wasn't just that Mary was pushing for it to happen – it was far simpler, and far worse than that.

Val needed him. That was it, at the core. She had screwed up in her job and she didn't seem to have anywhere else to go – in retrospect, he realized it must have been less than a year after Lindsey moved to California, and that would have made it all the harder for her.

And in the maze, just like that day at Pete's Coffee, he had known right then that Val needed him. Nick was good at being an anchor; it was his role with Josh. He planted his feet and let Josh whirl around him, and today Val needed his roots to ground her. And he understood why – kissing someone you didn't know well and certainly weren't attracted to was weird, but it was one of the few weird things he had direct experience with. Soothing her had felt like second nature, and then kissing her was even easier.

He needed to get himself together. Sure, that one kiss had made him feel more alive than he had in . . . honestly, he had no idea how long. Years, probably. Maybe ever? But it was unexpected, and Nick hated the unexpected. He liked predictable, comfortable, normal.

Val was none of those things. He needed to keep this clean; simple. Nothing good came of complications and falling for her would complicate just about everything.

Sure, fine, he liked kissing Val. And holding her hand. And touching her gently and casually during their double-date. That wasn't completely unexpected. She was pretty and she needed him, so of course he would feel protective of her. That was it. He was more than capable of shoving those minor feelings away, so that's what he would do.

His phone rang, startling him out of his stupor. He put it on speaker and shifted the car into drive.

'How'd it go?' Josh asked without preamble.

'How'd what go?'

Josh sighed, exasperated. 'Making out with your roommate to send pictures to a low-rent internet gossip site.'

'Fine.' There was a long line of cars to get out of the parking lot – not really a parking lot so much as a fallow field with some orange cones marking the exit lane – and Nick leaned back against the seat. 'It went fine. Just like when I had to kiss Luz that one time,' he lied.

Luz had played Crystal, their next-door neighbor on *Just Us Girls*, and Jakey had had a long-simmering crush on her. Nick and Josh had flipped a coin over who had to take the actual kissing scene – at twelve, neither of them was wild about their first kiss being onscreen – and Nick had lost. Luz was a good friend, but it was like kissing a sister, if he'd had one.

Josh made a noise like he didn't believe him. 'Except you haven't known her for six years, most of them during puberty where, let's be honest, none of us looked our best.'

'I live with her,' Nick said, redoubling his grip on the steering wheel and inching forward. 'It's the same thing.'

'It's really not, but sure,' Josh said. 'Are you okay?'

'Why wouldn't I be?'

'Because you sound like you're about three seconds away from ripping your steering wheel out of the dashboard.'

Nick rolled his eyes even though Josh couldn't see him. 'Why would I do that? It's not like I'm angry about anything.'

'No, you're not angry, you're freaking out.'

'Am not.'

'Are too,' Josh said in an equally petulant tone. 'I bet your knuckles are white, even if you're driving the way you always do.'

'And how's that?'

'Like a grandma.'

Nick's knuckles *were* white, but that was beside the point. 'I'm still not freaking out,' he insisted. He was, but that was also beside the point. It didn't matter how he felt, it mattered that people believed them. Specifically, their mother. Nick was getting sick of the daily texts, asking if he had reconsidered and reminding him of just how much money was at stake. Candy knew that would twist him up inside, which was exactly why she used it. When Nick had walked away from acting, their dad had walked away from all of them, leaving Candy and Josh with almost nothing.

'Okay, let's say you're not,' Josh replied. 'You still just made out with a woman you're attracted to. I doubt –'

'Who said I'm attracted to her?'

Josh snorted. 'Are you not? Because I've seen pictures of her, bro. She's hot.'

'You don't even like women.'

'No, I don't want to *sleep* with women. There's a difference. I am still perfectly capable of judging another human's attractiveness, just like you are. And don't try and distract me, because I'm not letting this go.'

'I'm not trying –'

'Yes, you are, shut up,' Josh argued. 'Are you, or are you not, attracted to Val?'

Nick was still two cars away from being able to exit onto the highway. 'She's pretty, sure.'

'Yes, we've established that. What I asked was, are you *attracted* to her?'

'What if I am? I'm not going to act on it.'

'Except you already are,' Josh countered. 'You literally just made out with her.'

'And?'

'And, I'm just saying. Kissing someone you're attracted to for reasons other than "we want to make out," would probably make anyone flip out a bit. Hell, it would make me flip out. And let's be real, I do a lot less flipping out than you do.'

'Well, someone needs to flip out when the situation warrants it.'

Josh sighed, sounding incredibly put-upon. Which was a bit rich coming from him. 'Once again, stop trying to sidetrack me. We're talking about you and Val.'

Nick echoed his sigh. 'Fine.'

'Fine. Now, I'm just trying to figure out if you're okay with this, or if it's gonna cause a crisis.'

Nick was already in a crisis, but it was too late to back out. They had already made out, and Val had already wormed her way into his heart. She didn't seem to want to be there, or at the very least, she was unaware of her presence.

He let out a long, slow breath. 'I'm okay with it,' he said, as calmly as he could. 'It's - it could get complicated, but I can handle it. And she's not attracted to me.' After the maze, Val had assiduously avoided eye contact with him, and had kept Lindsey between them at basically all times. She might have responded to his kiss, but she clearly didn't want anything more. 'We're both getting something we need out of this, and then we'll go our separate ways.'

'Are you sure?' Josh asked.

'Positive.'

'Okay, good, because we've got another issue. Jan's going to be sending you the stuff later, but I wanted to give you a heads-up - they want to do a reunion episode.'

'No,' Nick said flatly.

'Not like that, more like - just interviews. All of us on the old set, or whatever they can make up to look like the old set, I guess. I didn't ask about the set decor, to be honest. But they want to film it alongside the reboot.'

'Who's all in?'

'Sarah's in for sure,' Josh said. Sarah Wandsley had played their mom on *Just Us Girls*, but now mostly hosted Australian variety shows so she could be closer to her family. 'I know they're in talks with the rest of the cast, but you –'

'I'm the hardest one for them to get.' He sighed, thinking. Answering questions about his life was quite possibly his least favorite thing in the world, unless the questioner was Val. 'I don't love it, but – sure.' It would help out Josh, he reasoned, and anything that helped his brother on the path to financial stability was a good thing. He could handle one day of bright lights and questions.

'Thanks,' Josh said sincerely. 'And you're sure you're okay?'

'I'm fine,' Nick said, and he meant that with every fiber of his being. Because if they had to keep doing stunts like this, he wasn't sure his heart could take it.

Chapter Twelve

'Were you going to make dinner?' Val almost didn't hear Nick's question, what with her head buried in the fridge as she searched for something that both belonged to her and was edible. She was, unsurprisingly, coming up empty.

'I was going to eat something, yeah,' she replied, closing the fridge and starting what was probably a fruitless search through the pantry. *Make dinner* was an exceedingly charitable way to describe her process, but Val was coming to realize that Nick phrased things that way, not to mock her, like Caleb might have, but to be, well, nice.

She still wasn't quite used to that. Over near the stove, Nick shuffled his feet. 'I made chili this weekend and I have plenty, if you . . .?'

Val let his question hang in the air for a moment. 'If I what?'

'Do you want to eat some? With me?'

'You know, you're pretty awkward around me considering we're dating.'

Nick huffed out a laugh and started dishing out the chili, which honestly smelled close to heavenly. 'Yeah, I wonder why anyone would be apprehensive about asking you something, given how warm and cuddly you are,' he said, and Val had to do her best to hide the smile that wanted to spread across her face.

'Come on, I don't bite,' she teased. 'Not unless I'm asked.' About four seconds too late she realized that was probably crossing a line and opened her mouth to apologize.

But Nick beat her to it. 'I'll keep that in mind,' he said, and if she didn't know any better, she'd think he was flirting.

She took a seat on a stool at the breakfast bar and took a bite. 'Oh my god, this is amazing,' Val moaned, immediately going back for more. After her fourth giant bite she frowned down at her bowl, poking the spoon back and forth. Several things fell into place. 'Are you a vegetarian?'

'Yeah,' Nick said with a shrug, taking his own bite. 'Since I was a kid. Twelve maybe?'

The breakfast bar in the kitchen wasn't very long, and Nick's broad shoulders almost touched hers as they ate. 'Why?' she asked.

'Never really liked meat,' he replied with another shrug. 'And it's better for the environment.'

Personally, Val wouldn't be able to survive without the occasional hamburger, but she respected his stance. And his chili was incredible.

From his pocket, Nick's phone chimed with an incoming text, followed immediately by three more. 'You can answer that if you need to,' Val offered, even though she suspected she knew who was texting and exactly why he was ignoring it.

'There's no point, it's just Candace.'

'Did the Ohyesss photos help?' Val asked, looking into her bowl instead of making eye contact with him. If she did, she might blush.

'I assume that's what these are about,' he said. At Val's

pointed silence he acquiesced and pulled out his phone, reading in silence before sliding it over to her. 'Could have been worse, I guess?'

Mom
Looks like you had an eventful weekend.

I know you're trying to convince me the show isn't worth it, but let's be realistic about this. Joshy let it slip that you're helping him financially, and we all know how expensive that can get. A reality show would pay better than whatever you're making reading books, and all you'd have to do is drop some dead weight.

The studio is still fully on board. All we need is your signature.
Think about it.

Val's eyebrows hit her hairline. 'Whatever you're making *reading books*? Is she for real?'

Nick shrugged, resigned. 'Yes, she is. But I thought you'd be more upset about the "dead weight" comment.'

'I don't care what your mom thinks of me,' Val said, although she wasn't going to pretend that it didn't hurt a little. She had thick skin, but she wasn't made out of steel. 'Want me to tell her to go fuck herself? I will,' she offered. 'In fact, I think I should. That would sell it, wouldn't it? If I was really offended by what she said?'

Nick yanked his phone out of her hands. 'There's nothing to be gained by fighting with her.'

'Is that why you won't just tell her no?' Val asked, her mouth moving faster than her brain. 'I mean – crap, I didn't mean it like that,' she stammered. 'I just mean, you know, maybe standing up to her a bit more might change things.'

Nick surveyed her closely. 'Because you're so good at standing up to your own family?'

'What do you even know about my family?' she asked defensively.

'When you first moved in, you said it was that or living with your sister, and you said, and I quote, "I'd rather get a root canal than live with Christine." You don't come by that level of hostility without a lot of baggage.'

'Maybe my sister is just even more of a neat freak than you.'

'Doubt it,' he said, with more humor than she would have expected, considering he was reading her the riot act. He pocketed his phone and turned back to his chili. 'But trust me, engaging with Candy is a losing proposition. For everyone.'

Val was sorely tempted to point out that by pretending to date her, he was, on some level, engaging with her, but she also didn't want to come across as a dick. Her phone chimed and she groaned. 'Speaking of a losing proposition,' she said, and slid her phone over to Nick to show him Caleb's text.

Caleb
I didn't know Lindsey was in town
It would have been great to see her. Say hi to her for me next time you talk.

Nick frowned. 'Is he friends with Lindsey?'

'He knows her,' Val said, taking her phone back. 'Friends is stretching it, although come to think of it, he might not know how much she hates him, so yeah, he probably *thinks* they're friends. But that's weird, right? Wanting to hang out?'

Nick looked thoughtful. 'Maybe he's jealous. If he knows

Linds was in town, then he saw your Instagram pictures, so he knows we were out there together.'

'I doubt it,' Val said, shaking her head. 'He's just got major FOMO about everything.'

They ate in silence for a while, but it wasn't strained or awkward. It felt comfortable; lived in. 'Can I ask you a question?' he asked.

'I don't know, can you?' Val snarked, and then immediately caught herself. 'God, I'm sorry – my default mode is bitch.'

A half-smile crinkled the skin around his eyes. 'You said it, not me,' he said, and Val snorted. That deepened his smile, and Val was suddenly glad they were sitting next to each other and not across from each other, because she still wasn't sure she could handle it full-on.

'What's the question?' she said, more to break the moment than anything else. Otherwise, she'd just gaze adoringly at him and look like a creep.

'Oh,' Nick said, looking down. 'Now I feel weird about it. It's probably personal. And a downer.'

'You realize you can't just say that and then *not* ask the question, right? Because otherwise I'll be knocking on your door at two in the morning to find out what you wanted to ask.'

'Feel free to not answer,' he said. 'I was just wondering – what happened with you and Caleb? I know you said it was messy, but there were some weird vibes when we did that double-date.'

Their double-date was mostly notable by how *not* awkward it had been to pretend to date Nick. Caleb had of course gotten under her skin, but Nick had managed to soothe her, and Aaron and Pete showing up had also helped. But there was something steadying about Nick's presence and she wasn't used to that. She looked down at her nearly empty bowl. She hadn't talked much about her breakup with anyone but Linds; it was hard, explaining what she and Caleb had been.

'Well, for one thing, we were never officially together. He made it very clear what he was looking for in a girlfriend, and it was someone who was . . . not me. And I was fine with that – relationships are bullshit. But no matter what I did, I was too – I don't know, too much, I guess. Too messy, too late, too forgetful, too unwilling to take his business advice. Eventually I just got sick of fighting and feeling like garbage all the time, all for someone I wasn't even dating.' She chewed her lower lip for a minute, debating. 'I called it off a few times, but he always talked me back into it. And like, I didn't care at first. It was just hooking up, and it wasn't like I was in love with him or anything, but I also couldn't really shake him.' She laughed bitterly, shaking her head. Nick didn't join in. He just looked at her steadily, in a way that made her skin feel tight.

Val broke eye contact and fiddled with her spoon. 'Linds never liked him. She was so relieved whenever we broke up. She would try and hide it, but I always knew, and then I'd end up back with him, and she'd be disappointed, and then I'd feel –' She broke off, searching for the right words.

'You'd feel like a screw-up, and admitting she was right in the first place would make you even more of one,' Nick said gently.

'Don't tell me you've ever felt like that,' she replied. 'You alphabetize your *catalogues*, you are nothing like me.'

'To be honest, not exactly like that. But Josh – he screws up. A lot. And I'm the one who usually cleans up after him. I realized a long time ago that if he felt ashamed about his screw-up, it made the resulting catastrophe that much worse. And he never screws up on purpose, so making him feel like crap just compounds the problem.'

Val blinked. She'd never thought of it in those concrete terms, but he was right. About how she felt, and about how her catastrophes always, well, catastrophized.

'Yeah, that,' she said. 'In the end we broke up during a fight about my editing process. He hated it and thought it was stupid and I should just stop, and I realized I didn't want to spend my life being the backup girlfriend for a guy who didn't seem to like me very much.' Val let out a breath, feeling abruptly lighter than she had in a long time. 'So yeah, that's me and Caleb.'

'By editing process, you mean the fact that you listen to music loud enough that I worry about your eardrums?' he asked, humor bleeding through his otherwise neutral tone.

'Yes,' she said, and this time when she laughed it was genuine. 'I know, it's weird, but it works.'

Nick shrugged. 'Artistic processes often look weird as hell from the outside. You should see what some actors do to get into character.'

Val sat up straighter. 'Once again, you can't just say that and then not follow through. Weirdest famous actor you met – go.'

Nick thought for a second. 'Josh and I had this bit part in a movie when we were maybe seven, and the lead was – well, super famous. His character was supposed to be this hard-boiled detective, and he decided that part of his character's backstory is that he used to smoke, but he recently gave it up. A few weeks before filming, he started smoking regularly and at specific times. We would have to film according to his former smoking schedule, so his cravings would be hitting right when he was on set.'

'That is weird. Did it work?'

'It made him cranky as hell, and he probably could have just, you know, acted. Also, he smelled terrible, but I think that was the refusal to bathe,' Nick said, grinning around the glass of water he brought to his lips. 'And that didn't have anything to do with his process, that was just him being disgusting because he's richer than god and no one could force him to just take a damn shower.' Val laughed, and Nick nudged her with his shoulder. 'See? You at least wear headphones and turn your music down if other people are around.'

She nudged him back. 'You still didn't say who it was.'

Nick rolled his eyes. 'I gave you plenty of context clues; figure it out yourself.'

'Okay,' she said. Val opened the IMDb app on her phone and started typing in his name. 'You said you were seven? And you're thirty now?'

'Oh no, we're not – don't you dare,' he said, reaching over and snatching her phone out of her hand. 'My picture on IMDb is from when I was sixteen, and it's – uh, not flattering,' he said, but he was grinning.

And holding her phone far out of her reach. 'Um, you grew up on TV? I've seen your old show, so it's not like I *don't* know what you looked like.' She pawed at his arm and *Christ* he was weirdly ripped for a librarian. She had no hope of getting her phone unless she climbed him like a tree, which was not unappealing. 'Fine, I won't look if you just tell me the movie.'

Nick appeared to consider her offer. '*The Disappearance of Walter P. Cowling.*' Val hadn't seen that one – it was a cop thriller that was rated R and came out when she was still far more into *Lizzie McGuire* than anything else – but she did know who starred in it. She would have had to live in a cave not to know that; his Oscars loss that year was considered one of the biggest snubs of all time.

Her jaw dropped. 'Wait, you mean – *he* smells bad?'

Nick grinned, flipped her phone around smoothly in his hand and held it out. 'He's notorious for wrecking his trailers.

We're talking garbage everywhere. He's basically a trash can with an anger problem.'

Val set her phone down next to her bowl, face down so he would know she wasn't going to break her word. 'Now I want more gossip *and* more chili.'

'I can give you one of those.' And then Nick Ford did the unthinkable.

He *winked*.

Chapter Thirteen

Nick moved a book that Val must have been reading back to its proper shelf and whistled, which wasn't something he usually did, but he was feeling more relaxed these days than he had in a long time.

Because things with Val were good. Really good, in fact. He was suddenly comfortable around her in a way he never quite expected, and he wasn't about to look a gift horse in the mouth. Everything was going well, so of course there was a knock on the door. Not many people came to the house at this time of night, aside from a handful of overeager get-out-the-vote canvassers when an election was coming, but he went to open it cheerfully anyway.

He shouldn't have. On the doorstep was a blonde, white woman dressed head-to-toe in designer clothes, looking sourly at the pot of maroon and gold mums he had sitting on his front step.

'Mom?' Nick said, aware his jaw was hanging open, not to mention she hated it when he made that expression.

'Nicky honey, close your mouth,' she said, as if reading from a script. Everything Candace Ford did was like that, calculated and about as genuine as her brown-to-blonde ombre hair. 'That's no way to greet your mother.' She gave him an air kiss on each cheek and skirted him to step inside, clearly ignoring the fact that he hadn't invited her in.

'What – why are you here?'

'Can't your mom just come and say hello?' she replied, her nose wrinkling as she looked around the living room. His stuff wasn't designer, but it was plenty nice.

'You live about a thousand miles away,' he pointed out, but she ignored him.

'Where's your Golden Globe, honey?'

Technically, it wasn't *his*. The show had won for best comedy when he was nine, and considering most of Jakey's plot line that season involved adopting a dog and trying to keep it a secret from the rest of the family, it didn't really feel like he and Josh had earned that one. 'Somewhere,' he shrugged, which wasn't a lie. He hadn't thrown it away, but it was in one of the many boxes in his basement he hadn't opened in years.

'You should have it out! Think of how impressed everyone would be,' she cooed.

'Mom.' Nick cleared his throat and glanced at the clock on the oven. Val was off at her second engagement shoot for Autumn and Caleb, this time at their apartment, but she was going to be home at any minute. He didn't want her walking into a vipers' nest unaware. 'What are you doing here?'

'You weren't answering my texts.'

'So you flew here?'

'How else was I going to be able to talk some sense into you?' she said, settling into Nick's favorite armchair like it was a throne. It was going to reek of her perfume for days.

A panic Nick hadn't felt in years brewed in his ribcage. It was an anxiety unique to Candy, to the way she steamrolled over everything he wanted with a poisonous smile. That was why he tended to avoid her; in person he usually lacked the courage. When he decided to quit acting, Nick hadn't even told Candy he was applying to college. Jan had helped him fill out the forms and found a tutor to help with his essay, had even gone with him to Freshman Orientation that July. Josh had helped him pack, and Nick waited until the night before his flight to Minnesota to let her know. Their dad had already moved out by then, but Doug was always leaving and coming back, so Nick hadn't considered that if the family was losing half of their golden calf, Doug might just stay gone for good. But he had, and the resulting divorce had thrown Candy and Josh onto some very hard times.

Candy had simply scoffed at him and assumed he was bluffing. By the time she realized he wasn't, he was safely in a state he figured was one of the least likely places she would ever go willingly. And his bet had paid off, at least until now.

'I told you, I'm not interested,' Nick said with as much calm as he could manage.

'Yes, you did,' she said, eyes still scanning the room for flaws. 'You've been quite emphatic on that front.'

'I have a girlfriend, too,' he added.

'Mmm-hmm,' Candy hummed. 'So you say.'

'She's – I – what? What do you mean, "so you say"?'

'You've been public about it,' Candy replied. 'Very public.'

Nick's panic hitched higher, his stomach buzzing unpleasantly. 'I can't help that fans saw us. You know how they are.'

Candy pursed her lips. 'I do, but I also know you, Nicky. And I just find it curious that I hadn't heard a word about this girlfriend until after I'd managed to create this opportunity for you, and now you two are . . . everywhere.'

Oh shit. She didn't believe him, which meant everything

they'd done so far was for nothing. 'I didn't tell you I was dating Anya,' he argued, hoping to derail her into an argument about their past.

'You were fourteen, and exactly. You didn't tell anyone you were with her, which is why it's so strange that now you're suddenly on Ohyesss.'

Okay, that didn't work. 'Do you think I submitted those photos?' Nick asked.

She frowned. 'It doesn't seem like you, but neither does kissing someone in a cornfield or whatever that was.'

'Maybe you don't know me as well as you thought,' Nick said, crossing his arms.

She clicked her tongue and changed tactics. 'If the reboot falls through, Joshy might need your help again. And here I am, giving you a chance at good money on a silver platter, and all you can do is throw it in my face.'

'I never asked you to do this,' he countered.

Candy sighed exaggeratedly. 'Being a mother is so thankless,' she muttered. 'After everything I've done for you, all my hard work to get you that role, and you can't even do this for me?'

When she put it like that, it sounded like Nick and Josh had wanted to act, rather than just being good at following directions and playing pretend as toddlers. Nick in particular had been quick at memorizing lines, and that and 'be cute' was all very small child actors needed to do in a sitcom. Candy had lucked out and as a result her sons had been working since they should have been in preschool.

Before he could answer, the door swung open and Val barged in, dumping her messenger bag on the floor, and kicking her boot off so vigorously it hit the wall next to her. 'You're not gonna believe this,' she said, and just one month ago this obnoxious entrance would have made him grit his teeth; now it sent a surge of relief through his veins. Whatever Val didn't think he'd believe, he didn't know, because she stopped – one boot on, one off, motorcycle jacket hanging loosely from her left shoulder – and stared. 'Uh, sorry, didn't know you – we – had company?'

'You must be the girlfriend,' Candy said, her voice sugary-sweet. Nick caught the flicker of revulsion on Val's face, but she managed to arrange it into a look of mild surprise quickly. 'I'm the mother.'

'Oh – uh – oh,' Val said, throwing Nick an incredulous look. 'Nice to meet you. I'm Valerie.'

'Such a beautiful name,' his mom cooed, standing up and flicking her hair over her shoulder. 'I'm Candy.' Val went to shake her hand, only to go stock-still when Candace did her usual air-kiss instead. Nick had a wild desire to laugh while Val did her best not to look disgusted. She was not a hugger, this fake girlfriend of his. He liked that about her. 'I can't say you're what I expected,' Candy added.

Before Nick could protest, Val had stepped away from his mother and to his side, surreptitiously weaving her fingers through his. 'What were you expecting?' Val asked, giving his hand a surprisingly comforting squeeze.

'It's beside the point,' Candy said with a wave of her hand. 'I don't suppose Nicky has told you about the job I found for him?'

Val's face hardened. 'He has a job. He's a librarian.'

'Oh, it would just be temporary. Just a quick little reality show, maybe a few months, tops, and he could go back to – whatever it is he does here.'

'You don't know what a librarian does?' Val said, lifting one eyebrow skeptically.

Candy ignored Val's question. 'As I was trying to say, I'm sure you'd understand if Nicky had to go out to LA just for a little while, wouldn't you?'

Apparently, Candy was going to try and charm Val, and if Nick hadn't been halfway to a full-blown anxiety attack, it would have been hilarious to watch. 'A few months to be on a dating show, you mean.'

'Oh honey, it's all faked for the cameras,' Candace assured her. 'It'd be no different than acting.'

'A job Nick hated.'

Candy's patience started wearing thin. 'Nicky was young, and what I've done for him now is really something special.'

'I don't really think a rip-off of *The Bachelor* qualifies as something special, but okay.' It was strange, having someone who wasn't Josh or Jan standing up for him. Most people on set just let Candy do what she wanted, because her temper tantrums weren't worth the price of pushing back. 'If Nick actually wanted this, wouldn't he have said yes already?'

'Sometimes, my boys don't know what's good for them.'

'You think he doesn't –'

'I think he is easily led astray,' Candy snapped. 'And I *tried* to talk to him over the phone, but he wasn't taking my calls.'

'You know, most people would have just taken the hint,' Val said, visibly swelling with anger.

Candy blinked. Very few people spoke to her like that. 'Excuse me?'

'You heard me. He wasn't answering your calls because *he didn't want to talk to you*. It's not rocket science.'

'I'm his mother. There are things I'm owed.'

'He doesn't owe you shit,' Val snapped.

As good as it felt to watch Val make his mother angry, Nick

didn't have the same stomach for conflict. He squeezed Val's hand and she glanced at him, nodding almost imperceptibly before letting him take over. 'It's late, Mom,' he said, his grip on Val's fingers tightening. 'And we're not going to get anywhere by fighting right now. Can we talk about this tomorrow?'

'If you say so,' Candy said with a large, showy yawn that stretched the boundaries of believable. 'But there's no way a podunk town like this would have a decent hotel, so aren't you going to offer me a room?'

Val's eyes bugged out, clearly realizing they were screwed if Candy figured out Val still slept in her bedroom.

'We haven't straightened up Val's old room,' Nick replied as smoothly as he could.

'Yeah, and I – uh, sometimes I stay in there, when I'm editing. I stay up late and don't want to bother him, so I'll just crash there. And I have no clean sheets,' Val added quickly.

'I'm sure Nicky has spares, don't you, Nicky?'

Nick wanted to say no with every fiber of his being, but fully standing up to his mother was never something he'd been able to do. He could walk away from her and ignore her, but if the choice was conflict or acquiescence, he would choose the latter every time.

'They're in the hall closet,' he said, avoiding Val's eyes. 'I'll go get them.'

Nick shut the door firmly behind him, his mother now at least temporarily ensconced in Val's room. For her part, Val was currently standing at the foot of his bed, looking furious. 'Your mom's a real piece of work,' she spat.

'I would have gone with "bitch", but yes, I agree,' he said, sinking into his desk chair with a sigh. He ran his hand through his hair and did his best to block out the *Nicky, don't mess up your hair or we'll have to go back to the makeup trailer* that echoed through his head in Candace's voice.

Val snorted. 'Never would have thought you'd call a woman a bitch.'

'It's not a word I like, but – Christ, she brings out the worst in me.'

Val nodded. 'What was with calling you Nicky? No offense, but you're, um, not a Nicky.'

'None taken. I hate it, but – well, you saw her. Telling her to stop is just not worth it.'

'You really couldn't say no to her, could you?' she said, the concern in her tone making it hard for him to look up.

'Never could,' he admitted, forearms on his knees. 'It's a whole thing, to the point where Josh and I had to invent a girlfriend for me and rope you into it just to avoid this exact moment. I'd rather not get into it.'

'Do you want me to do it for you? I can just go in there and tell her to find a hotel. Although she might have a point – does Swede River even have one?'

'We don't,' Nick replied. 'Not one that would meet her standards, anyway. And if I tell her that, she'll just throw a tantrum.' He blew out a breath. 'But we have a bigger problem. She didn't just come to try and convince me to do the show; I think she came up here because she suspects something. That we're not legit.'

Val sank onto the edge of the bed. 'Oh, that's bad,' she said.

'Yeah.'

'Now what?' she asked. 'If she didn't buy the Ohyesss pictures, how do we prove it?' She made a disgusted face. 'Do we . . . ?'

'No, we are not pretending to have sex so my mom can overhear.'

'Thank god, because I was going to be really grossed out the whole time. I'd do it if that's what it took, but wow, I would not enjoy it.'

He chuckled weakly. Dealing with Candace was the absolute worst, but it did help to have Val by his side for once.

'What do we do now?' Val asked. 'For real.'

'I sleep on the floor, you take the bed, and I promise not to complain that you haven't done your dishes in three days as payment?'

'It's only been two days,' Val protested. 'And you need to promise not to complain about that for like, the rest of the month. Or just do them yourself.' Nick snorted and she rested her hand lightly on his knee. 'Are you okay?' Val asked softly.

He put his hand on hers, deciding not to think about the fact that there wasn't anyone around to see them and thus there was no point in keeping up the dating charade. 'I think so,' he said, automatically taking her hand when she turned it palm up.

'One last thing,' Val said, waiting until he looked at her to finish her sentence. 'You're not taking the floor. We're sharing.'

Chapter Fourteen

Val felt the first prickling strands of awareness and did her best to brush them away. She was warm and comfortable, her nose pressed against something solid, a quiet *thump thump* lulling her into a contented doze. The steady, warm wall she was cuddling with cleared his throat and she opened her eyes, realizing where she was all at once.

In Nick's bed, and *in his arms*. His nice, muscled, pleasantly heavy arms, one of which was draped across her, keeping her tucked under his chin. Her nose was against his sternum and her leg was tangled between his, and even with realizing all of this she did nothing to move. In fact, she wanted to stay there for ever and never get out. She wanted to stay nestled in Nick's arms, smelling his sheets, and listening to his heartbeat.

That probably wasn't the appropriate reaction. She shouldn't have insisted he stay in the bed with her, but like hell she was sleeping on the floor, plus she felt bad for the guy. His mom was terrible, and the thought of him sleeping on nothing but thin carpet after that whole disaster out in the living room had tugged at her heartstrings. They hadn't fallen asleep like this, but now they were cuddling, and she didn't have the heart to pull away.

Nick cleared his throat again and eased back, lifting his arm as he moved. Val wanted to whimper at the loss but kept her shit together, moving her head back to her pillow like this was all totally normal. She opened her eyes, blinking at the sun streaming in through his white curtains. It gave the whole room an ethereal glow, which didn't help make this feel any less surreal.

'Hey,' Nick said in a sleep-roughened voice. He smiled softly at her, apparently not at all weirded out by their little snuggle fest. Dust motes danced in the sunbeams behind him, his dark brown hair gilded with gold. His eyes were warm and gentle. Everything about him right now was giving her a melty feeling, like sinking into a hot bath after a long, cold day.

'Hey yourself,' Val whispered.

'Did you sleep okay?'

'Great,' she said, and it was strange, but she had. She normally tossed and turned and struggled to stay asleep, but last night she had slept like a log.

A log wrapped in Nick's arms.

A half-smile twitched at the corner of his mouth. 'You snore, you know,' he said, clearly trying to keep a straight face. 'You should probably get that checked out.'

'I do not,' Val protested, dissolving into laughter, and reaching out to smack his shoulder.

Nick caught her wrist playfully. 'Like a damn chainsaw,' he said, breaking out a full-blown smile.

Val's breath caught in her chest. She'd seen him smile before, but they were almost always shy smiles, reluctant smiles, smiles that flashed across his face before he looked away. They were nothing like this. He was breathtaking. That was the only way to put it.

Nick dropped her hand and carefully moved a lock of hair from where it had fallen in her face, tucking it behind her ear. His fingertips skimmed the shell of her ear and then trailed down the line of her jaw, as if he wasn't ready to stop touching her. 'I'm sorry,' he murmured. 'Is this okay?'

His thumb swept over the bow of her lips, and she parted them slightly, letting the pressure from his thumb turn it into a kind of gentle kiss. 'It is,' she murmured back. 'And you don't have to ask.'

Nick slipped his fingers into her hair, his brown eyes hazy. 'I feel like I need to. Like – I'm always crossing lines with you that I shouldn't.'

Val reached out to touch his hair, pleased to find it was as soft as she remembered. 'I'm not saying asking for consent is a bad thing. I'm saying – you have it.'

'I have it,' he echoed, eyes dropping to her lips.

'You do.' She licked her lips and took the plunge. 'I like it when you touch me.'

Nick's eyes fluttered closed, and he groaned. Val felt it deep in her belly, a knot of heat suddenly coiling and loosening. 'I had all these reasons this was a bad idea,' he rasped, and she shoved aside the stab of disappointment at the reminder that he saw her as a *bad idea*, 'but I can't remember any of them.'

'Then it wouldn't be your fault if you ignored them,' Val said, doing her best to block out all the doubts rushing in. *Being a bad idea* felt too much like Caleb, too much like her family – a sign that she was just not quite good enough for any of them. That she would never, ever measure up. She licked her lips again and watched Nick do the same, his head rising just a fraction of an inch off the pillow toward her.

Her heart was slamming against her ribcage so loudly she was sure he could hear it.

'Nicky? Where's the best place to order breakfast?' Candy's voice floated through the door, shattering the moment.

Nick flopped back on the mattress, covering his face with his hand. 'Now?' he muttered.

'Nicky?'

'She knows damn well there's no delivery out here,' he grumbled. 'I'll be right out,' he called, and Val decided it was time for her to do the sensible thing and get up. As tempting as that moment had been, she was done being with guys who saw her as a *bad idea*.

Better to just leave it as a fleeting moment.

Thanks to Nick's nightmare of a mother monopolizing her room, Val was in Nick's enormous sweatshirt and yesterday's pants, standing awkwardly next to the stove holding a serving platter while Nick made pancakes. Across the kitchen, Candace kept looking around like she expected to see a rat pop out at any second.

As mornings-after went, it was one of the most awkward of Val's life. She had lobbied to take Candy to Pete's for breakfast, which could also have the benefit of providing more witnesses to their relationship. But Nick said he didn't want to subject any more Swede Rivertonians to Candy than necessary, and Val had to admit he had a point there.

She shuffled her feet and wondered if there was something girlfriend-y she could do while Nick flipped a pancake over. She could touch his hair, maybe? But he was a lot taller than her, and she would have to put the platter down to reach. Granted, there was no reason for her to be holding the platter – he had plenty of counter space – but she wanted an excuse to stand near to him and not his mom. Just when she'd ruled out touching his hair and decided lightly touching his arm would suffice, Nick eased a series of perfectly browned pancakes onto the platter.

'Why don't you and Mom get started, babe? I'm almost done here.' Candy was busy nosing through a stack of mail (all Val's, obviously) and paid no attention.

Val raised an eyebrow at him. *Babe?*

Nick shrugged imperceptibly. *It felt right*, his expression said.

'Sure thing, babe,' she said, and a hesitant smile twitched across his face.

Nick had promised her before they came down that he could take the lead on the whole *acting like a couple* thing again, and that his flailing yesterday was because he hadn't expected to see her in person. Apparently, they were going to be a couple who called each other *babe*.

'Syrup?' she asked Candy, jerking her attention away from a piece of junk mail promising to help Val consolidate her student loans. 'And don't worry, I'm up to date on all of my utility bills.'

Candy looked at her sourly. 'Joshy said you two were roommates first.'

'Joshy's right,' Val replied brightly. 'That's how we met.'

'I just can't see my Nicky having a roommate. Especially one as eccentric as you.'

Val did not manage to hide her snort. 'Opposites attract,' Nick said, taking the stool next to Candy, but not before he had silently offered it to Val, and she had silently refused it. He could be such a gentleman it killed her sometimes.

He was also one hell of a cook. Val had to keep from moaning aloud when she finally took a bite, but Candy acted like it was nothing. 'I meant, I don't see Nicky agreeing to live with you in the first place, given your . . . differences.'

Candace was like a very rude dog with a bone, it seemed. 'She needed a place to stay, and fast. Her old place flooded, and she knew my coworker, Mary,' Nick lied smoothly. 'It was only supposed to be temporary, but then . . .' He trailed off and tucked into his plate, appearing perfectly nonchalant. But Val had seen how freaked out he was last night; he was a good actor, but she wasn't totally fooled.

'I'm only saying –'

'That you think we're faking it so Nick can get out of your stupid little dating show, right?' Val said, deciding to take the bull by the horns. 'We're not, and you fishing around is getting weird, okay?' She stalked across the kitchen to pour herself a mug of coffee, grabbing a second one from the cabinet for Nick. Candace could get her own damn coffee. 'I get that we don't like, fit, or whatever, but what do you care? When was the last time you had a conversation with your son that wasn't about something you wanted from him?'

Candy opened and closed her mouth soundlessly. Val walked around the breakfast bar to set Nick's mug down near his elbow. Nick slung his arm around her waist and tugged her closer, until she was half-perched on his lap. 'Pulling out of the show is not going to be easy,' Candy spat, narrowing her eyes at Val's new position. 'Things are a lot farther along than you seem to think.'

Val toyed with the hair at the back of Nick's head, acutely reminded of their moment that morning. 'And whose fault is that?' Val pointed out. 'Nick has said no every step of the way.'

'Just because he's –'

'It's a bad time,' Nick blurted. 'Just tell them you can't get me on board yet.'

Val's stomach churned. *Yet.* Yet was not *no*, it was *maybe later.* They couldn't pretend to be together forever, but it was an abruptly unpleasant reminder that this charade had an expiration date.

'You really don't care what a difficult position you're putting me in, do you?' Candy said. 'I can't keep putting off the studio.'

Nick had fallen silent and she wasn't sure he could keep going. But she certainly could. 'That's not his problem, and it sure as hell isn't mine.' She stood, putting a few inches of space between her and Nick. 'In fact, why don't you go get your things,' Val said, forcing herself to focus on the current conversation, and not the internal meltdown Nick was clearly having. 'It's a long drive back to Minneapolis, and we wouldn't want you to miss your flight.'

For once Candy didn't put up a fight. It didn't take long for her to get her bag from Val's room, and her goodbyes were perfunctory and stilted. Nick didn't go in for a hug, and neither did Candace. Val watched it all with her arms crossed, like a bouncer at a very uncomfortable nightclub.

Nick shut the door behind her and rested his forehead against it, breathing hard. They both waited in silence until Candace's rental car started. 'I'm sorry,' Nick said, more to the door than to her.

He turned, his eyes unexpectedly anguished. 'You've got nothing to be sorry for,' Val said, wanting to reach out and touch his cheek to reassure him, but contenting herself with just a brief brush of her hand on his forearm. Part of her wanted to ask what he planned on doing about the show after they stopped pretending, or if he was just assuming this would go on and on until they were fake married with fake babies. Another part of her wanted to ask why he couldn't have just told Candy no, and still another part of her couldn't figure out why it hurt so much to think about him eventually going on this dating show once he ran out of excuses.

She half-expected him to pull away from her touch. At the very least, she thought he wouldn't reciprocate, but at no point did she think Nick would fold her into his arms in a tight hug. 'Thank you,' he murmured from somewhere near the top of her head. His heart was beating under her cheek, and she wrapped her own arms around his back. He smelled like he had that morning, now with a touch of sugar and maple syrup, and Val closed her eyes. She was back in his arms, and she was going to let herself revel in it for as long as it lasted. 'Thank you,' Nick whispered again. He didn't make a move to let go and neither did she, melting into him while he held her like she was something precious to him.

And for one moment, Val let herself believe it was real.

Chapter Fifteen

Nick returned to the circulation desk, relieved that Charles Poulson had finally remembered his Gmail password. There was a lot more 'basic tech support' that went into being a librarian than he had ever anticipated, but unless the government started funding social services again this would just stay part of his job.

He had left his phone out on the desk when he was called away, and apparently while gone he'd missed several texts. Nick's heart sank when he realized they weren't from Val, and then immediately pushed that thought aside. He couldn't afford to fall for her, not when she needed him. She had needed a soft place to land and a way to work her way back into the photography scene and he had given her that, but nothing about her time in Swede River was permanent.

Nick did not handle heartbreak elegantly, so he did his best to avoid it at all costs. And Val had *heartbreak* written all over her – he was too staid, too boring, too stuffy for a woman like her. She deserved someone more vibrant and spontaneous, not someone who got tongue-tied around unfamiliar people and who had moved to a small town to basically avoid having to meet new people ever again.

Nick unlocked his phone and opened the string of texts from his brother.

Josh
OMG I JUST HEARD ABOUT MOM

WHY DIDN'T YOU TELL ME SHE WAS THERE?

Nick
It all happened really fast.

She was here and then she was gone, but not before she went full Candace Ford.

Josh
I think things must be bad for her? She seems extra desperate to get this show off the ground.

Nick
I was thinking the same thing.

Candace Ford does not visit states without beaches except under extreme duress.

Josh
And while we're talking about stuff you hate, I had a meeting with the writers' room and they wanted to know if you'd do a cameo as a cousin

Just walk through the door, let the audience go nuts for a while, and then say three lines and split

I know you just agreed to the reunion show and this is one more thing, and I'm sorry about that but man the fans would love it

Josh was right – fans would love it. And it wasn't like it was anything too difficult. No one would care if his line-readings were wooden – it wasn't as if he'd miss out on a job booking if people realized he wasn't actually a very good actor. No one cared if a librarian was a lousy actor; that was one of the many reasons he chose this profession. But returning felt like a much bigger deal than Josh was making it out to be. Answering questions with everyone else as himself was one thing, going back into acting, as brief as it would be, was something else entirely.

Nick
I'm going to pass, sorry

Just too complicated with everything

Nick waited for his brother to respond – Josh sent a yellow heart emoji – and went to pocket his phone when it buzzed again. His heart did a little leap at the name.

Valerie Costa
I'm trying this new thing called 'grocery shopping' and since you've been feeding me like three nights a week I think I should buy you some food

What food do you want

Carrots? Lettuce?

Peas?

Nick
Am I a rabbit?

Valerie Costa
I DON'T KNOW MAYBE

Nick chuckled to himself at her panic.

Nick
I was going to make vegetarian lasagna tomorrow. Do you want me to text a link to the recipe?

Valerie Costa
Depends

Are you gonna let me eat it

Nick
And here I thought you were being charitable? Isn't this payback for you eating all my food lately?

Valerie Costa
Details

But fine I'll buy it and not eat it

Nick
You're bad at knowing when I'm teasing, aren't you?

Valerie Costa
Not my fault you've got the sense of humor of a rock

Nick grinned to himself and found the bookmarked recipe to send her. Mary approached, pushing a cart laden with returns. The front left wheel squeaked with every movement, the sound unusually loud in the hushed room. 'You look happy,' she said quietly.

'Good day,' he shrugged.

'This seems like more than just a good day,' she countered. 'You've been smiling to yourself all week.' She paused and lifted her eyebrows slyly. 'Things with Val must be going well.'

Nick reminded himself that it wasn't *technically* lying to Mary to pretend to date Val. 'They are, yeah,' he agreed, and Mary's brown eyes lit up.

'I knew you two would be a good match. She's exactly what you need. You're too young to live like this, Nicholas, and Valerie is a burst of life. She's good for you.'

Mary wasn't wrong. 'She is,' he agreed, and at that moment, it didn't even feel like a lie.

'Thanks, Mary,' Nick heard Val say from near the door. Mary was headed out, leaving Nick to lock up before he went home to make the vegetarian lasagna he had promised Val.

'Everything okay?' he asked, double-checking that the printer had turned off.

'Just got bored,' Val shrugged, and boosted herself up to sit on the circulation desk. That was obviously not allowed, but it wasn't like any patrons were left to see her shocking breach of decorum.

Okay, maybe Mary had a point. Nick's general demeanor could be compared to that of a dour nun in her seventies; he could probably loosen up a little and not get itchy that his very pretty roommate was sitting in a place she shouldn't. Val cocked her head with fake confusion on her face. 'I was supposed to put all the fresh veggies in the freezer, right?'

Nick shook his head. 'Very funny,' he chided, circling back to behind the desk. 'But really, what brought you down here?'

She shrugged again, kicking the heels of her heavy boots against the desk with a loud *clunk* before turning around and sitting cross-legged on top of the counter to face him. 'I was bored waiting for you to come home and cook and realized I haven't really spent any time here aside from – well, that first day.'

'What brought you here? To Swede River that day, I mean.'

She gave him a puzzled look. 'I was literally run out of town.'

'Funny, I don't remember any pitchforks.'

'Yeah, well, they were metaphorical. But you know that. I distinctly remember telling you that the day we met.'

'Yeah, I know, I just meant – why here? Why not literally anywhere else?'

'What brought you here?'

'A posting on the University of Minnesota Library Sciences job listserv.'

'Okay, well, that's a better reason. I just drove until I had to pee, and I didn't want to buy a pop at McDonalds.'

'Ah, so it was the free bathrooms.'

'Exactly,' she said, and he'd never noticed it before, but she had flecks of green in her eyes when the light hit her just so. Her cheeks were pink from the brisk wind, and when she bit her lower lip almost shyly, Nick had some very work-inappropriate thoughts.

They still hadn't discussed the moment in his bed, when he'd nearly crossed every single line he'd ever drawn. When she had all but told him to cross those lines, even if it might make everything between them so much messier. And Nick loathed messes. He liked his life neat and orderly, which was why everything about Val was both so tempting and so difficult. He needed to remember she saw her time in Swede River as temporary; not get attached.

'What about you?' she asked as he checked the returns bin one last time. 'Aside from the job posting, why here?'

Nick sat down in the chair in front of her. 'There aren't a ton of library jobs, for one thing. For another – I always liked the idea of small towns, probably because they're so different from what I grew up with. The industry can be claustrophobic, but Los Angeles itself is just so *big*. It's hard to feel like you belong, and I think I just always wanted this – knowing that Margie Schumacher takes a walk at ten in the morning every day, that Pete and Aaron picked Swede River to raise Felix because it's halfway between their two hometowns and neither could bear disappointing their mothers by moving too far away. It's comfortable, and honestly, within a year of moving here I knew everyone, and everyone knew me. It meant I didn't have to go through that *do I know you?* dance, or the *oh my god you're Jakey* one that usually follows. It lets me just be myself, and not who I was.'

Val observed him quietly. She rearranged her legs again to drape over the side of the desk facing him, her feet now mere inches from his knees. Intellectually, he knew he couldn't feel them. She wasn't touching him, and it wouldn't have been her skin that touched him anyway, just her thick combat boots. But all the same, it was as if there was an electric current between them. Nick cleared his throat and moved to rest his ankle on his knee, rolling back a few inches in the process. It helped, but not enough.

She looked momentarily wistful, until her face cleared, and she hopped down. 'Let's go have you make dinner, I'm starving,' Val said with what was clearly forced brightness. Something he said must have wounded her. That made his chest want to cave in – no, it made him want to gather her to him and hold her there, but he knew that wouldn't be allowed. Or worse, that it would be.

Instead, he pocketed his phone and picked up his keys. 'Then let's go home,' he said, standing and holding his hand out. There wasn't anyone outside, so there was no reason for them to pretend, but Val didn't even hesitate. She slipped her hand into his and together they walked out into the evening sun.

Chapter Sixteen

'I really wouldn't have pegged you for a *John Wick* fan,' Val said, settling more comfortably against the arm of the couch. She had insisted he skip past the dog dying scene, which Nick had grumbled about but agreed to do.

Roommate Movie Night was her newest, dumb idea. She liked spending time with Nick, but she also felt like they needed to have a reason. Showing up at the library the other day had been one of her less-thought-out-impulses, and this was another one.

Nick clearly didn't *want* to be attracted to her, which meant of course she would start chasing him. Val had always been the type to press on her own bruises, after all.

'What type of movie would you think I like?'

'Probably more, I don't know, Wes Anderson? Or mumbly indies where everyone is washed-out and sad-looking and nothing happens except their lives get worse. Maybe those BBC period pieces where everyone whispers and fusses over their neighbor's money. Or nature documentaries.'

'You are not painting a very flattering picture of me, you know.'

'Oh, I know. But you have to admit, you're kind of stuffy.'

Nick snorted and hit play. 'Well, mostly I'm a Keanu fan,' he explained, draping his arm over the back of the couch. 'But I also like movies that are – elegant.'

Val lifted her eyebrows. 'And *John Wick* is elegant? Are we talking about the same movie? Where Keanu Reeves kills a bunch of people for two hours?'

'By elegant I mean it does what it means to do, effortlessly. It doesn't try to please everyone or feel like a bunch of execs got involved to make it a four-quadrant crowd-pleaser by watering it down. Movies are best when they succeed in achieving their goals, whether it's "let Keanu murder bad guys" or "let Reese Witherspoon get into law school".'

Val laughed. '*Legally Blonde* deserved an Oscar.'

'No argument here.' Nick tossed her a half-grin that made her heart do a stutter step. 'I also consider *When Harry Met Sally* and *Ever After* to be exemplary examples. And *Scream*.'

'I really wouldn't have thought you'd be a horror fan.'

'I like good horror.'

'Meaning not . . . *Terror at Camp Wowitan*?' Val asked mischievously. On screen, Keanu was smashing a concrete floor with a sledgehammer.

Nick turned his eyes to the TV but snorted. 'Hey, we had some excellent special effects and stunts. My decapitation was especially gory.'

'I notice you didn't mention the writing.'

'Because it sucked,' Nick said. He cocked his head. 'But are we going to roast my movies, or watch this?'

'Before we do, which movie of yours do you hate the most?'

Nick sighed and finally hit pause. 'Did you know that talking through a movie is considered rude?'

'You're the one who keeps volunteering information,' Val

argued, nudging his thigh with her foot. 'If you really didn't want to talk, you could just not.'

'You say that like it's easy to say no to you,' Nick said, stealing a glance at her.

'You do say no to me leaving my dishes in my room,' she replied. Her heart was hammering again, because this time there was no one else in the house to interrupt them.

'That's because I don't want ants,' Nick said, his face unreadable in the dim light.

She swallowed hard and forced herself to keep her voice light. 'But for real, worst movie. Go.'

He looked thoughtful. 'Josh and I were in *The Disappearance of Walter P. Cowling* and *The Volcano Boys* in the early days of *Just Us Girls*. *Volcano* got dumped straight to DVD, and we were only in that as the main character's little brother for a couple of scenes.'

Val furrowed her brow, thinking. 'Was that the one with the volcano? And the girl scientist?'

'Yes, *Volcano Boys* definitely featured a volcano,' he grinned. 'I don't think it was terrible, but it also wasn't good. *Disappearance* was awful to film and honestly, I've never watched it because we were too young at the time, considering all the murder that happened, and now I have zero desire to see myself on screen ever again, but given that he was nominated for an Oscar, it's probably at least not horrible. *Terror at Camp Wowitan*, though – if I hadn't already been thinking about quitting acting, that would have done it.'

'Why did you do it, then?'

Nick shrugged. 'I had to find out if I hated acting, or if I was just sick of the show. *Just Us Girls* was over, so that was my chance. I probably still would have left even if the movie was good, but it might have taken longer.' He sent her a sidelong glance that made her flush all over. It was devastating, how innocently flirty he could be. 'Is that all? Or do you have more questions about my life and choices?'

Val licked her lips and considered him for a moment. She knew instinctively that if she pushed – if she kept this flirtation going – it would go somewhere. They had been on a knife's edge in his bed the other morning, and yet again they were standing on a precipice. She could pull him over with her, or she could be responsible for once and stand back.

Val had very little experience being the responsible one. But she couldn't forget him calling her a *bad idea*, which still stung even if it was probably true. She was a Category Five hurricane at the best of times, while Nick was a sturdy oak tree that could withstand most winds – but not her. He didn't want her to throw him off course, and she didn't blame him. She might be able to convince him for a while, but in the end, he would regret her and that might kill her. Val was just going to have to tuck that little flame of longing away; bury it deep down until lack of reciprocation smothered it.

'Sorry,' she said, softening it with a smile. 'Go ahead and start it.'

Nick looked at her inscrutably and then turned back to the TV, hitting play like the electric current between them had never existed.

Chapter Seventeen

Nick couldn't move. He didn't dare, because moving would mean ending this moment and he just didn't have the strength.

Against his shoulder, Val breathed slowly and deeply. She hadn't started this close to him – when the movie began, he was on one side of the couch, and she was safely on the other. But then she'd gone to stretch her legs out. Nick had picked up her feet and placed them in his lap before he even realized what he was doing, but by then it was too late. Just like when she was in his bed, Nick couldn't bring himself to do the responsible thing and back off.

He had thought he was in the clear when she'd paused it to go get herself a glass of water from the kitchen, but then she had sat down next to him on the couch, without the buffer of a cushion and a half between them. She hadn't moved any closer, but she didn't move away, either.

Val had fallen asleep just over halfway through the movie with her head on the cushion behind her, but then not five minutes later she started listing to the side, eventually ending up with her head on his shoulder. And there he'd left her for the remainder of the movie, instead of doing the decent thing and waking her up. But now the movie was over, and he was rapidly running out of excuses. Liking how warm and soft she felt against him wasn't a good enough reason, not when she had made herself perfectly clear.

Nick had given her an opening, after all. He was flirting with her about as obviously as he could, and then gave her a choice – keep going, or stop. She chose to stop, and anything that happened after that, like not taking her feet out of his lap or sitting close to him, didn't change that.

Val's head lolled back slightly, and he knew it was time. 'Hey,' he whispered, but she didn't move. 'Hey,' he said, a little louder, and nudged her with his elbow.

She blinked sleepily up at him, her face softer than he'd ever seen it. Even in his bed the other morning, Val's eyes had been the tiniest bit wary, and he wished all over again he hadn't been so reserved and brusque with her when they first met. Maybe it would have been like this the whole time; easy and gentle and full of promise.

Her eyes focused on him, and her face brightened, just enough to send an arrow of longing into his heart. He wanted her to look at him like that all the time, not just when she was sleepy and able to forget how much of a colossal jerk he could be. 'Hey,' she said in a sleep-roughened voice. 'I guess I fell asleep.'

'John Wick killed a lot of guys,' Nick explained, unable to keep the grin off his face. 'And again, you really do snore like a freight train.'

'Shut up,' Val grumbled, smacking his shoulder and sitting up. He wished she didn't, but he wished for a lot of pointless things these days. She looked away, licking her lips, and taking a deep, steadying breath. 'I guess I should just go to bed,' she said, not looking at him.

No. Stay up. Stay with me. Come with me to my bed. Whatever you do, don't leave my side. Nick cleared his throat and lost his courage. 'Go get some sleep,' he said as lightly as he could. 'I'll go find some earplugs.'

With an eyeroll, Val stood up and left him behind.

Val was sitting on a stool at the counter when he walked into the kitchen. Nick had only lately stopped getting fully dressed for the day before leaving his bedroom; he'd been trying to make her feel at ease but realized recently that maybe his insistence on formality was making her *un*comfortable. Plus, it was nice to eat breakfast in his sweatpants and the U of MN T-shirt he slept in again. It had been even nicer to see her in his clothes after the night she spent in his room, but he wasn't going to let himself go there.

Because if he did let himself go there, he would wind up in a spiral of despair. Val was pretty, yes. He liked kissing her, sure. He found her funny and smart and charming and every other thing that made her nearly impossible to ignore, and that meant that he needed to stop thinking that as quickly as he could. No good would come of this, just heartbreak, because Val was not made for boring, grumpy men like him. She needed someone with more of an edge, someone who could keep up with her, not bring her down. In short, she needed someone who was most definitely not Nick.

She stole a glance at him and then darted her eyes back to her phone, a spoon of Cocoa Puffs halfway to her mouth. A look of fierce annoyance crossed her face. She dropped the spoon, splattering milk on the counter, and started furiously tapping with her thumbs.

'Everything okay?' Nick asked, pulling his granola out of the cupboard and yogurt from the fridge.

'Yeah, just – family stuff.'

'I can relate,' he said. 'Coffee?'

Val nodded, holding it out for him to refill before he poured his own cup. She stopped typing and watched him pad around the kitchen, chopping fruit and adding it to his bowl. 'How do you do that?'

'Hmm?'

Val gestured with her spoon. 'Have the energy to, like, make stuff to eat. All the time. I can barely convince myself it's worth it to eat, and you're like, cooking a gourmet breakfast every day.'

Nick leaned against the island opposite her. 'Putting fruit and granola into yogurt isn't exactly cooking. More like assembling.'

'Still though. I almost ate these dry because I was too lazy to get the milk.'

Nick snorted. 'I think it's because I spent so much of my life eating stuff off the Craft Services table. Once I was on my own, I had to learn how to do everything, and I discovered I liked it. There's something satisfying about it, you know?'

'Again, too lazy to put milk into cereal, so no, I don't.'

Nick could tell she was eyeing his bowl jealously, so he held out his loaded spoon to her. She lunged forward to swipe it like he might take it away, and he had to look away at the little moan of delight she let out. Nick plucked the spoon back and pointed it at her mock-sternly. 'Don't go thinking I'll be making you breakfast too, now.'

'I only eat your dinners like four nights a week,' Val said dismissively. Her phone buzzed again, and she shot it a dark look. 'Speaking of, any chance you have some sort of major Hollywood Thanksgiving Event that I have to be your girlfriend for?'

'George and Amal forgot to invite me this year.' He nodded to her phone. 'What's going on?'

Val sighed. 'I'm just not really looking forward to the annual Airing of Val's Failures.'

'It's really that bad?'

'No boyfriend, no real job, currently living with a roommate rather than having my own house, mortgage, husband, and two point five kids,' she said, ticking them off on her fingers. 'Oh, my car is a piece of junk, that's another one my dad's going to bring up. My brother-in-law will probably ask how my retirement account is doing in the stock market. He'll phrase it to sound like he's just making small talk about the economy or something, but he's trying to not-so-subtly remind me that I am screwed financially, which yes, I know.'

'Then don't go,' Nick suggested.

'That's not how my family does things. If I don't go it would be this *whole thing*. I would hear about *the year I skipped Thanksgiving* at every family event for the next twenty years. The Costas have the memories of elephants, but with more grudge-holding.'

'Haven't elephants been known to kill poachers years later?'

'Exactly. I have to go, or else they'll hunt me down. And my sister is currently texting me, pretending like she's trying to "nail down details" for Mom, but really she's just gathering ammunition.'

'Such as?'

'Christine knows I'm dating you. Well, thinks I'm dating you, and she wants to know if you're coming. I said I think you've got your own plans, and then she wanted to know what those plans were and if they were flexible.'

'You could always say –'

'Christine spends a decent amount of time following Hollywood gossip, so she already knows you don't speak to your parents and that Josh is spending Thanksgiving at a meditation retreat in Palm Springs.'

'He's not. Jan probably told someone that's what he's doing, and I have no idea what he's actually planning, but I promise you, he's not meditating. Smoking a ton of weed and talking about wanting to learn to meditate, maybe.'

'Are you going to see him?'

'We've never bothered.' Nick shrugged. 'Sometimes we FaceTime, if he's not too stoned to remember.' Nick had gone to Mary and Eng's house for Thanksgiving dinner a couple years in a row, but they were going to her daughter's in Florida this year, so he really hadn't considered making other plans. He looked down at his remaining yogurt and decided to say something incredibly, incredibly stupid. 'You could tell Christine my plans changed,' he said, not daring to look at her. 'And I could come with you, if you want.'

Val stopped her incessantly loud crunching. 'You would?'

'I would, yeah. If you wanted. If it would make things worse, forget I offered.'

'Are you sure?'

'If your family is the type to, like, try and sell the *National Enquirer* a story about me being a coke addict, then no, I'm not sure, but it doesn't sound like they are. And besides, I owe you.'

'My sister will probably brag incessantly to her coworkers that she met you, and my brother-in-law is definitely going to try and get you to tell him how accurate *Entourage* was, but otherwise they're your average boring, suburban family with a very disappointing youngest daughter.'

'I still don't see what's so disappointing about you,' he argued. 'All of that stuff you listed earlier is totally normal for someone in a creative field in their late twenties.'

'See, that's just it – I'm in a *creative* field. They all think I should just give up photography and take a job at the car dealership my dad works at.'

Nick lifted an eyebrow. 'No offense, but you'd be terrible at sales.'

'Right?' Val laughed bitterly. 'I think even they know that. My dad keeps bringing up the fact that the admin staff never stay long, and they want someone who could take that job and be "in it for the long haul."' She let her spoon clatter into her empty bowl and Nick wordlessly picked it up and set it in the sink, knowing all too well that if he didn't do that, it might very well stay there until dinner.

See? He was adapting.

'Would you want that? A steady job to supplement photography?'

'I don't,' she said. 'I get why people do, and there's nothing wrong with that. But I can't. It would feel like giving up, and besides, I'd have to move.'

'Where do they live?'

'St Cloud.'

Nick made a face. 'Okay, yeah, I see the problem there. But I can handle them, if you want. It's the least I can do after my mom kicked you out of your own bedroom.'

There was a flash of heat in Val's eyes, but it was gone before he could be sure it was even there. 'Then I'll tell them I have a plus one this year,' she said, and Nick really hoped he wasn't going to make things worse for himself.

He probably was, but he didn't care. Which should have been a sign that he was in deeper than he realized.

Chapter Eighteen

Val's childhood home loomed behind a vast expanse of perfectly manicured lawn as Nick pulled up against the curb. Frost had turned the usual emerald green of Dad's prized grass to a dull, washed-out brown, and the only decoration was the 'festive autumn wreath' Mom had hung on the door. Amy Costa had a strict *No Christmas decorations until Black Friday* policy and a well-established loathing of Halloween, which she felt was an incredibly tacky holiday, thus the seasonal fall decorations were somewhat lacking.

Nick leaned back behind her seat to grab the bottle of wine he insisted on bringing. He was wearing a dark green sweater over a button-down with dark jeans and it was exactly the sort of reserved, starchy nerd look she had come to expect from him. However, for some reason tonight it made her stomach feel all nervous and fluttery. Maybe it was that she knew he'd picked out his clothes to drive home the *partnered and stable* vibe she needed her family to pick up on.

Or maybe it was just that he looked incredibly hot; the sweater stretched tight across his broad shoulders and his hair dark and shiny. If someone looked up *hot nerd male librarian* in the dictionary, this outfit would show up. Was that a thing? It should be, in her opinion.

'Ready?' Nick asked, jerking her out of her reverie.

Val looked up at the pristine white colonial she'd grown up in. It hadn't been an unhappy childhood by any stretch, but she'd always felt a little bit separate from her family. Christine had always wanted what her parents wanted for them – a stable job, a family, a husband – but Val had never quite fit. She was too messy, too artsy, too averse to routine to settle into the life they so desperately wanted her to want. Her parents had never gone so far as to tell her she couldn't pursue her dreams, but they had also never missed a chance to remind her that she wasn't as successful as her sister.

Val didn't really think 'Human Resources Officer at a health insurance company' really counted as a wildly successful career, even if Christine seemed to like her job well enough. But it wasn't like she was making millions on Wall Street or saving little kids with cancer; she had a regular office job and a regular family and that was perfectly fine, just not for Val. Except Amy, Anthony, and Christine had never stopped trying to bring her back into their fold.

'As I'll ever be,' Val said drily. The grass crunched under their feet as they cut across the lawn – Val had insisted Nick park on the street so they could make a quick exit, if need be – and she took a deep, steadying breath as they reached the front steps.

Even though no one could see them yet, Nick took her hand warmly in his. 'It'll be fine,' he said in a low, soothing voice. 'I've got you.'

Val couldn't remember the last time she trusted someone who wasn't Linds to have her back, but before she could process that realization Nick started to knock and the door swung open.

'I cannot believe you're on time,' Christine said, instead of *Hello* or *Hi* or even *Happy Thanksgiving*. 'Must be his influence,' she added sweetly at Nick.

Nick nodded without even a glimmer of a smile. 'You must be Christine,' he said, keeping a firm hold of Val's hand as they stepped inside. Christine clearly noticed – her eyebrows hit her hairline and she shot Val a look – but any observation she was about to make was interrupted by the arrival of Ada and Milo, who burst into the foyer with excited shrieks of *'Aunt Val!!!'*

Val left her leather jacket on to greet her niece and nephew with their respective secret handshakes and then turned to Nick, who was watching them with a mildly amused look in his eyes. 'Nick, this is Ada and Milo,' Val said.

'Mom says you were on TV,' Milo said without preamble.

'I was,' Nick confirmed.

'Is that Val?' Amy Costa walked into the foyer with a look of exasperation. 'I wasn't expecting you for another half-hour.'

'You said to get here at five, and it's five,' Val countered, finally getting her jacket off and tossing it onto the bench near the door.

Amy rolled her eyes, like Val had done something wrong. 'Yes, but I didn't think you'd *be* here at five.'

Okay, sure, Val wasn't the most punctual. But her family was acting like she was completely incapable of making it even close to when she was supposed to, which wasn't true. 'Do you want us to go back outside and wait?' Val asked.

'Don't be ridiculous,' Amy snapped. 'I just wasn't ready to meet your guest. Christine, the timer is going off.' Christine hightailed it for the kitchen, and Amy's brow smoothed out as she put on her most welcoming smile, like she hadn't just been scolding Val for being on time. 'So lovely to meet you,' she said, shaking Nick's hand and accepting the wine. 'Anthony and Kev are in the family room with the game on.'

Nick looked bewildered. 'Oh, uh –'

'Nick doesn't watch sports,' Val explained.

'Is there anything you need help with?' Nick offered.

Amy blinked. 'My goodness, look at you,' she cooed. 'Someone raised you right.'

Val longed to point out that if *that* was true, then her own lack of punctuality would be Amy's fault, but she figured it wasn't worth picking a fight within the first three minutes of arriving. She had the whole night, after all.

'Aunt Val, you haven't seen my Minecraft castle yet,' Ada said, taking Val's hand. 'Can I show you?'

'One sec. Mom, did you need help –'

'Oh, don't bother,' Amy said as she turned to head back to the kitchen. 'I can't babysit you with the potatoes *and* finish the turkey. Remember what happened the last time I let you cook? Just stay with the kids.'

Nick waited until Amy had left. 'What happened last time?'

Val waved her hand dismissively. 'It was like, four years ago. I was supposed to be watching the stuffing, but – whatever, long story short, there wasn't any stuffing that year. Mom loves to remind me of the time I ruined the holiday.' Val caught the flash in Nick's eyes, and she suddenly regretted accepting his offer to come to Thanksgiving. It was bad enough that he thought she was moderately incompetent at adulthood; he didn't need to see just how convinced her whole family was that she was utterly useless.

At least Ada and Milo thought she was fun. She did have that going for her.

'We'll go say hi to Grandpa and your dad, then come find

you, okay?' Val said to her niece and nephew. She led Nick through the formal living room to the family room at the back of the house with her dad's massive TV and the sectional that took up about 80 percent of the floor space.

Anthony – Tony, to everyone who wasn't Amy – was sitting on the edge of a cushion with a beer can in his hand, clearly having just finished yelling at either the ref or the Packers. Kevin was at the other end of the couch, his blond hair perfectly styled. He was a CPA for the same insurance company Christine worked for, which was how they met, but he looked more like a trader on Wall Street. It was a deliberate choice, as far as Val could tell, but it wasn't one she'd make. 'Hey, sis,' Kev called. 'This your Hollywood boyfriend?'

'No, he's just some random dude I picked up on my way here,' Val deadpanned. 'And hi, Dad.'

'Hi, sweetie,' Tony said without really looking at her. 'Does your mom need your help in the kitchen?'

'I've been assigned babysitting duties,' Val replied. 'This is Nick, by the way.'

'Have you ever met Robert Downey Jr?' Kev asked.

'Um, no?' Nick replied.

'That's too bad. Iron Man's my favorite superhero.'

Nick sent her yet another confused look and she bit back a smile. For once, she wasn't the only one who had to deal with all of them, and there was some comfort in that. 'We're going to go find your kids,' Val said. Her dad was back to grumbling about a ref, not even acknowledging Nick, so they left without another word.

Val could hear Ada and Milo bickering in the foyer still, but before they left the living room Nick stayed her with a hand on her forearm. 'Are they always like this?' he asked, voice pitched low so no one could overhear.

Not that anyone would pay attention, but still. She appreciated the attempt. 'Ha,' she said humorlessly. 'Yes. *Val is a failure* is just about everyone's favorite topic. Which is why I'm about to go spend time with a nine- and eleven-year-old, because they at least think my screw-ups are cool.'

Nick looked like he wanted to protest, but instead he just followed her back to the foyer, where Ada and Milo where busy arguing about whose turn it was with the iPad.

'Um, excuse me, but I kicked your ass at Mario last Christmas,' Val said to Milo, following Nick and Ada – who were busy discussing the finer points of a Disney+ TV show about princesses that Val had never seen – into the dining room. True to form, Amy had set the table with elaborate place settings, and a massive centerpiece that would make it nearly impossible to see the person sitting across from them.

Val took a spot directly in front of the centerpiece and hoped Kev would sit opposite her, just so she would be spared any discussion of bitcoin during dinner. Unfortunately, Christine took that seat and Kev snagged the seat across from Nick, and sure enough, they had barely started passing the stuffing when Kev asked if Nick was familiar with cryptocurrency.

'I know what it is, yes,' Nick said pleasantly. 'But I tend to be pretty conservative with my investments.'

'Conservative with money,' Tony chuckled from the head of the table. 'How'd you end up with my daughter, again?'

Kevin was undeterred. 'You should consider –'

But Nick still had his eyes on Tony. 'What do you mean by that?' he asked mildly, scooping mashed potatoes onto his plate.

'Oh, you know,' Tony said, and Val felt herself starting to shrink back into her chair. 'Just how she is.'

'I do know how she is,' Nick said in that same pleasant, mild voice. 'She's a very smart businesswoman. Is that what you meant?'

Christine and Amy stopped chatting about Ada's soccer team, and even Kev put down his fork. An uncomfortable silence settled over the table. It was like the double-date, but at least that time Autumn had been oblivious. Now the tension was thick with *everyone*.

Amy recovered first, chuckling politely. 'Oh, you know,' she said in her *let's not make a fuss* voice. 'It's just that being an artist is no guarantee of steady income. You of all people would know that.'

'I do,' Nick said evenly. He was talking like they were making small talk about the weather or the Vikings' chances at the playoffs, but there was an unmistakable iron underneath that amiable tone. 'I also know how hard it is to cut off the creative side of you, and I've seen the damage it can do to people who deny it.'

Amy shifted uncomfortably, and uncharacteristically stayed silent.

'You quit acting for a steady nine-to-five job,' Christine argued. Val could only see the top of her head – light brown with vivid blonde highlights, because Christine got Mom's coloring while Val got Dad's – but she knew the look Christine would have on her face: skeptical but pleasant, like she was asking one of the kids to repeat an obvious lie they'd just told.

Speaking of, Ada and Milo were at a small card table tucked into the corner with a giant plastic mat underneath them, lest they accidentally spill cranberry sauce onto Amy's spotless teal carpet. Val desperately wished she was sitting with them, even if her knees would bang into the table every time she crossed her legs and it meant having yet another in-depth discussion of *Lord of the Rings*, which Milo was currently reading.

Next to her, Nick continued to surprise. 'I quit acting *because* it was just a job to me. Josh is the artist, I was just there for a paycheck. Creating art when your heart isn't in it is hard, so I left for something I wanted to do more. I also can't really imagine Josh being good at anything *but* acting. That's where his passion is, and he's lucky enough to be able to support himself by doing that. Just like Val.'

Once again, you could have heard a pin drop. Even Ada had stopped bickering with her brother about whether *Lord of the Rings* would be better 'with more girls in it' to listen. Val's usually sharp tongue was silent, and not just because it tended to fail her around her immediate family. There was an unfamiliar sensation in her stomach, warm and liquid and not at all unpleasant.

Tony attempted to rally next. 'It's not that we don't support her artistic side, we just think it would be better suited as a hobby. She can't just fiddle around with pictures for the rest of her life. What about when she has kids?'

'What about it?' Nick asked. Val wondered if her family could hear the danger in his tone, or if it was just her. 'Have any of you asked her if she even wants kids?'

Amy did her polite chuckle again, and Val knew her mother had clocked it too. 'I think you're getting the wrong impression,' she said soothingly. 'We absolutely understand why Val wants to do this job, we just think she needs something else, too. Something with a steady salary, something with health insurance. Anthony's dealership –'

'Have you asked her?' Nick said again.

'Sorry?' Amy said, setting her fork down with the tiniest *clink*.

'Do any of you care what Val wants to do? Have you asked her if she *wants* to move back here, away from her friends? Settle down, have kids?' Val's only real friend was Linds, who now lived in California, but she wasn't about to correct him. 'She has income, some good new leads, she's a thriving member of the Swede River community,' – *okay, that's a complete lie*, thought Val – 'and as far as I can tell, your only real objection is that she isn't doing what you want her to do. But what you want her to do would crush her, and I just can't imagine a family as loving as this one would want to hurt someone like that.'

Her family sat in stunned silence until Christine panicked and asked Tony to pass the salad. That was how the Costas operated, more or less – nitpick Val until it was untenable, and then pretend none of it had ever happened. They started chatting again, completely ignoring the previous five minutes, which underlined the sense of unreality of all of it.

Val swallowed hard, tears springing into her eyes, and below the table she reached for Nick's hand, giving his fingers a grateful squeeze.

No one, not even Linds, had ever done that for her before.

Chapter Nineteen

Val's door had been closed for several hours with barely any sounds emanating from her room, so she was either asleep (unlikely) or editing photos with her headphones blasting obnoxious music at earsplitting levels (probable and concerning). Nick knocked on her door, feeling absurdly nervous. They were friends now; asking her to come to the Swede River Sleigh Bells Festival wasn't weird or over the line. It was just a friendly roommate interaction, which she was free to turn down. Val's door flew open before he was even done knocking. She drew up short and looked flustered – maybe she'd just been leaving her room in her usual flurry of energy and hadn't realized he was there.

'Uh, hey,' she said, and if Nick had his way, he would ban her from looking so damn appealing in black joggers and a plain white T-shirt, especially because her bra was a bright, vivid red and the thin cotton of her shirt did almost nothing to hide it.

God, he was a pervert. Maybe he needed to move out and just leave his house to her. Nick wasn't sure where he'd stay – he'd rather get a root canal without anesthesia than move back to LA full time, but maybe Mary would let him move in with her and

Eng. They were still in the newlywed phase, which would be annoying, but Nick was reasonably sure he wouldn't fall in love with Mary because he thought her pajamas were hot.

Nick focused on Val's feet, which weren't *un*sexy, but at least wouldn't completely derail his train of thought. 'Hey,' he replied.

Val put her hand on his. Nick dragged his gaze up to her face, hoping his thoughts didn't show because right now they were a slideshow of every single time he'd touched her, either on purpose or accidentally. It was taking all of his energy not to think about what it was like to kiss her, because if he got hard in the middle of the hallway, she would think it was because she touched his arm, and then he would have to simply cease to exist. Diminish into the west, etc.

'Nick?'

Nick pulled his brain away from thinking about the fate of Tolkien's elves. 'Yeah?'

'Did you want something?'

'Oh, uh – right. It's the Sleigh Bells Festival tonight and I was going to go, and I was wondering if – you want to come?'

'That's the holiday thing, right? I assumed it was for families with kids and stuff.'

'There are some things that are for kids, but I don't think anyone would ban you from sitting on Santa's lap if you really wanted to,' Nick said, marveling internally at how quickly he could go from a stammering mess to bantering with Val.

'Given how things went at the Swedehearts' Dance . . . do you think it's a good idea?'

'It might not go over super well if you sit on Santa's lap, no.'

Val snorted. 'I meant going at all.'

'You're wondering if the whole town still hates you for being with me?'

'Yeah, that.'

Nick crossed his arms and considered it. 'I think Swede Rivertonians don't really handle outsiders well, but you've been here for a while, and as far as they know, we've been together for most of that time. If you're participating in town events, it'll look like you have some town spirit, which would probably go a long way.'

'I know, but – contrary to popular belief, I don't *like* being hated. I can handle it, but if it means a repeat of this fall . . .' She trailed off with a half-hearted shrug.

'You won Margie Schumacher over immediately,' he pointed out. 'That's about half the battle.'

'Still. It feels . . . daunting.'

'I'd be with you,' Nick said, and he wished he didn't sound quite so earnest, but it was hard for him to remain aloof around her, especially when she looked uncertain. 'And we could take a few photos of ourselves there for you to post to social media, just in case anyone at the studio is still keeping an eye on us.'

Something unreadable flashed in Val's eyes, but she nodded. 'That's a good idea,' she said, and then plucked at her shirt. 'I'll go change.'

Ten minutes later Val met him at the front door, stuffing her feet into her boots and grabbing her coat. 'It might snow later,' Nick said, and Val looked at him blankly. 'You'll want a hat,' he clarified.

She raised her eyebrows, amused. 'Sure thing, Mom.'

Nick rolled his eyes and grabbed her scarf from the hook while she tugged on her gloves.

He couldn't help but feel like he'd gone too far with her family on Thanksgiving. It wasn't usually how he operated, but like that dinner with Caleb, he couldn't watch Val – brash, confident, fiery Val – sit there meekly and have people rake her over the coals like she wasn't a fully formed adult capable of making her own rational choices. He also couldn't believe that they thought Val should be an administrative assistant at a car dealership, as if that wouldn't curdle her soul.

Sure, she was kind of a mess, especially when compared to that platonic ideal of suburbia. She was blunt in a way that clearly did not come from her family of origin, if her mother's impressive display of passive-aggression was any indication. But that explained why she could be so defensive, and with the way her sister fit in so naturally with their parents it made a certain amount of sense that Val had rebelled in the complete opposite direction.

What Nick couldn't understand, though, was why her family didn't like her very much. They cared about her, or at least they thought they did, but they also wanted to crush every little thing that made Val *Val*, which Amy would then probably sweep up and toss out immediately. And he just didn't get that.

Val had been unusually quiet on the drive back, and Nick had decided not to press it. Which meant it had now been a week and they were both acting like Thanksgiving had never happened, and that was weird. Right? It felt weird to him at least. He had no earthly idea how to broach the topic. *Sorry if I got overprotective of you when your family was being a bunch of jerks? Sorry if I keep forgetting this relationship is supposed to be fake, because I kind of wish it wasn't?*

Neither of those things felt like an appropriate thing to say to a roommate, so Nick had been following her lead and keeping quiet. It was fine; he was used to internal agony.

'I meant to say thanks. For Thanksgiving,' Val said, and let him wind the scarf around her neck. He was standing too close to her, and he really shouldn't have reached out and loosened her hair from where it was trapped under her scarf. But of course he did, because he always did the dumbest thing possible when it came to Val.

'It was nothing.'

'It wasn't nothing,' Val replied, her tone urgent and hushed. 'You know that. You have to know that.'

Nick was desperate, grasping at straws. 'It fit the role,' he said, and then immediately regretted it when he saw disappointment flash in her eyes. If Val was disappointed, that meant she might feel the way he did.

Except he couldn't afford to think that way. It would be too messy, too painful if he was wrong, and even if he was right – well, Nick had never been much of a risk-taker. And this would be the biggest risk of his life, bigger than walking away from a job that paid very well to become an anonymous librarian in an underfunded, overworked public library system.

He swallowed hard and tried to keep forging ahead. 'It's just what a real boyfriend would do. It would have been weird if I'd joined in.'

'Caleb would have,' Val said, shrugging.

Nick did his best to fight down the instinct to go wring Caleb's neck with his bare hands. 'He did that?'

'No, I meant, he would have if he'd ever been in that position. He never wanted to meet my family,' she added bitterly.

'Well, it's what a *good* boyfriend would have said.' He moved his hand from where it had been tangled in her hair and swallowed hard. 'We should get going, before all the hot chocolate is gone.'

Val let the moment pass without comment and fell into step next to him on the front walk. The air was crisp with the fresh scent of approaching snow, but for the moment, nothing was falling. Despite being only late afternoon, it was already fully dark, and they joined the trickle of people walking toward downtown.

Nick cleared his throat. 'You never did tell me what happened with the stuffing at Thanksgiving,' he mentioned. Now that he was over being mad at her family – or at least, not so mad he wanted to drive back to St Cloud and yell at them some more – something about it had been bugging him.

Val shrugged. 'I was with Caleb, but we were fighting, and he wasn't there, obviously. Mom had put me on stuffing duty, and I got distracted by texting him. I thought I turned the oven off, but actually, I'd hit *broil*, which is a stupid setting anyway. Who even uses that setting?'

'People who need to broil things,' Nick pointed out.

Val looked dubious. 'If you say so. Anyway, there was a minor fire, but whatever, I put it out right away. It was mostly just smoke. And then there was no stuffing, obviously, unless someone wanted to eat a pile of charcoal.' She laughed a little, but then looked over at him. 'Seriously, it was nothing.'

Nick chewed at his lip thoughtfully. 'I mean, sounds like it was a little more than *nothing*. Doesn't mean your family is right to keep beating you over the head with it, but – shit, you started a fire?' He felt bad when Val started to flush and hastened to explain himself. 'I don't mean to pile on you or anything, but – even if they treat you like crap, that does sound sort of like your fault.'

'What, are you going to ban me from the kitchen now?' she asked, a little waspishly.

'No, but I might put tape over the broil button to keep you from hitting it by accident,' he teased gently. Val snorted, so at least she wasn't too upset with him. A comfortable silence fell over them and they walked side by side, the air smelling faintly of woodsmoke.

They overtook Margie about a half-block from Main Street, resembling more a bundle of walking layers than an actual person. Nick held out his arm and Margie waved him off, preferring to look around him at Val. 'You need a hat, child,' she scolded.

Val frowned. 'Nick said the same thing.'

'Well, men are occasionally right. Like broken clocks.'

'I'm fine,' Val insisted. 'You two just like to fuss.'

That much was true, and Margie agreed, if her snort was any indication. Up ahead small booths for the various venders all decorated in white Christmas lights sprawled along both sides of Main Street. There was an oversized sleigh in the town square, complete with gigantic reindeer and a hand-painted *Swede River Sleigh Bells Festival* sign in blue and white arching over it all. The high school handbell choir was in the pavilion playing 'Jingle Bells' because Swede River was nothing if not on-the-nose when it came to town celebrations.

Margie spotted someone from the Senior Center who she needed to tell off, so Nick and Val joined the line at Pete's Coffee. By the time they arrived at the counter, Pete and Aaron were deep in a whispered not-quite-fight while Felix kept lunging out of Aaron's arms to try and grab a stack of paper cups. 'Just go ahead without me,' Pete was saying, catching Nick's eye apologetically.

'We were going to do this as a family,' Aaron argued. 'Sorry, guys, one second,' he added to Nick and Val.

'Do you guys need a hand?' Val asked.

'It's nothing, don't worry about it,' Pete said, turning to face them. 'Hot chocolate, cider, or coffee?'

'Hot chocolate,' Nick and Val replied at the same time, and then laughed. 'But really, did you need someone to step in?' Val offered.

'We're scheduled to take a sleigh ride in five minutes, but Livvy's handbell choir got started late and isn't done yet, so she can't take over,' Aaron explained.

'She's in handbell, too?' Nick asked. 'Is there anything Livvy doesn't do?'

'I don't think she's played football yet,' Pete said, handing over the cups and taking Nick's ten-dollar bill.

Val considered the chalkboard propped on the counter. 'Everything's five bucks?'

'Everything,' a bemused Pete replied.

'Well, you're looking at a certified Smorgasbord Cashier, who is also a certified Dartboard Cashier if we're counting high school gigs, and it's not like this involves making any drinks, so you guys go take your ride. I can handle this.'

'I couldn't –'

'Do you want to go, or do you want to argue with me?' Val asked, boosting herself up onto the counter and swinging her legs over. 'Go,' she said one last time, giving Pete a gentle shove. 'I promise, this will all still be standing when you come back.'

Pete pulled off his apron and hurried out of the booth after his husband and baby, leaving Val to look expectantly at Nick. 'Well, either order something else or get out of the way, you're holding up the line,' she said briskly. She rose on her toes to peer over his shoulder and nod to the next person in line. Nick stepped aside and watched her cheerfully greet Charles Poulson, check the steaming carafes behind her, and pour him a cup of cider. Charles jostled him slightly to get past, and Nick finally snapped into action.

He let himself into the booth from the side half-door, squeezing in next to her. 'You deal with people, I'll pour,' he said quietly, gratified by the answering smile that spread across her face.

It was hardly a two-person job, but it was fun. It was even more fun to watch Val interact with the steady stream of people who stepped up to order and did a double-take. Clearly, no one was expecting to see her working there, but unlike at the Swedehearts' Dance, the glares were few and far between. During a lull in customers, she poured an extra cup of hot chocolate and nodded to where Margie was sitting at a card table in front of the large sleigh, chatting with several other older women. 'Tell Margie this one's on the house,' she said, and rolled her eyes before he could protest. 'I already paid for it.'

Nick let himself out and walked across the square to hand it over. 'Val thought you'd want one,' he said, aware that Margie's friends were all eyeing him closely.

'She's a smart one, that girl of yours,' Margie said. The rest of the women nodded, taking their cues from the town monarch. 'Tell her thanks, and that I'll be in touch with her about New Year's Eve.'

Nick went back to the booth, where Livvy was arriving. 'Sorry, handbell ran over,' she said apologetically. 'Where's Pete?'

'Family sleigh ride,' Val said, plucking a candy cane from a jar behind the counter and leaning forward to hand it to an excited-looking toddler. 'They'll be back soon. Did you need a hand in the meantime?'

Livvy surveyed the short line and shook her head. 'Go enjoy the festival,' she said and tied on her apron.

Maybe it was his imagination, but it felt like Val was walking a little closer to him as they left. Every so often her shoulder would bump into his arm, but with thick coats between them Nick told himself it was a coincidence.

It *had* to be.

'By the way, Margie said to tell you she'll be in touch about New Year's Eve,' Nick said as Val examined a stand that displayed several elaborate gingerbread houses and, inexplicably, an entire rack of hand-knitted dog sweaters. 'You planning on throwing a rager with her?'

Val chuckled and moved on to the next booth, which was a bake sale fundraiser for the high school orchestra. 'She asked me earlier if I'd be willing to do the photos for the town New Year's Eve party.'

'And will you?'

Val shrugged. 'It's money, for one thing, and besides, you said I need to work at integrating myself into the town, so it can't hurt, right?'

Nick nodded, wondering why he wished it wasn't just a chore for her. It shouldn't matter to him if she liked being in Swede River, but earlier it had felt as if she wanted to belong, and he'd felt like everything was slowly falling into place. It was good to remind himself that wasn't what this was about before he went and did anything irrevocably stupid.

Nick waved to Eng, who was working a booth selling his sister's egg rolls. He bought one for himself and one for Val, while she scurried back to the orchestra booth to buy them both brownies. They walked together in a comfortable silence as a few thick, fluffy flakes came swirling down from the charcoal-grey sky.

As if on cue they both turned toward home, waving at Pete and Livvy as they passed, and Val called a goodbye to Margie. Flakes fell faster as they turned up their street, a thin layer of snow clinging to lawns like a lumpy blanket. It felt good, walking together like that, moving around the small foyer to hang up their coats and unwind their scarves, like two people who did things like this all the time. He liked feeling like they were a part of each other's lives, not just two roommates who had come up with a harebrained scheme to get themselves out of a jam.

Val climbed the stairs, Nick beside her, and drew to a stop near her door. She looked up at him with eyes that had gone soft. 'I've been meaning to say something,' she started, chewing her lower lip. 'About Thanksgiving.'

'I'm sorry for bringing up the stuffing thing.'

'It's not that – you might have a point, but you'll never catch me admitting that to Mom, or else I really will never hear the end of it.'

'Fair enough,' he said with a half-grin. 'So, what about it?'

'You stood up for me. I don't know if you know how rare that is.'

'I told you, it was nothing.'

'No, it wasn't. You were there for me, and it made me wish that this was – that it wasn't acting.'

Nick's heart responded before his brain could catch up. 'It wasn't acting.'

Val blinked and licked her lips. It seemed like she was standing closer to him, but he couldn't remember either of them moving. She opened her mouth to speak and then closed it several times, finally putting her hand back on his arm, this time closer to his wrist. 'It wasn't?'

This was his chance to take it back, to call on those supposed acting skills and make her believe he didn't care. But Josh was the natural actor, and Nick wanted – no, needed – Val to want it to be real, too.

Nick lifted his hand, fitting it along the curve of her jaw. Her skin was chilled from the walk but burned his palm anyway. His fingers tunneled into the messy waves behind her ear and her hand stayed wrapped around his wrist, almost like she was holding him there.

As if he would ever let go.

Val took a half-step back. He followed. Her shoulder blades bumped into the wall and Nick rested his free forearm above her head, caging her in. 'I'm not a very good actor,' he confessed, and Val made a noise that might have been a laugh.

She had tipped her head up to look at him and her fingertips traced the planes of his face. Nick closed his eyes and just let himself feel for a minute. His brain was always racing, always coming up with worst case scenarios, but right then, in the hallway between her door and his, everything went blissfully blank. He simply *felt*. The whisper of her fingers over his skin, the way they were somehow soothing and awakening at once. Her scent, warm and familiar, filling his lungs. Her silk-smooth skin under his palm. The little hitch in her breathing when his thumb swept across her cheek.

'Then I guess there's nothing stopping us,' Val murmured, and Nick was about to close the distance between them and do what he'd been aching to do since the corn maze when his brain kicked back into gear.

Nick hadn't ever felt like this before, and if it went further, he knew he was not going to get out of it in one piece. It was selfish, but it was the truth. 'Wait,' he said, hating himself but not able to stop.

Val froze. 'What's wrong?'

'Are you sure this is a good idea?' he asked, even though his forehead was now pressed to hers. Christ, he was stupid.

Val moved her head back to make eye contact with him. 'Are you honestly asking me? Because I've never had a good idea in my life,' she said wryly.

That tripped something in his brain. It wasn't just a bad idea; it was a catastrophically bad one. He couldn't see any positives, just the inevitable car crash of a breakup that would be barreling their way. She would move out, leave him and Swede River behind, and then Nick would have to rebuild his life after she'd just gone and blown a hole in it. He had never been a risk-taker, and this would probably be the biggest risk of them all.

Val would probably leave regardless, but it would be easier if he could keep his heart out of it. Or at least let himself pretend she didn't feel the same, because it was always easier for him to believe the fault lay solely with himself. But that didn't mean he hated himself any less for what he was about to do.

With tremendous effort, he dropped his hand and stepped back. 'Nick?' she asked quietly. He made himself look away because he couldn't handle seeing pain on her face. 'What's wrong?'

'I – I don't think we should,' he replied. 'It's just so complicated. We live together, so what happens if this ends? That would make it so much harder, and – it just seems messy.' His excuses sounded flimsy even to his own ears, but it was the best he could do. Every cell in his body was screaming for him to shut up, to kiss her, to stop *worrying* so damn much, but he couldn't.

'So, you – don't want to?'

'It's not a matter of want,' he admitted as his heart constricted painfully. *Of course I want you, but wanting you and keeping you are two very different things.* 'We can't. It's that simple.'

'I wouldn't exactly call it *simple*,' Val said with a bitter laugh. 'But if you don't want to, then – goodnight, I guess.'

She stopped with her hand on the doorknob and looked back, like she was waiting for him to say something. Nick opened his mouth and then closed it, because in the end, he was a coward.

He was going to hear the *click* of her door shutting for the rest of his life.

Chapter Twenty

Val bent her head against the wind as she stepped out of her car and hitched her bag a little higher on her shoulder. Livvy trundled past in her mom's minivan, the slush accumulating on the road sloshing messily. What had been soft, fluffy flakes during her photoshoot with Autumn was swiftly turning into a full-blown blizzard, which meant getting back to Nick's place had been way more difficult than anticipated. She had been beginning to think of it as *home*, but lately she had reverted to mentally calling it Nick's again. It helped remind her that 1) it was temporary, and 2) he didn't want it to get complicated.

She couldn't help it. That hurt. He wasn't wrong, but Val had never been good at calculating risks and choosing the least dangerous option. She always felt first and thought later, and yeah, that had created more than one catastrophe in her life. But using her brain rarely worked out in her favor – that was why she'd stuck with Caleb for so long.

Because Caleb was the Right Sort of Boyfriend. Or could have been, had it ever been that official. He was who her parents would have wanted her to be with, even if he'd never committed to her enough to spend a holiday with them. Caleb was successful at a job that required him to wear a suit sometimes and had the same general demeanor and sense of humor as Kev. Since Kev was considered the pinnacle of possible husbands by Christine and their parents, when Caleb had started flirting with her in college Val had thought *finally*. He was handsome and charming – and the sex was good, even when everything else was garbage. And then honestly, after a while, she kept it going because deep down, Val loathed herself and she had figured that was as good as it was going to get for her. Nick's wavering on her was way too much like Caleb's, with the added sting that Nick was an all-around better person than Caleb could ever hope to be.

It didn't help that Nick had a point when he said her mother had a good reason for not trusting her in the kitchen. Even worse, he'd been kind about it, like he was worried that telling her she was wrong was going to hurt her feelings. It had, obviously, which drove home both how different he was from Caleb, and how little of a chance she ever had of digging herself out of the hole she'd always been in. The weirdest thing was, it also made her want to prove that *wasn't* who she had been, or at least not anymore. Val had never quite wanted to change for anyone, so even the slightest hint in the back of her mind that she was considering it for Nick made her want to double down on the gremlin life.

Another gust of wind slapped her in the face, and she blinked against the wet snow gathering on her eyelashes, fishing around in her bag for the keys to the house. At least Caleb hadn't been at the photoshoot today, which was a relief. It had been a small product shoot for a parka Autumn had been sent by a prospective sponsor, and she needed someone to take pictures of her frolicking in the snow.

That was good, at least. It meant Val was becoming Autumn's

go-to photographer, which only meant good things for Val's career. When Autumn had posted photos of the engagement shoot with Caleb and tagged Val's professional page, Val had seen a sharp spike in her stats. She'd even been contacted by two couples who were getting married next summer and wanted to 'lock her down' in advance. It had also displaced most of the complaints from Terrible Bride in the top search results, which probably helped more than anything else. Val hadn't gotten the deposits from her new clients yet, but the invoices were out.

In short, everything was looking up, except for things with Nick. She still wasn't entirely clear on why he didn't kiss her – he wanted to, except he also didn't. It didn't make sense, and it still stung like hell. Val had never really been one to handle rejection with anything resembling grace, so she'd just avoided him ever since.

Naturally, that meant Autumn had wanted to talk to her about him. Livvy had posted a photo of her and Nick working the booth to the Pete's Coffee Instagram, which Autumn apparently now followed. Val and Nick were mid-conversation, Val half-facing a customer while he was pouring a cup of cocoa. They both looked happy, but more than that, they'd looked comfortable. Like a real couple, which meant it stung when Autumn squealed about how cute they were. But after talking about wanting to come down for Sleigh Bells next year, she'd stopped and cocked her head to the side. 'Cal was kind of weird about it, though.'

Val had paused at that. 'He was weird about the Sleigh Bells Festival?'

'Yeah, kinda. I mentioned that it would be fun for us to go next year, just how cute it was and how you guys looked like you were having fun, and I showed him the pictures on

Instagram, and then he like, clammed up. Got all grumpy about it, and said it looked boring.'

'It wasn't like, super exciting or anything,' Val had ventured. Something about the story bothered her. After the orchard, Nick had thought Caleb might be jealous of them, but she had written it off as Caleb getting annoyed when he felt left out of something. Except the Sleigh Bells Festival didn't have the sort of flash and glitz he looked for in a party and it wasn't like Linds was there that time. Maybe he was just dreading going next year.

'It looked so cute and cozy, though. I'm coming next year; Cal can stay home if he wants.' Autumn had laughed, and then returned to the spot they'd picked for another round of pictures. Maybe Caleb felt like Autumn was becoming their friend, which made him uncomfortable. Val had pondered that for a moment and then had turned back to Autumn, shaking Caleb off for the rest of the day, but left with a lingering queasiness that was mostly related to Autumn thinking she and Nick were doing well. In reality, they couldn't be doing worse.

It had been an awkward few days, that was for sure. Val stomped her boots on the welcome mat and shouldered the door open, hoping today was a day that Nick was stuck with an evening shift. She had been deliberately ignoring his schedule lately, because knowing when he worked meant admitting she was paying attention to him, which he clearly didn't want.

Or he did want, but he didn't *want* to want it, which wasn't much different, in her opinion. Rejection was rejection, and it hurt even if it was reluctant.

Val unwound her scarf and kicked off her boots, belatedly remembering to set them in the shoe tray Nick had painstakingly explained to her was there for that very purpose. She didn't fully see the point – the cramped entryway was going to be full of slush and melted snow no matter what – but she was trying.

However, the man himself was sitting on the couch right as she walked in, looking like the hero in a goddamn Hallmark Christmas movie with his cozy grey sweater, sitting in front of a fire – the nerve of him, honestly – reading with a glass of red wine on the end table next to him.

He glanced up and – oh, *shit*. He was wearing *glasses*. She knew he wore them, but knowing and *knowing* were two totally different things, and now she was even more weak in the knees for a man who wished she would just disappear.

'Hey,' he said, putting his finger between the pages and closing the book. 'I didn't realize you were out in this.'

Val shrugged and a clump of snow slipped from her hair to the back of her neck, sending shivers down her spine. 'It wasn't so bad when I left,' she said, running her hands through her hair and finding it completely saturated.

'You must be cold,' he said, and paused. After a minute's deliberation, he tipped his head toward the fire. 'If you need to warm up, feel free.'

Val was about to turn him down, if only to save her fragile heart from cracking a little more when he looked at her from behind those thick-rimmed glasses, but she couldn't bring herself to do it. 'My clothes are soaked, so I should change, but then – yeah, I think that would be nice.'

'Sounds good,' Nick replied, and the soft smile on his face warmed her thoroughly.

Val had sort of hoped Nick would have changed too while she was in her room, out of that soft, warm-looking sweater and into something considerably less appealing, like perhaps a black plastic poncho with a paper bag over his head. She was out of luck; he was still sitting there, now with a second glass of wine out on the coffee table. The bottle was next to it, and Nick almost never took bottles out of the kitchen.

Val was not known for making peace offerings, but she could recognize one when she saw it. Her hair was still damp, turning into the half-wavy, half-curly mess it became when water got too involved without proper styling products, but she hadn't wanted to waste time drying it before she came out. It had taken her long enough to pick out her clothes – a bright blue sweatshirt and black leggings, hardly groundbreaking – and it was taking all of her mental energy to keep from getting ahead of herself. *He wants things to be less awkward between us, that's all.*

Outside, the wind howled. Snow was flying horizontally now, and right as Val sat down the lights flickered. She hesitated, hovering over the cushion, but when they stayed on she proceeded. At least the fireplace was wood, so if they lost power they wouldn't freeze.

And if they lost power they might be forced to share a bed again, which really wouldn't be the worst thing.

God, *she* was the worst. Nick had made it perfectly clear he wasn't interested in anything, even if she didn't quite get his reasons. All she had to do was respect his wishes, and she could barely clear that low bar.

She picked up the glass by the stem and lifted it toward him in thanks. 'You didn't have to work the evening shift tonight?'

He shook his head. 'Not this week. Which is a relief, because blizzards like this tend to make it either eerily quiet or a complete zoo, and you never know which it'll be. With this hitting during the late afternoon, I'm guessing it's the latter.'

Val tipped her head to the side and watched his eyes track the fall of her hair over her shoulder. He had a thing for her hair, that much was clear. 'I guess I never really imagine the library as the sort of job that gets busy and chaotic.'

'Everyone thinks we read books all day,' he said ruefully. 'But it's a lot more than that. Snow like this means unhoused people are looking for temporary shelter, especially if the shelter is already at capacity, plus parents who bring their kids stock up on books before a snow day, or because they need somewhere warm and dry, too.'

'That doesn't sound like much of it has to do with books at all.'

'A lot of it doesn't, although the on-call social worker thing has way more to do with actual social services being underfunded, and libraries being one of the few public places people can access the internet if they don't have it at home.'

Val folded her legs under herself, if only to keep from stretching them out and resting her feet in his lap like she did that night she ended up falling asleep on his shoulder.

God, they were complete messes. It was unsustainable. Something had to break, and it was probably going to be her heart.

'You had a shoot with Autumn, right?' he asked, and Val decided to redouble her efforts to be a normal, platonic roommate-slash-fake-girlfriend, if such a thing existed. She explained why Autumn had wanted to do one like this last minute, and by the time her wine was mostly gone, it almost seemed like they could manage something approaching friendship. She could tell him about her job, he could tell her about his, and then they could go to bed – separately – like functioning adults.

She reached for the wine bottle on the coffee table, but it was too far away. Instead of standing up to get it like a normal person, though, Val slipped down off the cushion to sit in the small gap between the couch and the coffee table. She probably poured too much into her second glass, but it wasn't like she was going anywhere. There had to be five inches of snow on the ground already, and the storm was forecast to last all night.

The lights flickered again, and then the living room plunged into darkness. The firelight threw a semicircle of a warm, orange glow around the room, but Nick's face was hidden in the shadows. Outside, the sky was the peculiar shade of grey that only happened during snowstorms, where it was somehow brighter than it should be at that time of night. Silence settled over them like a blanket. The usual hum of the fridge had stopped, and the only sound was the *crackle-hiss-pop* of the fire.

'Should we be worried?' she asked.

Nick shrugged. 'They're usually pretty efficient at getting stuff fixed.'

'You'd think it would be slower, since it's such a small town.'

'You'd think, yeah. But the few times the power's gone out before, it's been back up in under an hour.'

Val leaned against the foot of the couch. 'Swede River just isn't what I thought it would be, even though it's also exactly what I thought it would be.' She laughed softly to herself and shook her head. 'I'm sorry, that doesn't make sense.'

'Actually, it makes perfect sense,' Nick said and moved down to the floor next to her. 'Probably warmer here,' he said, even though he had moved only a foot closer to the fire.

He was, however, now considerably closer to Val. Six inches away, to be precise.

Val held out the bottle and topped off his glass, more for something to do than because he needed a refill. Their earlier camaraderie faded away, replaced by something heavier, more potent.

She looked at him and he looked at her, neither of them saying anything. Nick's glasses were reflecting the fire, making it hard for her to read his expression, but then he carefully tucked a lock of hair behind her ear, and she realized she didn't need to see his eyes. She knew what they looked like and was glad she couldn't see them because his gaze would probably set her on fire.

Nick's fingers traced the shell of her ear, his throat working hard, but then his thumb brushed along her eyebrow and his brow furrowed, and she knew what he was wondering before he even spoke. 'What happened here?' he murmured.

She couldn't help it. She flinched, and he drew back his hand like he'd been burned. 'Sorry, I shouldn't have,' he apologized.

'It's fine, I just –' Val shifted so her back was against the couch again and dropped her head back on the cushion. 'It's a long story, that's all.'

He waited for a beat of silence to settle. 'I have time,' he said cautiously, and she loved that about him, the way he always seemed to let her take things on her own terms, at her own pace. He gave her space, and she never realized how much she craved that until she met him.

But she couldn't look at him, not while she told this story. 'No one really knows what happened,' she started, but then shook her head. 'No, that's not true. I do, and so does Caleb. But I never told anyone else the real story.'

Despite the gap between them, she felt him tense. 'Did he –'

'No, no, nothing like that,' she said hurriedly. 'And it's not even how I got the scar, it's everything after. I just meant –' She broke off and sighed. 'We'd been hooking up for about a year. And we were all just a few years out of college, trying to figure shit out. I shared this crappy two-bedroom apartment with

Linds. I had a part-time job as a cashier at Smorgasbord, plus another job as a local artist's assistant, which as you can imagine, I was terrible at.'

She paused, waiting. But Nick didn't chuckle at her joke, which made her throat thick. She cleared it and forged on. 'Caleb got his job right out of college, because his mom owns the whole company, but he took it really seriously and wanted to prove to all his colleagues he wasn't just a nepo baby.' Val could hear the pleading justifications in her explanation, but she couldn't help herself, it was a reflex when it came to Caleb. Above her, the fire made dancing shadows on the ceiling.

It was easier to look at them than at Nick. 'Anyway, my car was in the shop, so I decided to call a RideShare home from work, and some jackass ran a four-way stop sign and T-boned the car I was in.'

Nick sucked in a sharp breath but didn't speak. 'It wasn't catastrophic or anything, but I hit my forehead on the door and split my eyebrow pretty bad, and there was – god, there was so much blood. I legit thought I was dying there for a second, until I remembered that Lindsey said head wounds bleed badly but that doesn't mean they're always super dangerous. I mean, I know that head wounds are *bad*, but it wasn't *bad bad*.' She was rambling, she could tell, and she did her best to rein it in. 'But like I said, there was a lot of blood and a bystander called 9-1-1, so I ended up going to the hospital in an ambulance for stitches.' She traced the scar that still bisected her right eyebrow, a slim sliver of skin that refused to hide. 'I got four stitches and some topical anesthetic, and that was it. No big deal, really.'

She took a deep breath, because here came the terrible part, the part that still made her feel like something small and unwanted, tossed away carelessly, even after all this time. 'I was a little shaken up and didn't want to take another RideShare home. So, I called Caleb.' Val closed her eyes, even though she was still looking at the ceiling. 'I knew he had a meeting with a client at a property later that day, but, I had to mean something to him, right? I thought he could work something out, but he just told me that since I was fine and he had to get out to Maple Grove for the showing, I should just get over my nerves and take another RideShare. He had this whole speech about getting back on the horse or something, and it wasn't like I was *never* going to take another one, I just – I didn't want to right then, that's all. I was scared and rattled and I just wanted someone to take care of me, and instead – he made me feel stupid and weak. I ended up calling Linds and she had to argue with her boss to get off a little early at the lab. Eventually she came and got me. I told her that I couldn't get ahold of Caleb because he was showing some rural property that didn't have good reception, and as far as I know, she believed me.'

Nick didn't say anything. He'd gone deadly still, and Val couldn't bring herself to see the disappointment in his eyes. It was why she hadn't told anyone this story, especially Lindsey. Linds would have sat her down and told her in no uncertain terms that Caleb was a Grade A jackass who deserved to be dumped, but back then, Val wasn't ready to hear it, even if part of her probably already knew it. Self-loathing could really convince a person to do a lot of stupid things, and for Val, that stupid thing was protecting Caleb.

'I should have broken up with him right then. The fact that I didn't has always made me feel stupid in retrospect, you know? Like, I knew what I should have done, but I didn't, so however shitty he was, it was my fault too, for not breaking up with him. But in some ways it was easy with him, you know? I knew what to expect, and since it was never official it wasn't hard to pretend like it didn't matter that he didn't care.'

'Right,' Nick said, more under his breath than anything, and stood up. 'I'm going to go kill him,' he announced, and while she knew he wasn't serious – she had watched him gently trap a spider under a glass with a magazine and take it outside just three days ago – there was a part of her that wasn't totally sure.

And to be perfectly honest, that part of her? Super into it. But she made herself laugh and grab his hand, tugging him back down to the floor. 'He's not worth the arrest record,' Val pointed out.

'Can't get charged with murder if there's no body,' Nick countered.

'Mmm, pretty sure that's not true,' she said, and now her chuckle was genuine.

'Did I miss when you went to law school?' he grumbled, and the knot in her chest eased slightly.

'Okay, fine. How about the blizzard? Will that keep you here?'

'Maybe,' Nick said darkly, but he kept his fingers loosely tangled with hers. 'But seriously – I'm sorry. That was crappy of him. You –'

'Don't say I deserve better,' Val interrupted. 'I knew it wasn't working, but I stayed anyway. That's on me.'

'Sometimes we stay in things we don't want because it's easier than walking away,' Nick replied, with the air of choosing his words carefully. 'I had a hard time officially leaving acting, even though I knew it wasn't what I wanted. It meant leaving Josh behind, and even more than that, it meant giving up on the life Josh thought we'd both have. And I'm guessing Caleb was something like that for you.'

'Something like that, yeah.'

'Are you sure you don't want me to kill him? I wouldn't mind. I might enjoy it, even,' Nick said, and even though he was kidding, tears sprang into her eyes. She blinked, but one single tear betrayed her and escaped.

'Hey hey hey,' he whispered, destroying any illusions she had that he might not have noticed. 'I was kidding.'

'I know,' Val sniffed, swiping at her cheek with the back of her hand. 'I just – I'm not used to this.'

'To what? Someone being nice to you?'

'God, when you put it like that, I sound pathetic,' she laughed weakly, sniffing.

Nick caught another tear with his thumb. 'Don't say that,' he chided gently. 'If anyone's pathetic here, it's me.'

His hand was cradling her cheek, and she wasn't about to move, but she also wasn't about to stop arguing. 'You? The unquestionable grown-up who makes balanced meals and has a real job with benefits and made a deliberate choice to leave behind a life you hated? How is that pathetic?'

Nick licked his lips slowly. 'Because I've been falling for you for months, and this whole time I've been trying to tell myself it's pointless, but I can't help it.' His words pierced her heart and she winced at the reminder that his feelings were against his better judgment, but he didn't let her go and he didn't stop talking. 'You deserve someone so much better than me, someone more exciting, someone who doesn't alphabetize his books and iron his socks.'

'Wait, do you really –'

'I'm confessing here, shush,' Nick admonished with a tiny grin. His thumb swept along her cheekbone and Val swallowed hard. 'You need to know by now I'm falling pathetically in love with you, and I can't stop hating myself for not kissing you the other day. Not kissing you was the right thing to do, but Christ, Val, it kills me. It kills me to see you every morning and not have you, and every night I watch you go to a bed that isn't mine and that kills me, too. I'm dying over here and I can't even be mad about it, because – because it's you.'

It felt like she was drowning. She couldn't breathe and she couldn't even really think, all she could do was look at him and the way he was looking at her. 'I can't stop thinking about you, either,' she admitted, but her words felt clumsy after his. Nick had given a speech like he had a team of scriptwriters crafting a perfect, heart-wrenching monologue, and all she could say was *samesies*. She struggled to get her thoughts into a more eloquent sentence, but in the end, all that came out was, 'I want you too.'

Chapter Twenty-One

Without letting go of her face, Nick pulled off his glasses with his other hand and leaned in, closing the distance between them. Val was glad it was so dark in the living room, because otherwise he'd probably see the flush crawling up her neck. As it was, he could probably feel her pulse hammering and the tiny, uncontrollable shivers that were making her tremble.

All this, and he still hadn't kissed her. 'Is this okay?' he asked, his nose brushing hers.

'Kiss me,' Val begged, and the relief that surged through her veins when Nick finally, *finally*, pressed his lips to hers was palpable.

If she'd thought the previous kiss was a fluke, this proved it wasn't. He had a way of stealing air from her lungs and making her forget everything she'd ever known or thought. Nick's tongue teased her lower lip, asking a question he already knew the answer to, but she liked that he asked it anyway. Val parted her lips and met his tongue with her own, deciding that if they were going to do this, she was going to do it *right*.

She swung her knee over his hips and settled into his lap without ever once breaking the kiss, because if she stopped kissing him, even for a second, she was worried this would all evaporate like mist on a cold spring morning. Nick groaned into her mouth and dug his fingertips into her back, his hands just as hungry as his lips.

Val rocked her hips and he groaned again, pressing his forehead to hers with a harsh breath. 'Fuck,' he whispered, and anchored his hands on her hips. 'Do that again.'

She did, and this time they both moaned. Nick took her face in his hands again and pulled her against him, and at least he seemed as desperate for her as she was for him. She could kiss him for hours, she realized, just let herself get lost in his touch and the gentle way he nipped at her lower lip.

With a soft *click* the lights came on abruptly, so bright they both paused and blinked rapidly, trying to adjust their eyes. Nick's lips were swollen, and his hair was mussed, his eyes glassy and dazed. She looked at him and he looked at her, and right then, even though they'd been kissing for who knows how long already, it hit her. This was real.

It was happening. His dick was hard between her legs. There was no going back. She saw the same thought flicker across his face, but after half a second's consideration they crashed back into each other.

It was going to take more than just some lights turning back on to keep her away from him. The loose neckline of her sweatshirt had slipped down her shoulder and Nick followed it with his mouth, burning a trail of kisses down her neck. She clawed at the hem of his soft grey sweater, pulling it up over his head and then groaning in disappointment when she realized he was still wearing a white T-shirt underneath.

Val slipped her hands under his shirt, skinning her nails across his flat stomach, and Nick hissed. 'Damn, your hands are cold,' he scolded.

'Sorry,' she murmured against his lips, but she didn't really mean it and his answering smile told her he didn't care, either. Nick swept her sweatshirt off in one quick motion and then took her face in his hands again, kissing her for so long and so hard it was difficult to breathe.

She rocked her hips along his length and his fingers tightened on her jaw, his breath catching. 'We should – move,' Val stammered, trying desperately to keep hold of her train of thought. 'To a bedroom? Maybe yours?' She hadn't made her bed in at least two weeks, and she was reasonably sure there were several cereal bowls still piled on the floor next to her desk. She didn't want to risk Nick getting annoyed with her messiness now, not when things were – well, not when things were perfect.

Nick pinned his forehead to hers, breathing deep. 'Good idea,' he agreed, and then without warning he lifted her up by the waist and deposited her unceremoniously on the couch. 'Race you,' he said, and flashed a smile that made her forget her indignation.

But that smile *also* had the effect of letting him get a split-second head start. Val cursed and jumped up, sprinting after him in just her bra and leggings. She took the stairs two at a time in a vain attempt to catch up, but his legs were a lot longer than hers.

Nick got to his door first. He whirled around and caught her, tugging her against him as he walked backwards through the door. 'Too slow,' he said, clicking his tongue.

'You cheated,' Val pouted, unable to stop her giggle when Nick playfully nipped at her lower lip.

'Obviously,' Nick shrugged, but then he peeled off his white undershirt and Val forgot her next argument because – *damn*. Just damn.

'I – wow. Do all librarians look like this?' she asked, resting her hand just above his heart.

Nick barked out a laugh as he lifted her hand and wove their fingers together. 'Librarians are a very underrated species.'

'I'll never make that mistake again.' Val let him arrange her arms loosely around his neck and stepped closer. Heat radiated off his skin and she buried her face in his neck, breathing deep. She dropped her hand to the waistband of his jeans, waiting until she felt him nod. Popping the button was easy, and the rumble in his chest when she reached in and palmed his cock was delicious.

She did it again, easing his jeans down with her free hand and shoving his boxer briefs past his hips. As she had suspected, his cock was perfect – thick but not too thick, long but not bruisingly so.

Perfect, just like Nick. Val mentally banished that thought – she was already having enough trouble processing the fact that he'd dropped the L-bomb already – and curled her hand around him, stroking him softly.

She sank to her knees and lifted her gaze, pausing again until Nick nodded. It was just a tiny jerk of his head, the tendons in his neck corded with tension and his jaw set tight, but she loved it. She loved that he was barely restraining himself and loved that he – a man who clearly did not like or trust many people – was trusting her with this. It made her heart feel soft and tender, but the look in his eyes was pure fire. That heat raced along her spine, and she brought him to her lips for a slow, swirling lick.

Nick knotted his hand in her hair. But he didn't take control, just let her slide his cock into her mouth. He was hard and heavy on her tongue, a tang of salt to his skin that she suddenly craved. Val pulled back, almost to his tip, and then engulfed him again. She soon found a rhythm that, if the way he dug his fingertips into her scalp was any indication, he liked. She curled her tongue around the tip and slid her hands up his thighs, bracing herself, but before she could go farther Nick's hand was on her arm and he was pulling her up. 'Keep going like that and I'm going to come right now,' he growled.

Val smiled against his lips. 'Maybe that was my plan.'

Nick made a choked noise and cuffed his hand around the back of her neck. 'Not tonight. Tonight, I'm coming inside you.'

Val felt a surge of wetness between her legs. As if he knew what his words had done to her, he eased his hand under the waistband of her leggings, tracing her folds through her now-damp panties. 'Is that what you want?' he asked, and all Val could do was mewl helplessly and nod.

Nick pushed her down on the bed, crawling over her with a playful grin. This was a side of him she'd seen so rarely, open and happy and almost silly, and it made a pack of butterflies take flight in her stomach. He undid the clasp of her bra, easing it off her shoulders. Val pushed herself up on her elbows to kiss him, her hand curling around the back of his neck to keep him close.

He let her kiss him even as he peeled her leggings down, pulling back just long enough to toss them and her panties into a heap on the floor near her bra. She raised her eyebrows and clicked her tongue. 'Shouldn't you fold those or something?'

Nick snorted and gently pushed her shoulders back into the mattress. 'I mean, I could stop, if that's what you want,' he teased, skimming his hand up her side. His thumb brushed against the underside of her breast, and she let out a breathy moan. Her breasts weren't very large, and when he palmed it, his hand covered the entire mound easily. Still looming above her, he smirked. 'Do you? Do you want me to stop and clean up?' he repeated as she arched into his touch. He bent his head and drew her nipple between his teeth, and Val forgot the entire English language. She groaned and he laughed, flicking his tongue across her aching nipple.

His other hand drifted lower, sifting through the dark thatch of curls at the apex of her thighs. His touch was light, so delicate she wanted to cry, or scream, or maybe both. She settled for making a pleading noise that had him grinning against her other breast, and he eased his finger inside her.

She wasn't sure if she was the one who gasped or if it was him, but all the same there seemed to be a lot less oxygen in the room. 'You're perfect,' he muttered from somewhere near the curve of her neck.

Val planted her feet on the mattress, lifting her hips to chase his hand, letting him fuck her with his fingers until her thighs were quivering and she was panting, and then he pressed his thumb to her clit, *hard*.

She came with a wave of emotion that stole her breath away. Pleasure ripped through her, and a tear leaked from her eye, and the ragged moan that spilled from her lips might have been his name.

Val went boneless and Nick once again cupped her face to kiss her, his fingers sticky with her arousal. 'You're perfect,' he whispered again, his kiss soft and light as she returned to herself.

Her throat felt unaccountably thick, so Val just kissed him back and climbed on top of him. 'Condom?' she asked, hovering over him, and dipping down to nip at his collarbone.

'Drawer,' he managed, and sure enough, there was a stash of condoms tucked in the back of his nightstand. Val rolled one down, enjoying the way he threw his head back into the pillow at her touch, and then slung her leg back over his hips.

She went slow at first, wanting to savor the feeling of having him inside. There was a stretch, and then a fullness that felt so right she had to blink back more tears. Val wasn't weepy usually, but Nick had a way of mixing her up emotionally. Once he was fully seated, he gripped her hips with a tiny raise of his eyebrow before guiding her in a rhythm that was far faster and harder than she would have expected, but it felt so good. It was exactly what she needed, and if the way he was breathing was any indication, it was what he needed too.

Every rock of her hips took him just a little deeper, and every curse that fell from his lips felt like a kiss. His hand smoothed up her spine and back down, fingers digging into the flare of her hips with more pressure than she expected. But there was something perfect about the contrast; his gentleness mixed with the rough desperation in his touch. Heat started curling in her belly again, unspooling slow and steady, banking higher with each thrust inside her.

Nick came with a hiss, spilling into the condom and holding her still on his cock until he collapsed back against the bed. But before she could climb off, he licked his first two fingers and slipped them between her and his pelvis, letting her grind against his hand with his softening cock still inside her until the heat within her rose like a wave and she came again. This one was softer and less emotionally wrenching, but it rolled through her in endless ripples, like overlapping waves on a shore.

When she was finally done, Val let her head drop between her shoulders, her arms locked to keep her above him. He reached up, taking her chin between his thumb and forefinger to pull her into one more kiss, and she let herself fully collapse into his arms, exhausted and satiated and honestly, just a little bit scared of how much that had just meant.

Chapter Twenty-Two

Roses. That was the first thing that registered in Nick's brain, before he'd even opened his eyes. Something – something close – smelled like roses. Roses, and a sense of peace he couldn't remember having in a long time, if ever.

The source of both shifted in his arms, her head pillowed in the soft space between his shoulder and his chest. Outside the storm had abated and the sun was now streaming in through his white curtains, making his room bright and fresh like new-fallen snow. Val's hair fanned out across his chest, hints of auburn shining through in her dark, messy waves.

He smoothed a lock back from her forehead and tucked in his chin to kiss the top of her head. Val made a sleepy groan and he had thought that the noises she made *last* night were something he wanted to hear forever, but this was somehow better.

She lifted her head, smiling, and rested her chin on his chest. 'Morning,' she said softly.

'Morning,' he replied, his voice rough from sleep. He cleared his throat and carded her hair back. 'Storm's done.'

'That would explain the sunshine,' she replied, deadpan.

Nick didn't even bother to stop the smile on his face. He loved it when she teased him and loved it even more that he could just enjoy it. Sure, it might all blow up in their faces later, but for now, he was going to enjoy every single second he could.

'Smartass,' he said affectionately, and she moved in for a lingering kiss.

He ran his hands down her sides, intending to reposition her more fully on top of him to deepen the kiss, but she flinched and giggled when his thumb brushed the underside of her ribs. 'Sorry, ticklish,' she explained.

'Oh, my mistake,' he said, careful to keep his face impassive. He did it again – this time, three fingers lightly skating across the bottom of her ribcage – and Val squealed.

'Screw you,' she laughed, squirming away from him. She pulled the covers up over her head, leaving just one eye peeking out. 'I'm not coming out until you promise not to tickle me again.'

'Then I guess I'm coming in,' he said with faux seriousness, yanking the covers over his head and sliding halfway across the mattress. Under the sheets the glow from the sunshine seemed brighter and the fabric draped around them, ensconcing them both in a private cocoon. The air was close in there, but at that very moment there was nowhere else he'd rather be.

'No, please,' Val said through bursts of laughter, holding her hands out to swat at him. 'Please. Mercy, whatever it takes. I give up.'

'Okay, fine,' Nick sighed, but still slipped his arm under her back and hauled her over, trapping her underneath him between his legs. 'I'll have mercy on you,' he said, looking down at her with his elbows resting on either side of her head. 'When it comes to tickling,' he added, leaning down to kiss her. The sheet settled gently on top of him, feather light.

As he hoped, her body went languid with the first brush of

their lips. He pressed against her, and her arms came up to encircle his neck. He nuzzled at the spot below her ear, and she sighed, sibilant and contented.

He settled into the cradle of her hips, but before he could begin to work on his long, detailed list of things he wanted to do to her, his stomach rumbled. Loudly.

Very loudly.

Val giggled. 'Was that you or me?'

'Me,' Nick confessed, dropping his head to her shoulder.

'Hey, I'm hungry too,' she said, cheerfully consoling. She patted his back for good measure, throwing the sheets back and letting in a blast of cold air. 'I'll go make breakfast,' she offered.

'Do you even know how?' he teased, rolling to his side and dragging his hand longingly down her back as she sat up.

'No. I didn't say I'd *cook* breakfast, I said I'd *make* breakfast. I hope you like Cocoa Puffs,' she said with a mischievous grin. 'Now get dressed; *someone* in this house keeps the heat on way too low in the winter and you'll freeze if you're naked in the kitchen.' And then his shirt hit him in the face.

Nick looked down at what appeared to be a bowl of brown marbles in rapidly browning milk. 'I still can't believe you eat this every morning,' he said, poking at it dubiously.

'Come on, it's the breakfast of champions or whatever,' Val said from the stool next to him, nudging him with her shoulder. Rather than walk the five feet to her bedroom for her own clothes, she was in a sweatshirt of his that covered her hands and sweatpants that she'd had to roll up several times at the waist and ankles to even sort-of fit. It was adorable and incredibly sexy, and Nick was pretty sure he had completely lost it when it came to Val.

'Pretty sure that's Wheaties.'

'Whatever,' she said, cheeks already bulging. 'Just try it,' she urged, or at least he thought that was what she said – it was hard to tell, what with her mouth so full of food. He must really have it bad if her lack of manners wasn't just not bothering him but was in fact endearing. 'Come on,' she added, finally swallowing. 'It'll be just like being a kid again.'

He frowned down at the bowl, lifting a spoonful and letting it dribble back into the bowl. 'I've never had them before, and yes, I know how sad that sounds,' he added before she could say anything. 'But when you have to be in the makeup trailer at five-thirty for a seven a.m. call time, cereal isn't the most convenient thing in the world. I mostly had bananas, fruit parfaits, that sort of thing. And on the rare occasion we ate breakfast at home it was Fruit Loops, because my mom was convinced we'd be able to get an endorsement deal from them for some reason, and she wanted us to be able to say "It's all we eat for breakfast!" at any given moment.'

'Doesn't sound like she had a lot of faith in your acting abilities,' Val observed, getting down and grabbing the coffee carafe that had just finished burbling and hissing. She poured him a cup and slid it across to him before getting her own. 'I mean, no offense, but wouldn't have pretending been easier?'

'She really didn't,' he agreed. 'Or she did, but she needed an insurance policy, in the case of Josh. He's a better actor than me, but he also tends to say the first thing that comes to mind when he's asked a question.'

'Like when he said you had a girlfriend, and then you slept with me to make it true?' she asked, eyes twinkling.

'Exactly,' Nick replied with a grin. He took a sip of coffee and watched her add more – yes, *more* – Cocoa Puffs to her bowl.

Val focused intently on her cereal. 'I told Margie I'd do the

New Year's Eve event, by the way. It's not like I have plans, what with Linds in California.'

'I could go with you,' he said, trying to convey an awful lot of things with just five words. 'It's my town, after all. And we could take a few photos of ourselves there for you to post to social media. It would make it extra believable if we're tagged in a bunch of posts about a New Year's Eve party.'

Val didn't respond right away, and Nick had the uneasy feeling he had once again said the wrong thing. In an effort to change the subject, he decided to take the plunge and indulged in a bite of the pile of sugar that Val insisted was cereal.

And then – holy shit. 'This is *amazing*,' he mumbled around the vaguely chocolatey lumps of carbohydrates crunching under his molars. 'Oh my god, how have I never had this before?'

Her face cleared, a delighted smile lighting up the room. 'Right? It's amazing.'

'It's like chocolate crunchies with chocolate milk,' he said, now shoveling it into his face as fast as he could. He was maybe overselling it a little – it was delicious, but maybe not transcendent – but Val was smiling instead of looking vaguely hurt, so he was going to keep pouring it on.

It couldn't hurt, right?

Chapter Twenty-Three

'What do you do with Felix on a night like tonight?' Val asked as Aaron led her to the area set up as a photo booth. She was scheduled to spend the first few hours there, and then the rest of the night circulating and taking candids. The town would get them for their Facebook page, while Val would be able to host them on her website and offer partygoers the chance to purchase them as keepsakes, with the proceeds split evenly between her and the Swede River Senior Center. Val wasn't sure how many people would follow through on buying photos, but she did have high hopes for her tip jar while she worked the booth, at least.

'He's really responsible for a nine-month-old, so we usually just leave him pizza money,' Aaron said, and then chuckled, shaking his head. 'Livvy is with him. She's saving up for the Band trip to Washington D.C., so she's been taking any extra shifts she can.'

'She's in Band? In addition to Handbell Choir?'

'She's the Drum Major,' Aaron said proudly, like he was Livvy's dad too. A tiny pit in Val's stomach ached at that, the sense of belonging so many of the residents of Swede River had.

Things were getting better since the Sleigh Bell Festival, but there was a palpable feeling of loneliness that went hand in hand with seeing other people feel at home.

The New Year's Eve Ball was in the same old theater as the Swedehearts' Dance, with the autumn decor replaced by disco balls, gold streamers, and giant numbers representing the coming year. Everything was low-budget yet charming; it had the air of a party for people who genuinely wanted to hang out together and thus had clubbed together to make the decorations themselves. Aaron led her across the dance floor to the table set up with the usual silly props of feather boas, oversized glasses, and clown wigs. The first arrivals – a family with a couple of sullen-looking pre-teens – wandered in, and Val turned to Aaron. 'Hey, uh, quick question. Does the whole town still hate me?'

Aaron chuckled and shook his head. 'It wasn't the whole town, and give us a little credit; we've been a lot better since Sleigh Bells. Besides, no one hated you. I think people are just . . . wary.'

'And what about me made me seem like a threat?' Now that things with Nick were happening, she had a sudden urge to prove herself, which was both utterly foreign and completely beyond her capabilities.

'People didn't know you, that's all.' He shrugged. 'They just wanted to be sure you're here for real. That this isn't temporary, because if being here is temporary for you, then so's Nick.'

Val narrowed her eyes slightly. 'Is that why Margie asked me to do this? So I look involved?'

'No comment,' Aaron said with a smile. 'Also, you're a damn good photographer. A couple of our friends were asking who did our Chanukah card this year. It was the most compliments we've ever gotten.'

Val laughed. 'I think that was the baby, not me. But one last question – do I look okay?'

In a very uncharacteristic move, Val had agonized over what to wear to the New Year's Eve party. Usually when she worked, she wore the same uniform of dark pants and a black or white shirt. It helped her fade into the background, but she hadn't quite wanted to do that tonight. It had taken ages and at least three phone calls with Linds, but she had settled on a black jumpsuit that was not unlike The Fleabag Jumpsuit, with a few strategic-but-classy cutouts. At the very least it made her feel good about herself, which would help if the town ended up giving her the cold shoulder.

'You look like a million bucks,' Aaron replied.

'You're almost as pretty as I was in my day,' Margie Schumacher interjected from over Val's shoulder.

'Now there's a compliment,' Val said, turning around with a grin. 'And you look pretty damn good yourself.'

Margie was in a simple pink dress that looked lovely with her white hair. She preened a little and switched her cane to her other hand to pat Val's shoulder. 'I'm glad you're here,' Margie said. 'This town could use a shot in the arm like you.'

'Us troublemakers need to stick together, don't we?' Val said, and Margie laughed.

The family with the annoyed-looking pre-teens approached her hesitantly and Aaron and Margie melted away, leaving her to do her best. Val put on her most welcoming smile. She could do this – she had done this countless times before, so it was silly for her to feel like her future with Nick was riding on her being able to charm the town. For one thing, he'd never done anything to indicate that she had to get Swede River's approval to be with him, and for another, Val was not the type to try and seek approval. If she was, she would be the administrative assistant at St Cloud Motors, not a semi-flailing photographer in Swede River.

But Val still had the urge to make sure everyone in Swede River approved of her, so she coaxed the pre-teens into being goofy with their very relieved-looking parents. They thanked her sincerely as they left and soon enough, the trickle of arrivals turned to a stream, and most stopped by the photo booth on their way in.

In fact, it ended up being kind of fun. Margie set up shop at the table next to the booth and kept up a running commentary for Val between shots, explaining who people were and which families hated each other.

Val learned that there was a long-running feud between the Schmidts – the Gary Schmidts, not the John Schmidts, they were completely innocent – and the Jacobsons over damage done by a snowplow clipping a beloved oak tree back on New Year's Eve 2001, and now the whole town knew that if the Gary Schmidts were attending the NYE Ball, the Jacobsons would not come for love or money. That meant when Carina Jacobson, age seventeen, showed up with Ella Schmidt, age sixteen, on her arm a few hours in, Val was able to be shocked – shocked! – along with the rest of the town.

It felt good, honestly. It had been a long time since she'd tried to be part of something, and by the time Mary and Eng swung by her station to say hello and put on gigantic sunglasses and take a few adorably affectionate photos of them kissing and hugging, Val was feeling less like a sore thumb and more like someone who might, someday, belong in Swede River.

Nick arrived shortly after the Schmidt–Jacobson drama. Val spotted him the second he walked in, and a wave of warmth washed over her, anchoring her in place in a way that was both comfortable and unfamiliar. He said a brief hello – just a kiss on the cheek and a hand on her back – because she had a line five couples deep waiting for photos at that point. As the evening went on, she always knew where he was, even if it was just chatting with Pete or grabbing a glass of punch from the table near stage left. She wasn't intentionally keeping tabs on him, but it was like she was drawn to him in a way she couldn't fully explain.

Val shut down the photo booth when the line finished up and started circulating, snapping photos of dancing couples just like at a wedding reception. In a lot of ways, it was muscle memory for her, but it felt good – she liked seeing people happy, capturing those moments for them when they didn't even realize she was there.

A warm hand rested softly on her lower back. 'Can you get away for a minute?' Nick murmured into her ear.

Val felt an uncharacteristic blush on her cheeks, and she nodded. Nick wrapped his fingers around her wrist and towed her away, out into a chilly hallway and down to a door that was slightly ajar. It looked like a closet where the caterers kept their jackets and bags, but no one was in there when he pulled her in and shut the door.

'I'm flattered you want to fuck me in a closet, but I am kinda working,' Val said, even as she slid one arm around his back, pressing her chest to his. 'And if this was your plan, you should have told me to wear a dress.'

Nick shook his head. 'You make me sound like a horny teenager,' he scolded.

'I didn't say you wanting to have sex all the time was a bad thing.' Val went on her tiptoes and pressed a soft kiss to his lips. Nick carefully moved her camera to the shelf behind her, his hand still spanning the bare skin on her lower back.

'Stop distracting me,' he murmured, and pulled away.

'I know you have to shoot the countdown at midnight, so I thought we'd do our own,' he explained, and slipped his phone from his pocket. 'It's almost eleven, which means it's almost midnight on the east coast. If it's not too cheesy, we could do the countdown and kiss now, and then you won't be missing it while you're working.'

'And you won't miss it, you mean.'

'Guilty.'

Val's insides did that melty-liquid thing they always seemed to do around Nick. 'You don't need an excuse to kiss me, you know.'

'I know. But I wanted to be smooth *and* kiss you, and I think I succeeded,' he teased.

'I don't know if I like this cocky side of you,' she replied.

'Oh, I think you do,' he said, and then held up his phone to display a countdown. 'Ten,' he started, his voice sliding lower. 'Nine. Eight. Seven.'

She didn't even let him get to *six*. Val kissed him, every mushy feeling pouring out of her and into him. She barely even heard when his phone finished the countdown and started chiming. There was something about him that turned her into a marshmallow.

The rest of the evening was a hazy, pleasant blur. She circulated, took photos, and got to dance with Nick to at least two slow, romantic songs. Val laughed with her friends and got to kiss Nick on the cheek whenever she felt like it. When the ball shut down at two in the morning, Val walked out hand in hand with Nick in the gently falling snow, feeling more at home than she ever had before. She rested her head on his shoulder as they walked, smiling as she felt him brush a kiss to the top of her head.

It was, quite frankly, the best New Year's Eve ever.

Chapter Twenty-Four

'I'm sorry, you're doing *what*?' Josh's voice was just slightly obscured, so Nick repositioned his earbuds under his hat.

'Shoveling,' Nick said, scraping the shovel along the pavement in front of him. 'We got fifteen inches over the past few days, and there's a pack of kids down the block who have to catch the bus tomorrow morning, and I'd rather they not fall and hurt themselves.'

'Aren't kids that young basically rubber? And seriously, I do not understand why you willingly subject yourself to that weather. You could have moved anywhere, bro. Anywhere. And you chose Minnesota. Even Arizona would have been better.'

Nick snorted. 'You know how I feel about places with that much sun.'

'I do, and it's fucking weird,' Josh grumbled. 'Anyway, we had our first table read. Beth's the first cameo, so I got to see her again.'

'Holy shit,' Nick said, and tossed a shovelful of wet, heavy snow onto the growing snowbank to his left. 'How is she?'

'Ninety-six and still hilarious,' Josh said. 'I mean, you didn't hear it from me, but I'm pretty sure they put her in the first episode because they're worried she might die any minute now. I don't know if they should be worried, though, because she had more energy than I did. She says hi, by the way, and wants to know if you're done being boring.'

Nick smiled to himself. Beth Black had played the matriarch in *Just Us Girls*, a wisecracking broad with a lascivious sense of humor. She was a comedy institution, having been acting since the mid-twentieth century. Her presence was probably why the show had even been picked up since their pilot was notoriously hacky and bordered on unfunny. All Josh and Nick had had to do at that point was show up on camera a few times and mug cheekily, but over the years Beth had taken the boys – mostly Josh, since he cared more – under her wing. Not enough to get Josh steady work, since she believed actors needed to earn their stripes on their own, but she had been a helpful resource at least.

'Have you given any more thought to –'

'I don't want to cameo,' Nick insisted. It felt stupid to say it out loud, but returning, even for a cameo, felt like giving his mother what she wanted. Maybe he couldn't get her to leave him alone, but he could deny her this one small satisfaction.

Josh didn't push, to his credit. 'By the way, Jan is going to send you the info about the reunion show, and Beth wants to know if you're bringing your girlfriend along.'

'Nosy old coot,' Nick laughed. 'Tell her I called her that.'

'You tell her, I don't have a death wish. But will it just be you?'

'Honestly, I hadn't thought about it,' Nick admitted. It would be nice to spend that time with Val, and it would have the added benefit of dousing any remaining doubts anyone in LA might have about their relationship. 'I'll ask her.'

Josh waited a second, and Nick knew he was gathering his courage to be a nosy old coot himself. 'How is she?'

'Val? She's good. Great, actually.' He couldn't help it; he knew Josh would hear the grin in his voice, and there didn't seem to be much point in trying to hide it.

'Ooooooh,' Josh said, in a remarkable imitation of a studio audience watching a kiss for the first time. 'That good, huh?'

'Yeah,' he admitted. 'Things are – good.'

'I knew it,' Josh crowed. 'I knew it. You're really dating, aren't you?'

'We haven't had an official conversation about dating, but – yeah, we're together.'

There was an unusual pause on Josh's side. 'Since . . . New Year's Eve?'

'A little before that.' Nick stopped, resting his forearm on the shovel to catch his breath. 'Why? Have you been Instagram-stalking us?' Val had posted a handful of photos to her page after New Year's, although Nick hadn't looked at them. He wasn't caring as much as he should about whether people were buying them being together anymore, since all that mattered to him was that they were.

'Aren't I supposed to? To make it look real?'

'Yeah, but I never thought you'd pay attention to it.'

'You're my twin brother, why wouldn't I? You're half a country away, I take what I can get.'

Nick bit his lower lip, Josh's words stinging. Josh had inadvertently touched a nerve, because, well, Josh had always been there for him. As much as Nick had hated Hollywood, Josh had loved it. But Josh had his back when he decided to leave completely, and in return, Nick moved halfway across the country and never looked back.

That was why he was constantly bailing Josh out of his stupid financial mistakes; he owed him. It was the least he could do, considering he had blown up their lives.

That didn't feel like something he could bring up during this otherwise lighthearted conversation and anyway, what was there to say? *Sorry I moved away, so I'll clean up your messes for the rest of your life?* 'But yeah, things with Val are really good,' Nick said, and fortunately Josh didn't seem to notice his brief detour into self-loathing. 'What was the tip-off?'

'How you were looking at her in some of those New Year's photos she took of you. You're a better actor than you ever gave yourself credit for – you'd have to be, seeing as you're related to me – but you're not that good. You were . . . glowing.'

He'd felt like he was glowing that night, so that made sense. 'I'm really that obvious, huh?'

'Honestly? You weren't acting in the corn maze photos, either. But you clearly weren't ready to hear it then.'

Nick shook his head even though Josh couldn't see him. 'I wasn't,' he admitted. 'I felt like a creep. She pays me rent.'

'She likes you, and she's an adult woman who is more than capable of telling you to fuck off if she wants to. And she has. Several times.'

'I'm just saying –'

'No, you're trying to talk yourself out of being happy,' Josh interrupted. 'Knock it off.'

'Fair enough,' Nick said, because Josh probably did have a point. Nick didn't tend to trust feeling happy, so maybe he was just looking for an out. 'I should really finish shoveling.'

'It's barbaric that you even said that, but sure,' Josh agreed.

Chapter Twenty-Five

Val positioned herself on the open side of the table, the large pack of influencers lining up on either side of Autumn like a monochromatically dressed Last Supper, if the Last Supper also involved an enormous beauty queen crown and a sash that said *Bride to Be*.

'Ready?' Val asked, and started snapping photos, marveling at how easy it was to work with people who were deeply involved in the influencer community. Everyone knew their angles, and at least two people had helped position everyone in the best light possible. All Val had to do was let them know a picture was being taken, and they did the rest, including arranging themselves in order of color, with the magentas on the outside wings and the people wearing the palest shell-pink right on either side of the bride.

And at the center of it all was Autumn, absolutely glowing in her white outfit. Val took a few snaps from a couple of slightly different angles, just to give everyone the widest variety of choices, and then nodded to the server who had just entered the private room Autumn's friends had rented. Val moved out of the way, and everyone quickly retook their seats while artfully plated winter salads were deposited before each guest. There were a few beats of silence where everyone took out their phones to take a shot of their food, and Val grabbed the chance to take a somewhat meditative candid of the crowd. With the dramatic lighting of the room, it gave the impression of people being separate, but together. It wasn't judgmental, but it was illustrative.

'Are you eating?' Reese asked, tucking into their salad.

'Grabbed something before I came,' Val said, and let them pause to take a more-posed photo.

'You're the one with that hot famous boyfriend, right?'

Val had literally never felt so smug. 'I am, yeah.'

'And he's so nice!' Autumn yelled from down the table. 'Literally, the nicest child star you could ever imagine. Not messy at all, totally normal. You wouldn't even know unless you already knew. Oh, and Reese, you should see if he knows anyone who could look at your newest designs.'

'I do fashion design,' Reese said, proud and modest at the same time. They tucked a lock of their chin-length bob behind their ear, black hair gleaming in the light. 'There's not that much of a scene here, but I'm saving money until I can move to New York.'

'I honestly don't think Nick could help you there,' Val said apologetically. 'He's about as far out of Hollywood as you can be without moving to Siberia or something.'

Reese stabbed their fork into the salad. 'I mean, Minnesota, Siberia – what's the difference, really?'

'I think that's exactly why he moved here,' Val said, laughing. 'But his brother is still there, and Josh is the king of social media, so he'll definitely see some of these.'

'Don't worry about it. Autumn is always trying to sell my designs,' Reese said fondly. They were one of the three people in magenta, which was a hard color for anyone to pull off, but Reese was doing it with aplomb.

'How long have you known each other?'

'Since birth,' Reese said. 'Ride or die, me and her.'

Autumn was now deep in conversation with Addy and Emma, two of her influencer friends who Val vaguely recognized from Autumn's posts. 'You must be happy for her, then,' Val said carefully. She didn't want to be nosy, but she couldn't help it – she was feeling guilty as hell these days, lying to Autumn about her history with Caleb. And she felt even worse when she thought about how Caleb might be treating Autumn, but she kept trying to remind herself that she had no proof he was being terrible. Maybe he was a good boyfriend when he was *actually* someone's boyfriend, and not just their long-term hookup.

Maybe Caleb had been right all along. Maybe Val had been the problem. He could be charming and funny, and he was indisputably smart, so maybe it really was just that Val was too messy and complicated for him.

Reese's face was hard to read. 'They make a really cute couple,' they said. 'And she's happy, so I'm happy for her.'

Val decided it wasn't her place to push any further. Autumn had a solid group of friends, it would seem, so if there were any red flags, they would be on it. It wasn't her business, and as mercenary as it would seem, calling off the wedding now would lose Val a whole lot of money and social capital she really needed.

Several hours later, they had left the restaurant for the dance club-based scavenger hunt Autumn's bridespeople – her sister Summer (yes, really), Emma, and Reese – had orchestrated. The group was on their way to the third club of the evening, and Val was feeling looser than usual thanks to the vodka shots

Addy had coaxed her into taking. She had been taking photos but also joining them on the dance floor, and she couldn't remember the last time she had this much fun with a group of people.

It had probably been a happy hour with Linds's labmates, and right there – in the middle of an intersection of downtown Minneapolis on a cold January evening – the full weight of her loneliness over the past year slammed into her. She had thought she would be fine, mostly because Val had always operated with just one or two close friends, but losing Linds to the other side of the country also meant losing the slight tethers she had to other people. Val had never been much of a party girl, but that didn't mean she *never* wanted to get drunk and goof around with a bunch of people in her age bracket. Swede River was fun and was starting to feel like home, but that was just it – it was *starting* to feel like something approaching a place she belonged, which only underlined the fact that she didn't really belong anywhere right now. Maybe she belonged with Nick, but that felt like way too much to put on one person.

'I am so glad you could come,' Autumn said, slipping her arm through Val's. It was freezing and Autumn was in barely anything, just a gauzy white top and skirt, but she still radiated warmth.

'I mean, you are paying me,' Val said drily, even though she had to admit, it felt nice to link arms with her. She might as well admit she wanted to be friends with Autumn. But being legitimate friends with her would mean spending time with Caleb, and Val didn't hate herself that much. She wished she could just be friends with Autumn and eliminate everything to do with Caleb. That would have made everything so much easier.

'Yeah, but like – you're so cool. And I know everyone

keeps bringing up Nick, but it's not just that you're dating the child star we all wanted to marry when we were little. You're just so badass. You don't give a fuck, and I wish I could be like that.'

Autumn was being so sweet and genuine. It sent a pang through Val's chest, but before she could say anything, Autumn sighed and leaned into her. 'And I bet no one thinks you're stupid,' she said, clearly a little buzzed and wistful. 'People look at what I do and they think I'm this – this idiot. They think they can run my life, and what's worse is, they think I'll be grateful. I'm a grown-ass adult. I run my own business, and I'm getting married. I don't need your advice, just let me live my damn life.' The vehemence was unexpected, especially from someone as sweet-natured as Autumn.

'I don't think you're stupid,' Val said, patting Autumn's hand and shifting her camera bag to a more comfortable spot on her hip. 'I think you're awesome. And people underestimate *me* all the time. I'm a disaster. I'm constantly late, I'm messy, I'm forgetful, and in case you forgot, I got distracted and accidentally posted a nip-slip of a client a few months ago.'

'But you're an amazing photographer,' Autumn argued. 'I was right to trust you.'

Autumn's faith in her brought a lump to Val's throat, and suddenly, she was seized with a desire to confess her past with Caleb. She opened her mouth, trying to find the words. 'Hey, Autumn! Get your ass over here, this guy says he'll buy us all shots if we come into this bar,' Reese called before Val could figure out a good way to say *I used to sleep with your fiancé, and he treated me terribly. I didn't want to lie to you, but I did and now I feel crappy about it.* Autumn squealed happily and ran toward them, and the moment slipped away.

* * *

There were some distinct advantages to dating her roommate, Val decided. Like being able to laze around in bed at two o'clock on a Wednesday afternoon because neither of them had to work. Val was almost done editing the bachelorette party photos, which was taking slightly longer than she'd planned thanks to the unpleasant jolts of guilt she would get whenever she thought about Autumn and Caleb.

But her messy relationship with her client and her ex had absolutely no place in her brain when Nick was lying in her bed, relaxed and smug. She adored this side of him, this confident, teasing man who was still somehow just as sweet in bed as he was out of it. Val had never been uncomfortable in her own skin – in fact, her problem was that she was maybe a little too comfortable, and thus unwilling to change at all – but she still marveled at how centered she felt around Nick; how calm. It was like she was able to breathe freely after holding her breath for who knew how long, and the relief made her almost giddy.

And Val was never giddy. Happy, sometimes. But not giddy.

'Jan called yesterday,' Nick was saying, doing that thing he always did and tucking her hair behind her ear. He had rolled to his side, the sheet draped dangerously low on his hips, and her eyes kept tracking the obscenely perfect planes of his chest and stomach. At some point she had pulled on his T-shirt for a quick run to the bathroom, but she was already wondering if she should get rid of it, if only to feel even more of his skin against hers. 'She's getting the flights set for LA next month.'

'Mmm,' Val hummed, only half listening. She was too busy trailing her fingers along the curve of his biceps and remembering what he felt like inside her just ten minutes ago.

'Would you want to?'

'Would I want to what?' Val asked, unable to hide the fact

that she hadn't been paying any attention to his words, just his body.

'Do you find me distracting?' Nick asked instead of answering her question.

'I do,' Val said with an eyeroll. 'So go ahead and repeat yourself before I forget what we're talking about again.'

Nick laughed, and her stomach did that flip-flop thing it always did around him. He cupped his hand on her cheek and tugged her down for a lazy kiss that once again wiped her mind completely clean. 'Would you want to come with me?' he asked, his voice lowering to almost a whisper.

Val valiantly attempted to regain her train of thought. 'Where? To LA?'

'Yeah. For the taping. Not on camera, but just – to see. Meet Josh, maybe some of the old cast, that sort of thing.'

'When is it? I have to shoot Caleb's bachelor party on February nineteenth, and I've got a wedding in early March.'

'It would be in between there. We're taping the reunion show February twenty-second, and there's going to be a small cast party the twenty-fourth.'

Val did some mental calculations about what was left in her bank account, and what would be coming in with the bachelor party and wedding. 'The studio would pay for it. Jan finagled a plus one for me on everything, including flights,' Nick said, reading her mind like always.

'What's the weather like there in February?'

'It'll be warm. It's more like late April, here.'

'You mean no parkas for a week? Sign me up,' Val said, laughing.

Nick was looking at her strangely, and she suddenly felt self-conscious. 'What?'

'I love it when you do that,' he said.

'Do what?'

'Laugh.'

Val frowned. 'That makes it sound like I don't ever laugh.'

'That's not it – it's not that it's infrequent, it's just that sometimes, you laugh and I get a glimpse of you, and it's just –' Nick broke off and leaned over the edge of her bed suddenly, tossing a hoodie she'd left on the floor onto her desk chair with unnerving accuracy before grabbing the strap of her camera bag. He hauled it up onto the bed with them, ignoring her squawk of surprise. 'I can't explain it, you just have to see it.' He unzipped the bag and pulled her camera out – delicately, to his credit – and squinted down at it. 'Okay, how does this thing work?'

'You have to take the lens cap off first,' Val said to cover the way her heart was pounding. Nick slipped it off and put it carefully on her nightstand, on top of the three books that had been there since two days after she moved in, three water glasses (only one empty), and a pile of crumpled receipts from the pharmacy down the street.

To his credit, she could tell he was trying not to say anything, so she took pity on him. 'I know, I know, I'm a human trash panda,' she said.

'I'm just not used to it,' he said fairly. 'But it's not bad. It's different.'

'How do you manage to be so diplomatic?'

'I grew up in a town where pissing off the wrong person meant I'd never work again, not to mention with a nightmare of a mother, so I got very good at saying *Your room is like a storage room at a frat house* while sounding perfectly pleasant.'

'Screw you,' she laughed, slapping him lightly on the chest. He caught her wrist with his free hand and placed a kiss on the center of her palm.

'You know I'm kidding, right?' he said, holding her hand

just above his heart. She could see in his soft brown eyes he was completely sincere.

'I do.'

'Good, because I would also like to state, for the record, that I spent the first two months you lived here afraid we'd get ants.'

'I am *not* that bad,' Val laughed, but then she looked at her desk where there were two bowls and a plate sitting, all in various stages of dirty. 'Okay, fine, maybe I am.'

She glanced back at him, still laughing, just in time to hear the shutter snap. Nick looked at the image and smiled to himself in a way that made Val's stomach flutter. She tugged the camera out of his hands and set it down next to the bed in one of the only clear spaces on the floor. Then she launched herself at him, kissing him hard enough that she forgot that odd, vulnerable feeling.

Chapter Twenty-Six

Nick perused the chalkboard above the counter, wondering if he should switch from his usual two orders – Earl Grey tea or drip coffee, black – for something a little different. It was too cold for a blended, sugary drink, but maybe something with caramel might be nice. He'd been venturing farther outside his comfort zone lately, even going so far as to swipe some of Val's Cocoa Puffs for breakfast that morning. Something warm and sweet sounded good to him now, when just a few weeks ago he probably wouldn't have even considered changing his order.

Outside was the flat, iron grey of February, where the sky was only differentiated from the ground by virtue of being a handful of shades darker than the grey of icy snow mixed with slush from the road. Charles Poulsen finished paying and stepped aside. Nick blinked, wondering if he'd somehow gotten incredibly mixed up about his days – it was possible, considering how little sleep he and Val were getting. 'Livvy? Don't you have school today?'

Behind him, the bell jingled, and a gust of cold air buffeted his back. Livvy grinned good-naturedly. 'Inservice day,' she announced, just as Pete came down from their apartment above the shop.

'Be prepared for the library to be overrun with kids who have too much energy and parents who don't want to deal with standing outside in the cold at a park,' Mary said from behind him.

'Did you want tea or coffee this morning?' Livvy asked Nick, scooting to the side to let Pete through.

'Actually, I think I'll go with a caramel macchiato,' he said, and to their credit, it was clear that Livvy and Pete were doing their best not to exchange mutual looks of surprise.

'Want a scone with that?' Pete asked, reaching into the pastry case, and picking up a blueberry scone. 'We haven't had a chance to catch up in ages, either, if you'd want to stick around?'

Nick looked over his shoulder at Mary. 'Depends, is my boss going to write me up for being late?'

Mary clicked her tongue. 'You have never been late a day in your life, young man,' she said with faux sternness. 'I think I can spare you just this once.' She checked her watch. 'And we have at least a half hour until we need to unlock the doors.'

'Then you should stick around too,' Pete said, automatically reaching for a banana nut muffin for Mary.

The three of them settled at a table near the window while Livvy got to work on cleaning the notoriously finicky espresso machine. 'How are things?' Pete asked, starting in on his scone. Nick took a bite of the one in front of him; Pete really was a fantastic baker.

'They're good,' he said, unable to wipe the smile off his face. 'Really good.'

Mary smiled indulgently. 'And how's Josh? You haven't mentioned him lately.'

Nick had gotten into the habit of filling Mary in on Josh's

latest shenanigans when he first moved there, but lately his life was revolving less around Josh, even though paradoxically that was *because* of Josh. 'He's good. Filming the new show is taking up a lot of time, which is good for him. Plus, the earliest buzz has been good, although you never know until something's out how the audience will feel about it.'

'You've changed lately,' Pete said. 'Not that you needed to change, or anything, and it's all good, but – wow, Val really is bringing out a new side of you, isn't she?'

'I thought there'd be something there,' Mary said with just a hint of smugness. 'It was an elegant solution to your money problem, but I could see it right away. She's who you needed.'

'I was a little surprised by how quickly you two got together, though,' Pete added.

'Agreed,' Mary replied. 'I thought it would take much longer.'

'You wanted us to get together, but not that quickly?' Nick asked. He wasn't entirely surprised Mary had had somewhat ulterior motives in convincing him to let Val move in, but he still had questions.

'You're a cautious man,' she said, shrugging. 'Two months in seemed sudden, that's all. Especially since you had been complaining about her just a week or so before the Swedeheart's Ball.'

Nick's stomach gave an unpleasant jolt. Somehow, in the glow of finally being with Val for real, he'd managed to forget that he had been lying to his friends for several months. He shifted and looked outside, watching the Huff family load both toddlers into their car across the street. Sylvie and her older brother Sammy were regulars at the library's story time hour, and Nick considered asking Pete and Mary if they thought the Huff kids were going to start preschool soon. But they were far too savvy to fall for such an obvious change of subject, which barely ever even worked with Josh.

He lifted his mug, half obscuring his face, and made himself sound completely neutral. 'Like you guys said, she's bringing out a different side of me.'

Chapter Twenty-Seven

Val took the picture just as the three men in front of her tossed their Jaegerbombs back. The bus was stopped at a red light, and the entire interior smelled like a mix of cologne, alcohol, and sweat.

It was gross, and way too much like college for Val's taste. It was also unsettling, because aside from Caleb's younger brother, whom she'd only met once in passing at Caleb's apartment, she didn't know any of the guests. She had been assuming his bachelor party would be an uncomfortable reunion of all his friends who had known about her but probably never learned her last name, but instead it was all strangers. Caleb seemed to have completely reinvented himself in the interim, with a crew of nearly identical white bros who all seemed to work in real estate. They had the sort of life Caleb had always wanted – rich, carefree, and above all, respectable-looking. Appearances had always mattered to him, even if his *overwhelming attraction* to Val, as he once called it, had overruled his *better judgment*.

God, what a dick. Sometimes she thought about all the time she wasted with him and wanted to kick herself.

There was a shuffling of seats as several guys got up to refill their drinks, and Caleb sat down heavily next to her. 'Are you having fun?' he asked solicitously. 'You could have a drink, if you want.'

Val had happily had a few drinks with Autumn and her friends, but it felt different with this group. They were a little too loud and quite frankly, a little too *male*. Being around that many cis men made her uneasy, even if she didn't feel like she was in danger. It was more the abundance of testosterone and alcohol that put her on edge.

Well, that, and the way Caleb kept looking at her. She had felt his eyes on her since she got on the bus at the scheduled time – she hadn't joined them for their drinks at a virtual-golf-bar, whatever the hell *that* was, because Autumn rightly called it *too boring to even bother* – and now, an hour in, it hadn't abated. 'I'm fine,' she said tightly, with an attempt at a smile.

'Is something wrong?' Caleb asked, and this was the problem with him. He wanted to be a nice guy – he just wasn't. He wasn't cruel, but he wanted so desperately to be the good guy that he was willing to screw over anyone who made him feel otherwise. And that had been Val's fatal flaw, to him: she kept making him feel like the bad guy, so he had to make sure she understood she was the problem. Or at least that was how Linds had explained it to her once, and it had the ring of truth.

'Everything's fine,' she said as pleasantly as possible. 'Really, it is.'

'Are you good, though? This isn't . . . weird?'

'Caleb, I agreed to this. I'm a big girl, I knew what I was getting into.' *Not to mention you're the one who made this way harder than it needed to be.*

'No, I just meant – in life. Are you okay? Are you happy?'

'I am,' she said, forcing a smile onto her face, not because it wasn't true but because she desperately wanted to be doing anything but having this conversation.

'It's just – him? That's not who I saw you with. He's just so – not you.'

She couldn't help it. 'And who did you see me with?' she asked, her voice poisonously sweet.

Caleb shrugged. 'Someone else, I guess. He's so much like me, you know? And you never could really commit to me, so it just seems weird you can commit to him.'

That is not at all what happened with us, but okay. 'He's really nothing like you,' Val said cheerfully, unable to stop the words that came out of her mouth next. 'For one thing, he actually cares about me.'

Caleb had the gall to look wounded. 'You always mattered to me,' he said softly.

Val narrowed her eyes. 'How much have you had to drink?'

'A few beers at the driving range,' he said with a dismissive wave of his hand. 'I just – I don't like how we left things.'

'And who's fault is that?'

'I'm not saying I was perfect –'

'Good, because you weren't.'

Caleb sighed. 'Can we just put away the bullshit for a minute? I'm trying to actually say something,' he snapped.

Val's retort was on the tip of her lips, but she held herself back and gave a sharp nod.

'You and I were a mess, and now you're with him, and I'm just wondering how we went so wrong.'

Caleb sounded genuine, and Val had an uncomfortable realization. She didn't *want* to share it with him, necessarily, but she felt like she should. He had been a part of her life for years, after all. 'You never wanted to be the bad guy, and I think

I kept trying to make you one,' she admitted. 'I'd pick fights, just so I could try and make us equal.'

And you fell for it, every time, she wanted to add, but that felt – unnecessary. Maybe she didn't have to stick a knife into everyone all the time; maybe she could just let things be.

Caleb nodded, his mouth opening like he wanted to say something. But the party bus lurched to a stop and the group started filing off, cheerfully yelling about which bar they were going to hit up first. One of the guys grabbed Caleb and hauled him up, saving her from having to continue that weirdly personal conversation.

Val exited the bus, relieved to be free. But Caleb was waiting at the foot of the steps and pulled her aside. 'Hang on a sec,' he said, eyes darting around. He looked over his shoulder, but none of his friends seemed to have noticed he wasn't with them. 'There was something else I wanted to say,' he said, putting a hand gently on her forearm.

Val wanted to wrench it away, but she didn't. It could make a scene and honestly, she still needed this job if she was ever going to be fully back on her feet professionally. One more angry client would destroy her. She clenched her jaw. 'What?'

'I wasn't honest before.'

'When?'

'When Autumn hired you,' he replied, still holding her arm. She wanted to step back, but it was like she was rooted to the spot.

He wouldn't, she thought. *He's a coward, not a cheat.*

'I didn't think – I knew I couldn't handle it.' Confusion must have registered on her face because Caleb shook his head. 'You know how you and I are, Val. You're bad for me, but – I could never resist you.'

She swallowed hard. *Yikes*. Caleb was playing all the old hits, tap dancing on her insecurities, and then offering her a compliment just after he knocked her down. Her head was spinning, her earlier categorization of him as 'a coward, not a cheat' being proved wrong with astonishing speed. 'Caleb, I –'

But she didn't get a chance to fully refuse him because he kissed her. On the *mouth*. It took Val a heartbeat to realize what was happening, and then she pushed him away, slapping him with her palm before her brain caught up. A pack of college students stumbled past them on the sidewalk, shouting and laughing, and Caleb looked stunned. 'What the *hell*?' she spat. 'I have a boyfriend, and you have a fiancée.'

'I know, but Autumn, she's so safe. So predictable. And you –'

'Don't. I'm not getting on this merry-go-round again,' she said, knowing what he was going to say.

'Valerie, you know –'

'No, I don't know,' she said, cutting him off. 'Or more accurately, I don't give a fuck. I'm out, and you can take the rest of the photos yourself.'

She turned away and marched down the street, stunned.

Did that really happen? Did Caleb really kiss me? Val thought over and over again as she stalked down the street and turned the corner onto a quieter side street. Downtown veered between crowded and busy, like on the streets lined with bars and clubs, and quiet and half-deserted, and she had just found the latter. She stopped and leaned back against a wall, trying to figure out what she was going to do next. Her car was in the parking lot of that golf bar where she met them out in the suburbs, and that was going to be a stupid-expensive RideShare.

Plus, she'd just lost the rest of the money from Autumn and

Caleb. There was no way she was going to keep working for him, not after that, but that meant she was forfeiting the rest. And that was not a small amount to give up – just thinking about how hard it would be to make that much money now made her stomach churn.

'Val,' Caleb called, rounding the corner. He looked panicked, like a deer in headlights.

'I don't fucking want to talk to you,' she hissed. 'And I quit, by the way.'

'Don't,' Caleb said, dangerously close to begging. 'I shouldn't have tried that, okay? I'm sorry.'

'Sorry doesn't cut it. How could you do that to Autumn?'

'It was a mistake. I've been drinking, and I got nostalgic, and when I get nostalgic, I make dumb choices.'

Val didn't really like being considered a 'dumb choice' but at least he was consistent. Drinking made Caleb emo, and during their first (or maybe second, she couldn't quite remember anymore) breakup, he'd called her to drunkenly beg for another chance more than once. 'It was a little more than that,' Val said, crossing her arms.

'Please don't tell her,' he pleaded, eyes wet.

'How are you going to explain me quitting, then?'

'You don't quit,' Caleb said. 'I'll – I'll pay you an extra fifty percent, instead of thirty-five. All you have to do is not say anything.'

Fifty percent. That wasn't nothing, and for a relatively simple ask: all she had to do was *not* tell Autumn the truth, which technically, she had already been doing. This was just one more thing to keep from her which, yes, was crappy, but Val was already being shitty to Autumn. What was one more thing, compared to being able to pay her bills without stressing?

Caleb could tell she was considering it. 'Please, Val. It would just hurt her.'

'You should have thought of that before trying to kiss me,' she said, but the earlier chill had left her tone. It would be an awful thing to do, but the money he was offering – it was so much, and she remembered all too well how it felt to have almost nothing when she arrived in Swede River.

'I know,' Caleb said, and he sounded moderately sincere. 'It was just a slip-up, I didn't mean it. And if you keep working and stay quiet, no one would need to get hurt.'

'Nick –'

'Doesn't need to know,' Caleb interrupted. 'It would hurt him too, wouldn't it? And it was nothing, so – why hurt him, over nothing?'

Val bit her lip. It felt like she was back in the quicksand with Caleb, an unfortunately familiar sensation, but at the same time, he had a point. Nick would disapprove of her keeping it from Autumn, since he knew Autumn now. He would want Val to tell her because it was the right thing to do, and if she didn't, he'd be disappointed in her. Val could handle a lot of things, but that? That might kill her. She'd finally found someone who didn't make her feel like a constant screw-up, and if he knew she was even considering this offer, that was out the window. She liked the way Nick looked at her, and the thought of losing that was physically painful.

'Fine,' she said, jaw still clenched. 'But I'm still going home tonight, you can figure out what to tell Autumn about why the pictures end early. And you're going to pay for my RideShare back to my car.'

Caleb let out a long breath. 'Thank you. I owe you one.'

'No, you owe me money,' she countered. 'This isn't a favor – this is a business transaction.' The second the words were out of her mouth, she felt a little better, because she was right – she wasn't keeping this from Autumn out of loyalty to Caleb, she was keeping it from her because she couldn't afford to turn it down.

And what Nick didn't know couldn't hurt him.

Chapter Twenty-Eight

Nick pulled Val out of the way of a family with four kids, approximately eighteen suitcases, and zero plan to adjust their trajectory. She had been digging in her purse for something and had been on the verge of being flattened by the eldest kid. 'Didn't want you to get trampled,' he said, letting go of her upper arm. It shouldn't still feel so *tingly* to touch her, but it did, and he never wanted it to stop.

'Sorry,' she said, finally emerging from her bag. 'It just feels so weird to be without my camera that I keep thinking I forgot something. Which I did, but on purpose.' She grinned at him, and he took a deep breath, reminding himself that there was no reason to be on edge.

Val had seemed a little distant lately, which, when coupled with his constant, low-grade anxiety about anything and everything Hollywood-related, had sent his worries into overdrive as they flew. *Maybe she's having second thoughts about me, maybe she doesn't want to be here and be my real-slash-also-fake girlfriend, maybe she's looking for a way out and can't figure out how to tell me, maybe maybe maybe.* Those thoughts were irrational, he knew that. He just needed to shake his doubts and get his head on straight.

'Where is Jan meeting us?' Val asked as they stepped onto an escalator.

'The parking lot nearest baggage claim,' he replied, and felt his chest ease as she leaned against him. It was fine. The distance he'd felt between them since Caleb's bachelor party was entirely in his head. 'You'll like her. She's mean, but funny.'

'Mean but funny is my general vibe, yes,' Val agreed.

Together, they stepped out into the warm California sun. 'It is a lot quieter than LAX would be, you were right,' Val said, harkening back to a conversation they'd had a few weeks ago.

LAX tended to be a zoo even at the best of times, and everyone was on the lookout for celebrities, which meant his chances of being photographed by a stranger got higher every minute. Then there were the photographers who tended to lurk by the exits, who were a loud, noisy, and rather unpleasant bunch. Most of them stuck to the celebrity terminal, but a few would hang around the regular exits, just in case someone famous was slumming it.

'Yeah, LAX is a nightmare,' Nick said. The Burbank airport was much smaller, and as a result a lot less stressful for him.

Val had her face turned toward the sky, soaking in the sunshine. Seeing as it had been fifteen degrees and cloudy when they left Minnesota, he couldn't blame her. Being reminded that springtime and warmth did exist when it felt like winter was reaching endless proportions was always a shock to the system.

Nick scanned the space in front of them, looking for Jan's familiar tall frame and shock of grey hair. 'Jan's got a Volvo,' Nick explained, but then his eyes snagged on a sign.

DUMBASS and *DUMBASS'S GIRLFRIEND* were written on poster boards being held up by someone in the crowd of chauffeurs. Val was laughing before Nick could see the poster-holder's face, and then he cracked up despite himself.

Of course it was Josh, complete with a hat that was probably supposed to look like a limo driver's. 'Where's Jan?' Nick asked, fighting his way through the crowd and hugging his twin.

'I told her I'd handle it,' Josh said, and broke away to scoop Val up in a hug like they were old friends. 'Don't worry, my license got un-suspended.'

Val's eyebrows hit her hairline. 'Can Nick drive instead?'

'It was just speeding tickets,' Josh said. 'And Nick drives like a grandma. Do you want to get to the hotel today, or three days from now?'

'It's not going to take three goddamn days for me to drive to the hotel,' Nick grumbled.

'Might take three hours, though. But trust me, I've never been in an accident.' He paused. 'Okay, I haven't been in an accident *lately*, and none of those were my fault.'

'Reassuring,' Val muttered under her breath. 'Do you trust him?'

Nick considered it. Josh wasn't lying – his last two accidents hadn't been his fault, and that meant he had been driving safely for at least three years if he didn't count the twelve-month suspension. Which yes, was just speeding tickets.

'I trust him *enough*,' he said, and that was apparently all Val needed to hear.

They followed Josh past the shuttle bus stop and through the surface parking lot. A woman in her late thirties was walking a few paces away, stealing glances at the brothers every few seconds. Nick felt a familiar tension rising in his gut and saw the moment that the recognition clicked. He braced himself, but all she did was shoot him a kind smile and climb into her SUV, apparently uninterested in an autograph.

Nick had forgotten that not *every* interaction in Hollywood was full of people clamoring for his signature, or wanting something from him, or just wanting to be near him because being famous was its own sort of currency. He'd been away for so long that only the bad memories stuck around; the times he'd felt suffocated and used and like little more than just a money-making robot. But there were plenty of days in Los Angeles like this, where someone would notice him and then go about their day with hardly another look.

When he had moved to Minneapolis for college, and then to Swede River to work in the library, it had felt like a breath of fresh air. But when someone *did* recognize him, as infrequent as it was, it could sometimes be even worse than in California, because people were far more prepared to see a celebrity out shopping in Los Angeles, and significantly less so at a circulation desk in a small Minnesota town. Nick had only had a handful of encounters like that over the years, but sometimes they could be . . . a lot. Too much, in fact. It was good for him to remember that sometimes, people in Los Angeles could be chill while people in Minnesota weren't.

It made him feel a little better about the visit, or maybe that was just having Val at his side, happily bantering with his brother like they'd been friends for years.

Chapter Twenty-Nine

Nick seemed unaccountably nervous as they approached the stage door. Val had gotten used to the fact that he simply seemed to vibrate at a different, much more tightly wound frequency than she did, but this was another level, even for him. 'You okay?' she whispered, and he tightened his grip on her hand.

'It's just – been a while,' he whispered. 'I haven't seen anyone since the finale wrapped.' The person at the door checked their IDs and ushered them in. Up ahead was a facsimile of the old *Just Us Girls* living room, with stools lined up for the actors. People were milling about, some clearly working while others wandered around with food in their hands and chatted with each other amiably.

Val swallowed hard and did her best to hide her nerves, to keep from setting Nick off further. She didn't care that much about impressing actors and famous people in general, but she was more nervous than she should have been about meeting the cast of *Just Us Girls*. These weren't just any actors, they were everyone's beloved TV family. Josh was easy for Val, because his catty sense of humor blended with hers, but Beth Black, comedy icon? Sarah Wandsley, everyone's favorite TV mom? It was important to her not to mess this up.

'Well, this is . . . the set,' he said, gesturing to the space around them. 'Did you want to meet everyone?'

'Is that okay? Like, aren't you guys technically working?'

'Honey, nothing about acting is work,' Beth Black said from five feet away with her famous cackle. 'You must be Nick's girl.'

Usually, Val bristled at being called a girl, but she decided she could make an exception for a ninety-six-year-old comedy legend. It was like Margie all over again, or maybe Val just had a weakness for sassy old ladies. 'Valerie Costa,' she said, shaking Beth's hand.

Nick furrowed his brow. 'You're saying hello to her first?' he asked Beth in a surprisingly jovial tone.

'Of course I am,' Beth snapped. 'She's a guest in our house. Did I teach you nothing, young man?'

Nick pretended to think. 'Does how to sneak out of the house count? Because you definitely taught me that.'

Beth guffawed, and Sarah Wandsley put down a cup of coffee and hurried over on impressively high heels. 'Nick! There you are,' she called with an Australian accent. Val had vaguely known she was Australian, but it was still a shock to her system to hear it. Nick dropped Val's hand for the first time and met Sarah in a hug, a smile breaking out across his face.

'Sarah, this is Val,' he said when he pulled back. His hand found hers again, but he didn't seem nervous anymore – just like he wanted to touch her.

'Lovely to meet you,' she said warmly, and then looked around. 'Where's Josh?'

'Late,' Nick said ruefully.

'That was how I knew which twin I was working with,'

Sarah stage-whispered to Val. 'If I could see one of the boys on set on time, it was Nick. Late, it was Josh.'

'Who did you like working with better?' Val asked with a mischievous grin.

'We liked our Jakeys equally,' Beth sniffed. 'Even if Josh did have a better sense of humor than this one,' she whispered loudly.

Nick shook his head fondly, and Val was happy to see that the tension had left his shoulders. He might not have enjoyed acting, but these people clearly cared about him. It was good to see that, and even better to see him remember it.

More people were coming up to greet him, and Val took the opportunity to brush a kiss to his cheek and head back outside. The taping was supposed to take most of the day, so she killed time on the studio lot as best she could, joining a tour with a group of Australians who were quite enthusiastic about *The Nerds on the Second Floor* and one sullen teenage girl who only wanted to see things related to *Wolf Boys*, a show Linds loved about sexy werewolves. It was interesting learning about how shows were filmed, and Val had probably more questions than the intern leading the tour had banked on about how they rigged lights to shoot outdoor scenes on an indoor soundstage. But after that was done and she had bought several cheesy mugs and a T-shirt featuring half a dozen shirtless men (pre-werewolf transformation, presumably) for Linds at the gift shop, there wasn't much more to do.

Val shifted the shopping bags to her right hand and tugged the lanyard with her security pass out of her jacket as she approached the stage door, having successfully wasted close to three hours. She probably didn't need the jacket, but it felt weird to be outdoors in February in just short sleeves. Which meant she was now slightly sweaty, but oh well.

Just like earlier, the person at the door checked it, glanced at her face, and then triple-checked to make sure the *filming* light was off above the door before letting her in.

Josh spotted her first just as her phone buzzed with a text, probably from Linds wondering if she'd gotten any autographs yet. 'Val!' Josh yelled from a good twenty feet away, striding over and scooping her up in a hug like he hadn't seen her the night before.

Josh was the exact inverse of Nick, personality-wise. Where Nick was shy, Josh was gregarious. Nick over-thought every single word that came out of his mouth, whereas Josh could probably stand to think just a little more about any word coming out of his. But Josh's messiness was part of why she was with Nick in the first place, so Val couldn't really be too critical. Besides, she liked him. He was like her, and that made her feel a little bit less like a false note in Nick's otherwise well-orchestrated life. 'How was the tour?'

'Cleaned out the gift shop,' Val said, holding up her bags.

'What'd you get me?' Josh demanded, peering inside and making a face. '*Wolf Boys* merch? Really?'

'There is nothing wrong with genre TV,' Val argued.

'No, those assholes passed on me,' Josh replied. 'I was up for the pack leader role, what's his name – Terrance?'

'Oh, that would have killed Lindsey,' Val said. 'She loves that character.'

'And I would have been so much better at it,' Josh said, somehow managing to say something arrogant as hell and have it come across as just charming.

Nick came over and stood behind Josh, rocking back and forth on his feet with his hands stuffed into his pockets and smiling shyly at her. It made her heart feel swollen and painful, and for a long time that was a feeling Val had run from. But with Nick, it made her want to run to him, which was scary enough in and of itself, but even scarier was the fact that she wasn't scared.

Her phone buzzed in her pocket again, and she gave Nick a quick peck on his cheek. 'How's it going?' she asked.

When he looked at her like that, it felt like there was no one else in the room, maybe even the world. It warmed her right down to her toes, and she was smiling more than she ever did. Her phone buzzed once more, and she made a mental note to tell Linds to calm down. 'It's been good,' he said.

Josh's phone chimed and he stepped away to check it just as Sarah approached again. 'This is the most talkative we've ever seen him,' she said. 'You must be good for him.'

Nick draped his arm over her shoulders and tucked her against his side, which was a lot of PDA for him. 'She is,' he said, just soft enough that it felt like he was saying it only to her. Her phone vibrated against her side, three times in quick succession, and Val felt a bloom of uneasiness in her stomach. Linds wouldn't blow up her phone this much unless there was something really big going on.

Before she could address it, Josh came walking over with a hard look on his face. It was so unlike him that it took her a second to realize it was directed at her. Val recoiled, but Nick was busy talking to Sarah about someone they had worked with years ago and didn't notice. 'What?' she asked.

Josh's eyes stayed cold and implacable. 'Something you'd like to share?' he asked, and Val's stomach plummeted. She didn't know what it was, but Josh – he knew something. Something *bad*.

Nick finally turned back to them and noticed the change in temperature. 'What's wrong?' he asked.

Josh looked around and jerked his head toward the door. 'Outside,' he said tersely.

Val stumbled as she followed him, Nick looking confused next to her. 'What's wrong?' he asked, catching her by the elbow. Val shook her head and pulled her phone out of her pocket, hands suddenly shaking as they stepped into the bright California sunshine. Surrounding them now were the looming, barn-shaped filming stages, stretching up and down the avenue like a firing squad.

'Josh, seriously, what's going on?' Nick asked as Val frantically skimmed Linds's texts, her eyes snagging on words that made her heart race and stomach sink.

Caleb. What happened. Ohyesss. CALEB, REALLY? were the only words she managed to process before she put together what must have happened. She opened Instagram and found Ohyesss's most recent Story.

She felt like puking. She was definitely going to puke, because it was there, for all of Ohyesss's 2.5 million followers to see. It wasn't the clearest photo ever, but it was clear enough.

Val, pressed back against the party bus, kissing Caleb.

She tucked her phone back in her pocket with fingers that had now gone completely numb. Nick had the picture on his phone too, but it wasn't from Instagram, which meant it had already breached containment and was circulating everywhere. His face was cold, and his voice was colder. 'Mind telling me what the hell is going on?'

Chapter Thirty

'You have to let me explain,' Val said desperately.

Nick's brain was encased in concrete. He wasn't sure what there was to explain – the picture had been fairly self-explanatory – but Val looked so frantic he couldn't help but nod.

'I didn't kiss him,' she started, and when he lifted his eyebrows in disbelief, she shook her head. 'I didn't. He kissed me. He had been drinking and he was rambling about our past, which is typical for him, honestly, and then out of nowhere he kissed me. I shoved him away, slapped him, and came right home. I swear.'

It was hard for him to piece together her explanation over the roaring in his ears, but Nick nodded. 'How did it end up on Ohyesss?'

'I have no idea,' she said, and dug her phone out of her pocket. 'Linds has been texting though, and –' she squinted, thumbing quickly through a long string of texts – 'it sounds like someone took that photo of Caleb because they recognized him from Autumn's stuff, and then someone found another photo from that night with me in the background, and, well, you know how stans are.'

He did. They could be well-meaning, but they were also one

of the most invasive types of people on the planet, especially when they were trying to solve a mystery. Combining the fans of two different people was combustible even at the best of times, and he probably should have seen this coming. Between his fanbase and Autumn's, the chances of Val and Caleb being recognized was probably higher than either of them thought.

But the kiss was only part of his problem. 'Why didn't you tell me?' he asked, voice breaking slightly.

'Yeah, why didn't you tell him?' Josh chimed in.

He wished his brother would go away and let him handle this alone, but he was working very hard on not falling apart and that meant he had no energy to fight with Josh about whether this involved him.

'Now's your chance to explain yourself,' Josh said to Val, who huffed out an annoyed breath. That in turn annoyed Nick, because of course Josh wanted an explanation. She had no right to be irritated by that.

'This is between me and Nick,' Val replied.

'I see,' Josh said, uncharacteristically quiet.

Nick broke himself out of the mental spiral he was in – *she lied to me, she kissed him, she didn't want me to know, she didn't trust me enough to know, everyone knows now, everyone on the cast saw us fight, everyone knows everyone knows everyone knows* – and shook his head. 'Let me handle this, Josh,' he said.

He was never that harsh with his brother, not even when his self-funded venture went belly up and Nick had had to find a roommate to help him pay for his mess, but he couldn't help it. He was melting down and there was no way to stop it.

Josh held his hands up in surrender, face skeptical, and backed away. Val waited until he was out of earshot to resume her explanation. 'You were sleeping when I got home. It wasn't important and it wasn't worth waking you.'

'And once I was awake?'

She shifted from foot to foot, looking away. 'I don't know. Not important, I guess.'

Something gnawed at him. 'Not important?' She knew how much honesty mattered to him. Hell, the reason he had let her move in was because she felt trustworthy.

But she was lying to him now. He was sure of it. 'What aren't you telling me?' he asked, and she chewed her lower lip, studying her feet. 'Val, please,' Nick begged.

'Caleb asked me not to say anything.'

'You did this for him?'

'No,' she said in a rush. 'Of course not.'

'Then why keep his secret?'

More lip-chewing, and the pit in Nick's stomach grew wider. 'He – we made a deal.'

'A deal.'

'My silence for an extra fifty percent on top of my wedding fee.'

'And I was included in that silence?'

Val opened and closed her mouth. 'I didn't keep it from you because of that,' she said quietly, and entirely too late. 'I just – I didn't want to hurt you, and you'd be mad at Caleb, and want me to tell Autumn, and then – you'd look at me like this.'

'Like what?'

'Like you're disappointed in me. Like I let you down.'

'Well? You did.'

'Exactly. Which is also why I needed the money.'

'You took the money as an insurance policy? Against me?' He couldn't say why that hurt almost as much as the lie, but it did.

'No, of course not,' Val said, and she wasn't sounding apologetic anymore. She sounded mad. 'Not like that, anyway. I don't have a ton of experience with dating long-term, and if we break up, I'll need it.' She crossed her arms more tightly. 'And if you're going to act like this over one single screw-up, it looks like I was right. I'm not doing that again.'

Nick blinked at her. 'Wait, are you comparing me to *Caleb*?'

'I'm saying I'm not going to be treated like some irredeemable mess. I shouldn't have agreed to his terms, no, but you can't even bring yourself to look at me.'

That much was true, but it was because Nick could barely focus on anything other than the shock and anger overwhelming his nervous system. 'Can you blame me?' he snapped. 'You've been lying to me for days.'

Val opened and closed her mouth. 'Because I knew you'd react like this. And like I said, I'm not doing this again.'

'You don't want to be with me anymore?' he asked dully. He was trying to process it all, but it was too much.

Val swallowed hard. She clenched her jaw and lifted her chin. 'Not if it means being treated like this. And if this is how it is – I'm out.'

He had known Val could be cold, but this cold? It nearly burned. 'If that's what you want,' Nick said, doing his best to sound just as detached as her.

He hated the look in her eyes – and he hated himself even more because he wanted to make it go away at any cost, even his own pride. But he held his tongue.

'Then I'll be gone by the time you get home,' she said, and it threatened to break him. Nick couldn't trust his voice, so all he did was nod. Val waited, like she was expecting him to say something, and when he didn't, she looked at the ground and nodded back. He turned on his heel and marched away without another word, refusing to look over his shoulder. If she wanted to be cold, he'd be cold.

Even if it broke his goddamn heart.

Chapter Thirty-One

Nick did his best to keep himself together through the rest of filming, but Sarah had given him an extra-long hug before resuming, and Cassidy, who played Jakey's oldest sister Charlie, had given him a sympathetic look like he was a kicked puppy, so apparently, he hadn't hidden his humiliation very well. The host had guided the remaining questions to the rest of the cast, leaving him to dwell on his own.

He couldn't get past it. Val had deliberately lied to him. It wasn't that he cared all that much about the kiss, since anyone with eyes and half a brain could see that Caleb had never completely gotten over Val, and by the same token could see that she was utterly, completely done with him. No, it wasn't that. It was that she didn't trust him.

Besides, Val knew how much he hated this sort of attention, and still she took the most selfish route possible that meant he was going to have to deal with this without any forewarning or plan. And it hurt. It hurt she didn't trust him, and that she chose a payout from a crappy ex-boyfriend over honesty. People who put their own feelings – and money – ahead of honesty were the sort of people he distrusted the most, and it hurt that Val could be like that, even sometimes.

Josh guided him off the set, uncharacteristically quiet, and then drew up short just outside the door. 'What are you doing here?' Josh asked, and Nick looked up just in time to have his last remaining shred of restraint tear in half.

'Oh, I had a meeting,' Candy said breezily, but there was a look in her eye that Nick didn't like. 'Did you boys have a good day filming?'

'What do you want, Mom?' Josh asked, sounding as exhausted as Nick felt.

'Can't I just check in on my boys?'

'No,' Nick said flatly. For half a second, he wished Val was there to help him ward off Candace's worst tendencies before remembering why she was gone. 'You want something. What is it?'

Candy's eyes flashed. 'Fine. I saw that your little girlfriend went and cheated on you, and I figured the dating show would be the perfect revenge. I have the contract in my car. You deserve better than that, Nicky, and I can help you find it.'

Nick stared at her. 'Are you kidding me?' Even a shitty mom would at least express *some* sympathy and not immediately capitalize on her son's heartbreak. 'What is wrong with you?'

'It's an opportunity, Nicky. Think about it – you can show her what she's missing, and she'll have to watch you find someone else to love along with millions of other people.'

Quite frankly, the idea made his stomach churn. He hadn't sorted out what he was feeling about Val yet – anger and betrayal, yes, but sadness and grief and regret too – but he knew he didn't want to punish her.

Candy used his silence to push her case further. 'Come on, like I said, it's just in my car. Sign it now, and you can –'

'Why's it in your car?' he asked.

'I didn't know if you'd be done filming, so –'

'No, I mean – why do you have it with you at all? How did you get here so fast?' There was something off about the whole situation, something he couldn't quite grasp yet. And then – 'Did you do this?'

She tossed her head. 'Don't be ridiculous. How could I have convinced that little photographer to cheat on you?'

The fog in his brain started to clear, replaced by pure fury. 'What did you do, Mom?' he asked, and waited.

'Nothing, Nicky, I swear. I know someone who's got an in with Ohyesss, and she gave me a heads-up that they got a submission about you, that's it.'

'And you didn't try to get them to not publish it? You didn't stand up for me?' he asked, even though his mother's betrayal paled in comparison to Val's.

'Keeping the truth from you would only be counterproductive.'

'Meaning what? You *told* them to publish it?'

'Can you blame me? I saw a chance,' Candy continued, glancing at Josh, who was staring at her with his mouth agape. 'I only want what's best for you, and what happened . . . I know you're probably upset, but think of it as an opportunity. Didn't I always tell you not to waste an opportunity?'

'This is my fucking *life*,' Nick roared. He'd never once actually yelled at his mother, but she had – finally – gone too far. 'You ruined my life, just so I'd do a show?' This whole mess was Candy's fault. If she hadn't pushed him to do the show, he never would have needed to use Val as a cover. And if he hadn't pretended to be with Val, then he wouldn't have gone and fallen in love with her. His heart would still be intact, along with his privacy. All of that, blown to hell, just because Candy wanted to use him. Again.

'It's hardly ruined,' Candy said dismissively, but she looked worried. 'In fact –'

'No,' Nick interrupted. 'Whatever you're going to say, save it. I should have told you from the start: it's not happening. Ever. With Val or without her. In fact, just – leave me alone. I don't care what you do, but I'm done with you.'

'Nicky, sweetie –'

'You should leave, Mom,' Josh said quietly. 'Now. And don't try and contact us.'

Josh had always been the one to try his hardest to please her, and Nick saw when the blow registered. Josh took him by the elbow and pulled him away, leaving their mother behind them in the fading twilight.

Josh slammed the brakes and barely avoided rear-ending the car in front of them, snapping Nick out of his spiral. He couldn't believe he'd told Candy off, any more than he could believe she'd been behind blowing his life to pieces. It wasn't that he thought she didn't have it in her, it was that he thought she was smarter than that.

'Where the hell are we?' he asked, looking at the sea of tail-lights out the windshield. 'Don't you live east of the studio? Why are we going west?'

'I was wondering when you'd notice,' Josh muttered. 'You could get murdered, not paying attention like that.'

'If my own twin decided to murder me, I'm pretty sure I'd just be dead, attention span or no.'

'Well, with that attitude, yeah.'

'Fuck you, I just got my heart broken.'

'I know, I watched it happen,' Josh said, his tone becoming

abruptly gentle. He turned into a small surface lot and killed the engine.

Nick blinked. He hadn't been to this beach in probably a decade, not since the night before he left LA for good. It wasn't the flashiest beach, and it didn't have a boardwalk like Venice or a pier like Santa Monica, but it was within walking distance from the grim, dingy, ground-floor two-bedroom apartment they'd lived in for the first few years in Los Angeles, and a short drive from the spacious McMansion their parents had bought when *Just Us Girls* got picked up for syndication.

The first time Nick and Josh ended up at the beach was right after the second season finished filming, but before they had been picked up for a third. Their parents had been fighting about it – Doug wanted them to audition for a movie, Candy wanted them to wait on the series getting picked up, not to mention Doug was sleeping with a cocktail waitress and all the money from the first two seasons was already gone – and Nick couldn't take it anymore. He slipped out the sliding door to their minuscule patio (which had nothing aside from a reclining lawn chair for Candy to sunbathe on) and had started running. He didn't even know Josh had followed him at first, and then they'd simply sat there, watching the waves in silence, until they didn't dare stay any later.

The fight was over by the time they got home, and the only indication Candy and Doug had even noticed that they left was a breezy *Where have you been? Dinner's getting cold* from Candy. Dinner that night had been pasta and marinara sauce, which was one of the only things Candy had ever learned how to cook. Doug didn't even bother; on nights he had to feed the boys it was fast food or pizza.

From then on, whenever things reached an intolerable pitch

for Nick, he had headed to the beach. Josh either came with him or found him there later, ready to tell him that the fight was over, and it was safe to go back home. Once *Just Us Girls* really took off, they moved to an Italianate monstrosity – every freaking thing was marble – where the beach was no longer within walking distance, but there was usually a driver on call.

'You coming?' Josh asked, standing outside his car with the door open. 'Or are you just gonna sit there and be depressed?'

'Not sure what difference it makes, being depressed in a car or depressed on some sand,' he grumbled, but followed Josh out. The salt air filled his lungs, and the distant roar of the waves tugged on something deep inside. He'd forgotten how healing the ocean could be.

Automatically, the brothers walked to a spot just out of the reach of the waves and sat down. Josh kicked off his shoes and Nick followed suit, digging his toes into the cool sand. 'So. Who do we tackle first, Mom or Val?' Josh asked, arms linked around his knees.

'What if I don't want to talk about either of them?'

'Then we sit here until you do,' Josh said, unusually serious.

'Fine, then Val,' Nick said. Josh remained silent and Nick sighed. 'There's not much to talk about. She lied.'

'But she didn't cheat.'

Nick snorted. 'That's a pretty low bar.'

'Still. If you're thinking she's like Dad, she's not.'

'I know that,' Nick snapped. He dropped his head forward, forearms resting on his knees. 'It's that she didn't tell me, and –' He blew out a breath, because saying it to Josh made it real, more real than when he'd been fighting with Val about it at the backlot. 'He offered her money. To stay quiet. I think it was mostly to keep it from his fiancée, but she kept it from me, too.'

'And that's worse?'

'She didn't trust me,' Nick replied. 'That's what worse. She chose money and a lie over honesty.'

Josh leaned back on his hands and straightened his legs. 'I don't know. She didn't tell you her ex tried to kiss her, and you're mad. Her reasons why she didn't tell you don't matter that much.'

'They do, though.'

'Okay, so what would be a good enough reason for her to keep that from you? What could she say that would make you not mad at her?'

Nick shifted uncomfortably. 'She didn't just lie, she lied so she could get paid,' he argued, aware he wasn't answering Josh's question.

'Ah,' Josh said in a low voice. 'You're not mad at her for being like Dad, you're mad at her for being like Mom.'

That can't be it. Can it? 'It's not that simple,' he said. 'And since when did you become a shrink?'

'Since I auditioned to play one on an HBO show and Jan told me I had to actually research the part this time.'

'When was that?'

'Six years ago, and nice try, I'm not letting you get me off track. Although I would have killed as that therapist, despite being "too young to be believable", according to the casting director.'

'They had a point; twenty-three is pretty young for a therapist.'

'I could've been a prodigy. But like I said, nice try. You know Val isn't Mom, right?'

Nick tossed him a withering look. 'Yes, I know that.'

'That's what this is about though, isn't it? Mom spent most of our childhood lying her ass off about us, for money. For chrissakes, she told that music exec you were *almost there* on choreography, when we all knew that was never going to happen.'

Josh sighed. 'And she's the reason you and Val are fighting in the first place.'

'She didn't make Val keep it from me. If she'd just told me, it wouldn't have mattered what Mom did.'

'Yeah, but what Mom did was seriously messed up. Messed up enough that you yelled at her, which I never thought you'd do.'

'It was a long time coming.'

'It was,' Josh agreed. 'I just never thought it would happen. I figured she'd be eighty years old and we'd both still be ducking her calls and pretending that Jan has something in the pipeline for us but it's top secret so we can't say what it is.'

'Is that what you told her?'

Josh shrugged. 'A couple of times, yeah. She never bothered me the way she bothered you, though. And at least I wanted this life.'

Nick decided that if they were going to have this conversation, they might as well talk about all of it. 'I always felt like a screw-up,' he admitted.

'I'm sorry, I must have misheard you. You, the screw-up? Have you *met* me? Do you want me to remind you of all the times you had to bail me out of a jam?'

Nick chuckled reluctantly. 'I did, though. When we were kids, it all came so naturally to you, and I had to work at it. I hated it, which made me think – for a long time, I thought I was just always going to feel like a failure. It wasn't until that tutor we had during the last seasons –'

'You mean the super dorky one you had a big crush on?'

'She was not dorky. She was smart.'

'Dorks *are* smart, dumbass,' Josh retorted.

Nick's laugh was a little more genuine that time. 'Anyway, I didn't realize I could be bad at acting but good at other stuff until then.'

Josh looked back out at the water. 'What do we do about Mom, then? Block her number and hope she gets the hint? Finally do what we've wanted to do for a decade and cut her off completely?'

The thought of not having to deal with Candace ever again made the vise around his ribs loosen. 'That's probably it, yeah. But if that would make it harder for you, I don't want that.'

'It's not like I really enjoyed spending time with her,' Josh said thoughtfully. 'I mostly just did because, well, she's our mom, you know? Dad's been out of our lives for a while, but she just hung on like a barnacle with a very expensive purse. If you're done with her for good, I am too.'

'You don't have to,' Nick said, throat tight.

'Sure, I do,' Josh said. 'What she did to you was supremely messed up, and she's not even sorry.' Josh cleared his throat and blinked hard. 'But we should be talking about Val. How did you guys leave things?'

Right. Val. The tightness in his chest returned. 'She's moving out,' Nick said, and it felt like someone had carved a big, gaping hole in his lungs to say it out loud.

'Jesus. You have one fight and that's it?'

'She was the one who brought up breaking up.'

'And naturally, you had no choice but to go along with it.'

'What was I supposed to do? I can't stop her from breaking up with me.'

Josh rolled his eyes. 'Of course not. But you could fight for her. Let yourselves have a fight, hash it out, make up. Like couples do.'

'She left right after.'

'And you didn't stop her?'

'Whose goddamn side are you even on?'

'Believe it or not, yours. You guys are good for each other, even if you both run when you're scared.'

'I'm not scared, I'm humiliated,' Nick replied. 'There's a difference.'

'I mean, sure, but also no. You didn't like how you were feeling, so you freaked out and broke it off completely, just like how you left –' Josh paused and chewed on the inside of his cheek. 'How you left Hollywood,' he finished.

Nick didn't think it was possible for the hole in his chest to get bigger, but it did. 'You think I left you?' he asked quietly.

Guilt threatened to swallow him whole. This was what he'd been afraid of all these years, why he had been so determined to constantly rescue Josh from whatever mess he got himself into. Getting confirmation that his fears were right was almost more than he could take.

Josh was silent for a long time. The waves crashed and receded, crashed and receded. Out on the horizon, a tanker slowly chugged past, hardly more than a shadow studded with lights against the water. 'I know you didn't. Like, intellectually or whatever. And I knew you wanted out, but – when you left, I didn't think you were *leaving* leaving. You basically never come back here. And of course our jackass of a dad picked that time to walk out for good, so – it was a lot.'

'I didn't mean –'

'Look, I get it. This was always my dream, not yours. Well, Mom's too, but that's not the point. The point is, you hate Hollywood and that's a part of me, and –' Josh broke off, shaking his head.

'I must hate a part of you too,' Nick supplied. 'Is that what you were going to say?'

'I know it isn't that,' Josh said. 'But I feel like it is anyway sometimes.'

Nick tossed his arm around Josh's shoulders. 'I didn't know it felt like that,' he said. 'I'm sorry. I really am. I was afraid you'd feel that way and I tried to make sure you knew I didn't, but I guess I didn't do enough. And Dad leaving – I've always wondered if that was my fault, too.'

Josh sat in silence for a long moment. 'That's why you always bail me out, isn't it?'

'It's not the only reason,' Nick said finally. 'Part of that is because you're my brother.'

'And part of it is a guilt-debt,' Josh replied. He kept his eyes laser-focused on the waves, his throat working hard. 'You shouldn't.'

'I wanted to –'

'I know what you wanted, okay? I can't say I didn't suspect it and that I haven't appreciated it, but – that's not what brothers do.'

'We take care of each other.'

'Yeah, because we love each other, not because we're trying to make ourselves feel better. And Dad – he'd had one foot out the door as long as I can remember. He was leaving, whether or not you did. Don't blame yourself for that.'

Nick gave his brother a long look. 'You've changed,' he said softly. 'More than I realized, I think.'

Josh chuckled, not bitterly, but not happily either. 'I've been doing some growing up, yeah.'

'I'm sorry I didn't notice it. And I'm sorry about the money. I'll stop.'

'Don't be that sorry,' Josh said, a grin playing at the corner of his lips.

Nick laughed. 'How about I do the cameo, instead?'

'And watch you act again? I think I'd rather have the money,' Josh said, committing to his grin. 'But if you're honestly in for it, I think it would be good for you. Not to remind you of what you missed, but as like, closure or something.'

'Closure. I like that,' Nick said soberly. 'But you're still my little brother. I'm always going to look out for you. That won't change.'

'Three minutes doesn't really count,' Josh said. 'And maybe it's my turn to look after you.'

'How so?'

'By telling you to get your head out of your ass. Val needs you to say you're sorry, and then she'll feel safe enough to say it back.'

'How well do you even know her?' Nick said, not quite willing to let Josh win completely.

'She's a human disaster. We recognize our own kind.'

Nick huffed out a laugh. 'She's probably already on a flight home, though. And I don't know if she even wants me to apologize.'

'Then you go get on a plane yourself and find out.'

Nick stood at the bottom of the walk, looking up at their front door. Of course, that would be when he realized it – it was *their* door, not his. *Their* house. Their *home*. Now, when it might not be anymore.

The flight back had been a nightmare. Part of Nick had hoped he would find Val at the airport, but she wasn't at the gate, and he watched carefully as everyone boarded to no avail. Whatever flight she was taking wasn't his. He was more jittery than usual on the plane, glowering at a flight attendant who sent him a flirty smile and curtly refusing a drink. It also took forever, like the pilot had decided to take them on the scenic route. He kept drumming his fingers on his knee and then realizing he was doing it, only to find himself fidgeting again two minutes later.

The drive to Swede River hadn't been any better. Unlike the

flight, it had gone by far too quickly, because now that he was getting closer, he was still not sure what he was going to say. *Don't move out, stay and fight with me? I'm still pissed at you, but I'm not so pissed I want you to leave? I'm sorry I made you feel like you couldn't trust me?* Nothing sounded right, and by the time he passed by Pete's, Nick knew he was going to have to do the unthinkable: he was going to have to wing it.

In short, he was a wreck by the time he got to their front door, and the lack of sleep thanks to Josh's oceanside pep talk didn't help.

But the second Nick stepped inside, he knew something was off. The house felt cold and quiet, his footsteps echoing like it was an empty warehouse. 'Val?' he called, stomach churning. 'Val, are you here? We need to talk,' he called, wincing as he remembered the way they bickered about that exact phrase once. 'I mean, I want to apologize,' he corrected, but it was like his heart already knew what his brain couldn't admit. There were no boots strewn haphazardly by the door, no stack of junk mail she'd 'get to later.' The signs were there, but reading them outright would be too much. He needed to see it for himself.

Nick walked up the stairs, heart already turning to glass. He felt fragile, breakable. Val had always made him feel strong, but not anymore. He put his hand on her doorknob. 'Val?' he asked, slowly turning the knob and easing the door open.

But it was empty. No mess, no exploding drawers, hell, she'd even opened the shades. Light streamed in like it was mocking him, dancing off the bare floor. It was as spotless as the day before she moved in, and that, more than anything else, was what made his heart shatter.

Val was gone, and she wasn't coming back.

Chapter Thirty-Two

@Idriveafordbrother
She's such a skank

@Nickjakeyfan91
I'd kill myself if I hurt Nick

@Kramerfamstan
If that bitch had any integrity she'd unalive herself right now

@justusjakeys
Slut

@jakeymyman
I hope she chokes

@Idriveafordbrother
Someone find me her new address so I can burn it down

'If you're on Twitter reading mean tweets about yourself I'm grounding you from your phone,' Linds said, walking the five feet between her kitchen and her bed. When she had told Val she was moving into a studio apartment the size of a shoebox, Val had assumed there was some hyperbole in there.

But no, it was barely more than a glorified closet, and with the two of them packed in there like sardines it was almost overflowing. Linds deserved sainthood for agreeing to let Val move in with her on all of twelve hours' notice. After the fight in the studio backlot, Val had decided to hell with budgeting and charged the first red eye to Minneapolis she could find to her credit card. Being back home – Nick's place – had hurt like all hell, but Val shoved that feeling aside and started packing. Then she dumped anything she couldn't fit into a suitcase at her parents' house while they were at work, and she was back on a plane to California by the next evening.

The whole thing had taken barely twenty-four hours. It felt surreal to think about, if it could be surreal and more painful than anything she'd ever felt in her life at the same time. She couldn't get over how quickly Nick had turned on her, and the cold, harsh man that afternoon bore almost no resemblance to the sweet, shy Nick Ford she had come to know and – well, she wasn't going to go there.

No, that wasn't quite true. He was like the Nick Ford she thought he was initially; an uptight, critical jerk who snapped at her about cereal bowls being left too long without being properly rinsed out. Val thought she had uncovered the real man underneath, but apparently, she had been right the first time.

Linds plucked the phone out of Val's hand and flopped down next to her on the bed. 'You have to stop it,' she scolded. 'Reading mean tweets is only good when it's a hot celebrity on late night TV having to read things that are actually just unhinged thirst tweets.'

Val threw her arm over her face and groaned. 'Put "celebrity" on the list,' she said, motioning to the whiteboard tacked at the foot of the bed. Linds had been using it for studying, but now half of it was dedicated to a list of currently banned words: *Nick, Ford (person or vehicle), gossip, influencer, Caleb, Hollywood.*

Linds crawled to the bottom of the bed, scribbled 'celebrity' and recapped the marker. 'It's going to be hard to have a real discussion about this when you're ready with those words banned from the apartment.'

'I'll never be ready,' Val replied. She had crumbled into Lindsey's arms, weeping, the day she arrived, but that was the only time she let herself cry. Ever since, all she'd done was ignore texts from her family, wallow in self-pity, and look anxiously at her bank account. And read mean tweets about herself from Nick's surprisingly active fanbase.

'Okay, if you're not ready to talk about . . .' Linds paused, searching for an acceptable word. 'The Incident,' she settled on, 'then can we talk about the other casualty?'

'You mean Autumn?' Val said, rolling to her side as Linds lay down with her face just three inches away on the other pillow. Seriously, the number of people who would be willing to put up with their broke, dumbass friend living in their tiny studio and sharing a bed indefinitely was minuscule, but Linds hadn't so much as broached Val figuring out where she'd go from here. She just let her crash and let her be.

Until today, apparently.

'Yes, I mean Autumn. You really liked working with her, didn't you?'

That was the thing – Val felt terrible for how it all shook out for Autumn, since she was the most blameless person in all of it. If Val hadn't been such a crappy human and agreed to lie in the first place, Autumn wouldn't be in this mess. Maybe she still would have married Caleb, which was awful in a different way, but at least that would have been her choice and wouldn't have resulted in massive humiliation.

'I did, but I also lied to her and kissed her fiancé.'

'You did not kiss her fiancé, you got kissed *by* her fiancé. Against your will. And then you hit him for it.'

'Things I guarantee she doesn't know,' Val retorted. 'And if I were her, I wouldn't be all that enthusiastic about hearing me out, since again, I have been lying to her from the beginning.'

'I maintain the blame for the lying falls mostly on Caleb, as he was the one with the preexisting relationship with her and held financial power over you.'

'Are you sure you don't want to go to law school?'

'Very sure. I hate writing papers. Anyway,' Linds said, eyes going soft. 'What if I told you there might be a way for Autumn to know the truth, but you wouldn't have to be involved?'

'How? Telepathy? Magic?'

'Close. The internet.' Lindsey sat up and reached for her phone, quickly tapping through a series of photos. 'I've been Instagram-detecting since this all went down, and I found someone with a public profile who was out in Minneapolis that night, but clearly has no idea who any of you guys are.'

Val looked at the grainy image on Linds's phone. It was from a different angle and a bit farther away, but she recognized the party bus in the background. Linds must have tried to zoom in, which generally just made things blurry, contrary to what TV would have people believe, but it was clear enough, especially if you had seen the other photos of Val and Caleb. It was mid-slap, her hand just about to connect with his cheek. It wasn't particularly ambiguous, and unlike a few other photos that online sleuths had found from that night, it was clearly taken at the exact right moment. There was even the same woman in the skintight green dress to Val's left, posing with her friends for a selfie.

'What do we do with this?'

'Same thing we've always done, Pinky,' Linds paraphrased. 'We send it to Ohyesss and hope they publish it.'

'You think Autumn will see it?'

'I think her followers will make sure she does,' Linds replied. 'Those of us who are terminally online always find out about this stuff. I don't want to do that without your approval, though.'

'Honestly, I don't see how this could make anything worse. So yes, let's do it.'

Linds tapped some more and looked up, a small smile on her face.

'There. Done. And now, for the elephant in the room.'

'No,' Val moaned, covering her face with a pillow. 'Not ready.'

'Will you ever be ready?' Linds asked quietly.

'No.'

'Then we might as well get it over with now,' Linds replied, and cleared her throat. 'Did Nick really throw you out?'

'Not in so many words,' Val said, words muffled by the pillow.

Lindsey plucked it off her face. 'That's a no, then.'

'He implied it.'

'How?'

Val blinked hard, and Linds reached out and took her hand. Val squeezed it, her throat thick. 'The way he looked at me. I just – there's no coming back from that. I can't see that look on his face ever again. I had to leave.'

'So you're avoiding him,' Linds said, settling herself cross-legged on the bed.

'Obviously,' Val snarked.

'And this is different from how you dealt with Caleb – how?'

'He's nothing like Caleb.'

'Obviously,' Linds echoed. 'I don't have a desire to put his head on a pike. But you can't deny there are some similarities to your approach, here.'

'I never cried about Caleb.'

'No, but you never loved him, either. You did, however, run away every time you two had a fight.'

Well, shit. Lindsey had a point, and Val couldn't do anything about it except glare at her. 'It's not like I can un-run away,' Val protested feebly.

'True,' Linds said. 'I just wanted to name the pattern. Sometimes that helps, according to the psych class I took last semester. Just think about it, okay?'

'Okay,' Val begrudgingly agreed.

Linds smiled softly. 'Now, it's time you got out of bed and did something. Come on, we're going to get sushi and then you're going to shower while I look over stuff for my test tomorrow, because you're starting to smell.'

'I am not.'

'It's harder to smell yourself than someone else. It's just science,' Linds said, and took her by the hand. 'C'mon, lazybones, let's get going,' she said, and Val let herself be hauled out of bed.

Three days after Linds had submitted the photo to Ohyesss, Val got a one-sentence email from Autumn.

Is it real?
  -A

That was all it said, but it was enough. Val opened her laptop and started typing, ignoring the clammy feeling in her palms. She was going to have to be vulnerable, and she generally would have preferred having to discuss crypto with her brother-in-law for six hours straight than do that. But she owed Autumn the truth, at least.

Autumn,

Yes, the picture on Ohyesss is real. Both of them. But there's a lot more to the story if you'll hear me out. If you don't want to, just delete this email. Either way, I won't contact you again unless you want me to.

I don't know what he's told you, but here's the truth: Caleb and I were on and off for a long time. We weren't ever officially together, and he made it very clear he didn't see anything long term with me. Someone with more self-respect probably would have walked away sooner but, well, you've met me. We were done a year and a half when I met you, and I didn't realize my Caleb was your Cal until he showed up.

It doesn't matter how or why we decided to lie to you, because in the end, we did. It would have been so easy to tell you the truth, and I should have. For that, I really am sorry. My reasons aren't important, because I hurt someone who was becoming my friend, and I wish I hadn't. And then the bachelor party happened, and I have no excuse for not coming clean right then.

I'm not going to ask for forgiveness because honestly, I don't deserve it. But for what it's worth, no, I didn't want to kiss him; yes, I slapped him in response; and yes, I wish I had told you. I'm not telling you any of this to make you feel bad for me, but so you at least know our friendship wasn't a lie.

Sorry one last time,
Val

The light from Linds's one window had shifted across the bed by the time Val hit send. Her phone was lying next to her, cold and silent, but she figured if she was dealing with one huge, emotional thing, she might as well deal with another. She found the right contact and hit call.

Amy answered on the first ring. 'Valerie? Are you okay?' she asked breathlessly. In Val's opinion that was a little dramatic. Sure, she hadn't answered most of her mother's many, many texts, but she had sent one that said *Taking a trip to California to hang out with Linds. I'll be back for my stuff in a few weeks.* They knew where she was, that she was safe, and it wasn't like they talked to each other constantly. Honestly, if she hadn't left her stuff at Mom and Dad's, they probably wouldn't even know she was gone.

'I'm fine, Mom,' Val replied. 'Like I told you.'

'Christine said there was internet drama,' Amy said. 'That you – cheated? And now you've run away? None of this is like you, Valerie. What's gotten into you?'

'I didn't cheat on Nick,' Val said, closing her eyes to keep ahold of her temper. This was intended to be a semi-peacemaking call, or at least not one that would start a fight. Linds had gently reminded her she couldn't ignore her family for ever unless she wanted to cut them off completely. That felt drastic, and besides, it would mean cutting off Milo and Ada, and Val couldn't imagine that. 'And I didn't run away. I'm an adult. I took a trip.'

'You left all your things behind.'

'I had to move out of Nick's place.'

'You said you didn't –'

'And I didn't,' Val interrupted. 'It was a misunderstanding, but we still broke up, and I didn't want to live there anymore.' She blinked back the hot tears that always threatened when she thought about Nick. 'I'm just calling to tell you I'm okay, and you can stop texting.'

'If you need a place to stay, or a job, your room is still here and your dad can always find you something,' Amy said.

'I don't need a job,' Val said tightly. 'How many times do I need to tell you that?'

'I'm just –'

'I know. You're trying to help. But you're not, okay? I'm not moving back to St Cloud, and I'm not going to stop being a photographer.'

'It's just not practical,' Amy said, defensive. 'It's so hard to make a living that way.'

'I am making a living, though. Maybe not the one you and Dad want for me, but I'm not Christine. I won't be, and I think we'd all be a lot happier if we stopped pretending I might be someday.'

Amy sighed. 'I just didn't want to see you fail.'

It was going better than she had rehearsed with Linds, but that didn't mean it was easy. 'I know, but in doing so, you made me feel like a failure. All the time.'

Silence stretched thin on the line. 'Okay.'

Okay? That was it? It was better than nothing, but Val had hoped for a little more. An apology, maybe. 'Okay,' Val said back.

More silence. 'We're sorry,' Amy added. 'Your dad and me. Like I said, we just didn't want to see you fail.'

'Right. Well, can we just agree that we'll drop it? The whole

Val-needs-a-job thing? It's getting old. And tell Christine that, too.'

'If you're sure,' Amy said reluctantly. 'Ada's got her spring concert coming up. Will you be home for that?'

'I'm not sure,' Val said honestly. She hadn't broached leaving with Linds yet, even if she knew she couldn't crash with her indefinitely. 'If I can't be there, tell her I'll watch the whole thing if Christine records it for me, okay? Or if they stream it somewhere, I'll watch it live.'

'Okay,' her mother replied. It was a hesitant detente, but it was at least better than open warfare.

'I've gotta go,' Val lied. 'Bye, Mom.'

'Goodbye,' Amy said. 'And Val?'

'Yeah?'

'I love you. I really do. I'm sorry if – it doesn't always show.'

'I love you, too,' Val said. 'Talk to you later.'

It was still late afternoon and she looked outside, deciding it was time to rejoin the living. She slipped into her boots and jacket and headed out, with no destination in mind, feeling lighter than she had in weeks.

Chapter Thirty-Three

Nick fluffed the throw pillow on his favorite armchair and did the little hand-chop thing he'd seen on multiple home renovation shows. That was about all he could bring himself to watch without Val, because nothing else seemed funny or entertaining without her. He could manage to watch half a dozen interchangeable white couples where the husband was a contractor and the wife was an interior designer who said things like 'greige' and 'pop of color' until he fell asleep, though, so that was what he did. Plus, it had taught him how to properly stage his pillows.

'Okay but like, are you *sure* sure,' Josh said on speakerphone. 'Because you don't have to do this. The show has good buzz, and Jan has a whole strategy planned out for me. If all goes well, I might even be in the running come awards season.'

Nick hadn't seen any of *Just Us Boys* yet, but Josh was right about the advance chatter. Reviews were saying things like *charming* and *hilarious* and *comfortably familiar without feeling dated*, and people were excited about the reunion show that would be debuting on the streaming service the week before. Nick would have been well within his rights to bow out now.

But that talk on the beach had made him realize some things. Nick had healed a lot since his time in Hollywood, yet he hadn't really moved on. He had simply stuck it in a box labeled *Josh* and ignored it, and that plus what his new therapist Dr Brunswick called *a persistent fear of attention* had kept him stuck in a rut. Val had even been a shield for him, helping him deflect the spotlight elsewhere. *There's nothing wrong with that per se,* she had said last week. *You need to examine why you did it though. And what you needed from it, so you can figure out how to break out of this pattern.*

That was why he had to do this, but the reporter was arriving any minute now. 'It's time,' Nick said. 'I'm ready.'

He could almost hear his brother's smile through the phone. 'Happy for you, bro,' Josh said. 'But have you thought about –'

'Reporter's here,' Nick lied, and hung up. He knew what Josh was going to say (*have you thought about reaching out to Val, I know you miss her*) and he didn't want to discuss that with him just yet.

The doorbell rang, making Nick slightly less of a liar, and he went to open it. On the doorstep was a young Black woman hitching her tote bag higher on her shoulder. 'Nick Ford?' she said with a bright smile. 'Michele Zeller. It's good to finally meet you in person.'

'Likewise,' he said, letting her in. He had had a handful of Zoom calls with Michele over the past few weeks, but today was going to be the bulk of the interview. She was writing a profile on him in *Elle*, arranged by Jan – with his permission – to publish right before the reunion show started streaming. It hadn't been as difficult as he thought it would be, to talk about his reasons for leaving and not going back. He was happy with his life and his choices, and it felt good to talk about them. The idea of other people reading his thoughts still made him cringe, but Dr Brunswick had encouraged him to think about how those words might make other people feel. If it gave someone the courage to walk away from a job or relationship that was destroying them on the inside, maybe that would be worth it.

Michele looked his shelves up and down, head cocked to the side. 'What's your system?'

'Alphabetized by genre. You're in the mystery section right now,' he explained, and had a vivid memory of Val teasing him about his system, even as she did her best to follow it.

He missed her so much it hurt.

'Should we get started?' Michele asked, and Nick reminded himself that a) he had okayed this interview and b) Michele was kind. He had read a few of her pieces before he agreed to do the profile, and each of them had been warmly human portraits of people that managed to demonstrate their humanity without seeming like a press release. He trusted her, at least as far as he trusted a journalist, and besides, it was time. There were things he needed to say, if only to say them out loud. Whether or not Val read them was up to her.

Nick sat down in the armchair, squashing his carefully fluffed pillow, and Michele took a seat across from him on the couch. 'Let's begin.'

Chapter Thirty-Four

Val adjusted her lens to bring the bird – it wasn't a robin or cardinal, but that was as far as her bird-identification knowledge extended – into better focus. The tree was in full bloom – yet another reminder that California's version of spring was an entire galaxy away from Minnesota's, which was probably still buried under a foot of snow. The sky above the park was bright blue, and off in the distance the Golden Gate Bridge stood astride the bay while seagulls wheeled above it. She wasn't much of a nature photographer and didn't have any plans to be, but it felt good to be taking pictures of things that weren't people and weren't staged. It reminded her of being in college and discovering that she was quite good at some things, photography being one of them.

She snapped the photo and kept walking along the path, past a playground loaded with toddlers and some teenagers lazily tossing a frisbee around. Linds had required her to start taking a Stupid Daily Walk for Her Stupid Mental Health, partially for her own good and partially, Val suspected, just to get the apartment to herself for an hour. Val didn't blame her for it, and knew that pretty soon, she was going to have to figure out a long-term plan. California was just too damn expensive and Lindsey's apartment just too damn small for this to be sustainable for much longer, but going back to Minnesota meant facing up to a few too many things. Autumn hadn't replied to her email, which wasn't a surprise, and Nick had been radio silent too.

She owed him an apology; she knew that. But it was hard to get past the way he'd looked at her that day, so utterly devastated by her latest screw-up. Finding the courage to get over that – she wasn't sure she could.

Except. Just yesterday she had been scrolling through photos on her computer, looking at the shots she'd taken on her walks, when she stumbled on the photo Nick had taken of her. On the surface, it was just a simple snapshot – she was laughing in a nest of sheets wearing his slightly faded maroon T-shirt. Her eyes were down, away from the camera, but there was so much *Nick* in it. Not his face, obviously, but she could see herself through his eyes. She looked beautiful, and she looked loved.

Loved. Tears pricked the corners of her eyes and she made herself navigate away from the photo, but for the rest of the day she couldn't stop thinking about it. Neither of them ever had addressed the fact that he had said he was falling in love with her the night they first slept together, and now they never would. But the whole time she was fiddling with the photos of birds and flowers, she couldn't stop thinking about the way Nick saw her.

It hurt to see herself that way. She didn't like it, even though she could admit now she craved it. With Caleb, she'd always felt like she was striving for his attention, like it was a prize just out of her reach, and if she just worked hard enough, she'd get there some day. That was a feeling she was used to, of knowing she wasn't quite living up and needed to try just a little harder to prove herself.

But Nick never made her prove herself. He saw her for who she was, good and bad, and he could still take a picture of her that made her practically glow. She wished she could go back to that moment and undo everything that came after.

Val slipped her camera back into its bag and shoved her hands into her pockets, deciding she'd given Linds long enough. At the exit of the park was a newsstand, which she only ever noticed because it constantly surprised her that a newsstand still existed. She hadn't read a paper magazine in at least a decade, if not longer, and mostly she just remembered Christine's *Seventeen* and *Self* magazines littering their bathroom floor when Val was a kid.

Maybe it was because she had been thinking of Nick that she noticed it, or maybe it was a rare moment of the universe deciding not to screw her over. Either way, it was his name on the cover of a magazine featuring a starlet from the latest comic book movie that caught her eye: *Nick Ford opens up about life, libraries, and love.*

Val thought it might be a hallucination at first. Nick, giving an interview? To a magazine? Of his own free will? That didn't seem like him at all. She stopped and grabbed it off the shelf, rifling through the pages until a set of familiar bookshelves nearly stopped her heart. She skimmed it, looking for a sign that he had been kidnapped by aliens, but quickly realized it was a full, in-depth profile. Heart pounding, she paid the man behind the counter and went back into the park, searching for the interview again. She swallowed past the lump in her throat and blinked back tears when she looked at the photo accompanying the article. It was of him – the only one, as far as she could tell, as the rest were of his house. Those hurt almost more than the picture of him; homesickness threatened to drown her, rising in her chest like a tidal wave. She missed the couch and lying there while he made dinner, she missed sitting at the counter and bugging him while he loaded the dishwasher and griped about how many mugs she had left in her room.

Mostly, she just missed *him*. But she missed Swede River, too. She imagined Nick strolling around the neighborhood, saying hi to everyone, talking to Pete, maybe even introducing the journalist to Mary and Eng. She missed him, yes, but she missed it all.

She missed her home. Val found a bench in the sun, sat down, and started to read.

Nick Ford is a notoriously private man. While his twin brother Josh has become something of a Hollywood mainstay, when Just Us Girls *went off the air, Nick did one critically panned horror movie and disappeared. As it turned out, he left for a life of normalcy in a small town in Minnesota. At his request we're withholding the name of the town where he works as a librarian and owns a modest home that is positively overflowing with books, but it's clear this is the life he was meant to lead. He takes me for a walk toward the end of our interview, and it seems like every person in town knows and loves him. Nick is reserved, but he still has a friendly hello for the man behind the counter at the coffee shop, and stops to chat with a family whose daughter is away on a band trip. It's a far cry from the glitz of the Emmys and fashion shoots with The Gap, but the famously quiet Ford brother opened up over a cup of tea in his cozy living room. This is a man who knows who he is, what he wants, and has very few regrets about the life he left behind.*

'Acting wasn't something I ever chose for myself. I started acting before I could even read, and for a long time, it was the

only life I knew. Josh thrived on it, but I always felt I was just barely keeping up. Acting as a child is about instinct and mimicry, but as you get older it takes a different type of thought process and emotional intelligence. Josh has always understood people in a way I never quite managed. My acting always felt forced, and as we grew up, he was able to shift with the demands of the profession while I struggled.'

It's no secret that the Ford brothers have a challenging relationship with their parents, especially notorious Stage Momager Candace. While Nick doesn't speak much about her – he's clearly a circumspect, private man – neither does he hold back about where their relationship stands. 'I don't speak with her anymore,' he says bluntly, pouring me a second cup of coffee in his almost preternaturally clean kitchen. It's the afternoon of our second day together, and I already feel like an old friend of his, stopping by for a cup of coffee and a chat. 'We had been low-contact for a while, but as of this year we're no longer in touch.' I ask if he holds any resentment toward her for pushing them both into acting when it was clear that only one twin enjoyed it, but he merely shrugs. 'My parents – my mother, really – made the choices they thought were best at the time. It wasn't for me, so I've now chosen differently.'

It's remarkably diplomatic, considering all the rumors about Candace's over-involvement in their lives. There was even a short-lived attempt at a dating show featuring both brothers, if my sources inside a studio are to be believed; a dating show Candace herself pitched without any buy-in from either Nick or Josh. Nick demurs when I bring that up, although he does surprisingly confirm a different rumor – he will be appearing on Just Us Boys, *Josh's new Netflix reboot. 'Just a cameo,' he says with a self-effacing grin. 'Enough to show people that I definitely made the right choice in leaving Hollywood.'*

I laugh, and his brown eyes crinkle warmly. 'You can't be that bad,' I insist.

'Oh, believe me, I can,' he chuckles.

By this point he's making me dinner, a vegetarian chili that is the perfect mix of homey and delectable. I must confess at this point that I, like a lot of other women my age, had a poster of the Ford Brothers up in my room, but even in my wildest pre-teen dreams, I never thought I'd be sitting in his kitchen, a stack of books he's loaning me at my elbow, while he makes me dinner. He's dressed like a small-town daydream in dark jeans and a henley, and as dusk falls and we split a bottle of wine in his cozy living room, I bring it up: the minor internet meltdown about him, his one-time girlfriend, an Instagram influencer, and the influencer's fiancé. There were photos on gossip sites that seemed to imply a kiss, and then a few weeks later more surfaced that showed a different side of things.

He's reluctant to talk about it directly, but eventually seems to realize either he answers my questions now or deals with more internet speculation. 'I don't like talking about my private life,' he says in a deep baritone that would probably surprise most of Jakey's old fans. 'And I want to remind my fans that I would appreciate it if they respected my privacy above all else. But I also don't want someone I care about to be painted as a villain when she's not. The first photo that came out wasn't the whole story, and I do want to say categorically that she did not cheat on me.' I ask about his wording there – someone I care about, present tense – and he goes quiet for a minute. 'We're not together anymore, if that's what you're asking,' he says, and looks deep into his wine glass, like the answers might be at the bottom. 'And the reason we're not together is my fault. I loved her, but I let her down. I had a choice to believe her and trust her, but I let my own stuff get in my way. So, I lost her. And that's on me.'

I ask if that choice had to do with the photo of her kissing another man, but he demurs. He also refused to let me use her name in this article, although anyone with the ability to google would be able to figure out who we're talking about. I decide it's time to bring up another internet rumor, one that you'd have to be Extremely Online to know about: was his relationship always real, or was it a cover at first, as many of his most devoted fans suspected?

To my surprise, he almost smiles. 'Honestly, and with all due respect to my fans, that's none of your damn business, guys. What I had with her was real, and that's all that matters.'

Well. It's not a confirmation, but it's not a denial, either. I ask if there's anything else he's willing to say on the matter, and he hitches up the sleeves on his grey henley as he leans his forearms on his knees. 'I miss her. I doubt she'll ever read this article, which is why I feel like I can say that. I let her down, and I'm sorry. I miss her every day, and probably always will.'

Chapter Thirty-Five

Thunder cracked and Nick turned the page of his book, despite not actually having managed to read a word. His concentration was horrible lately, and the raging early spring storm outside wasn't helping.

Maybe Pete and Aaron were right; he needed a cat. Or a dog. Something to talk to, because despite having lived alone comfortably for years, Nick was lonely. A few months with Val and he'd suddenly become *social*, needing to talk out loud about his day. A cat or dog wouldn't talk back, but at least it would satisfy this new urge to chatter.

Or maybe he could just get used to being alone again. He had been fine for a long time, after all. He'd be fine again. Eventually.

His friends had been cautious around him ever since he returned from California without Val. They had found out what happened thanks to Mary's youngest daughter, who had filled them in on the internet blow-up. Nick's first day back at work, Mary had gently probed to confirm it, but she had assiduously refused to take a position. Pete and Aaron had been similarly diplomatic, and Nick had gotten the impression they had decided to specifically avoid taking sides. The rest of the town hadn't been quite so circumspect, and at least two patrons had, unprompted, announced to him they were *on his side*, which was also part of why he'd given the interview. He couldn't change how protective Swede River could be, but he could at least let them know it was unnecessary.

The first knock was so quiet he thought he'd imagined it, but then, right after a booming clap of thunder, he heard it again.

He threw open the front door and there, on his doorstep, looking like a drowned rat, was Val. Hair was plastered to her cheeks and forehead, and her clothes were completely sodden. Her chin was determined, though, and her eyes were blazing.

'What are you doing here?' he asked above the noise of the storm.

'I've got some shit to say to you,' she replied, crossing her arms.

'Then come in,' he said, his heart doing an abrupt series of somersaults. His interview with *Elle* had published earlier in the week, and he wasn't going to pretend like he didn't hope she would read it, but he also didn't know if she would. Or if she did, that she would come back. He had wanted the chance to let her know he was sorry, but that was it.

'No,' she said, and took a step back, farther into the rain.

'It's raining,' he said, a little stupidly, considering she looked like she'd climbed out of a swimming pool and a crack of lightning had just flashed above them.

'I'm aware,' she said with an eyeroll. 'But no, I'm not coming in until I say my piece.'

'That's ridiculous,' he argued. 'Come inside.'

'No,' she said flatly, and took another step back. Now she was a couple feet away, and she had to shout to be heard over the storm. 'I'm staying here until I can say it all.'

Nick nodded, his heart and stomach at war. His heart was hopeful; she'd come back from wherever she was hiding to talk to him, which had to mean *something*. But his stomach didn't like that she was keeping her distance from him; maybe she was still pissed. It would be warranted. He'd been a dick.

Val took a visibly deep breath, lips pursed momentarily. 'Did you really apologize to me via *Elle* magazine?' she yelled.

'Yes?' he replied, still not sure whether this was a good thing or a bad thing.

'And what if I hadn't noticed your name on the cover? What if they hadn't put it there? Would you have ever reached out to me to say it in person?'

'It wasn't about getting you to forgive me. And anyway, Jan had my name on the cover as part of the agreement for the interview,' he explained.

'That still depended an awful lot on me noticing it,' she called with narrowed eyes.

'I know, it was a stupid plan,' he said, shoulders slumping. 'Can you please come inside so we can stop shouting? And you maybe won't die of hypothermia.'

'No,' she insisted. 'I can't. I don't – I don't trust myself around you, and I have to say this stuff first.'

Oh. Nick's stomach lost the queasy feeling, replaced by butterflies. He suddenly recognized her bluster for what it was – Val putting on her armor one last time, just in case. He needed to let her keep it on until she felt safe enough to take it off. 'Proceed,' he said, and leaned his shoulder against the door jamb.

She gave him another almost-dirty look, and it was hard for him to smother his smile. 'Okay, did you mean it?' she asked, and another lightning bolt split the sky.

'That I'm sorry? Of course. I should have listened, or at least not reacted so quickly.'

'I know I shouldn't have kept it from you,' she replied. 'I should have apologized, but instead I ran, and I'm sorry.'

Nick shrugged. 'I drove you away.'

'Don't let me get out of this without taking any responsibility,' she chastised. 'I messed up, and I know it and own it. Linds told me to notice my patterns, and this was – Classic Val. But I don't want to be that person anymore, and I wanted you to know that.'

'Fair enough. You fucked up, and then I made it worse.' He took a deep breath. 'And one more thing – that picture on Ohyesss was my mom's doing.'

Val blinked. 'Um, what?'

'She got a heads-up that they had it, and she let them go ahead and publish it anyway.'

'Holy shit,' Val said, eyes wide. 'What did you do when you found out?'

'I told her to never talk to me again. Josh cut her off, too.'

'Wow.' She paused, processing, and frowned.

'You know, I imagined this being a lot harder,' she said sourly.

Nick let the corner of his mouth hitch up. 'Sorry?'

She sighed in exasperation. 'You're really going to beat me at groveling?'

'I didn't know this was a competition,' he said, his smile getting wider. 'C'mere.'

Val hesitated, so he reached out and grabbed her arm, yanking her closer. 'I said, come here,' he repeated softly.

Her arm was freezing and soaking wet, but he knew the goosebumps prickling under his palm weren't from the cold. Nick tunneled his fingers into her hair, brushing their noses together. 'Don't tell me what to do,' Val grumbled, but he could feel her softening, leaning into him. A gust of rain spattered against them as Nick brought his mouth down on hers.

Despite the chill and rain, Nick felt like he was standing in front of a roaring bonfire. Val kissed him back immediately, drinking him in like she was stranded in the desert, and he was her oasis. He knitted his fingers into her wet, tangled hair and she threw her arms around his neck, chasing his lips with each breath.

Nick stepped back inside and pulled her with him.

Chapter Thirty-Six

Val listened to Nick's heartbeat, letting the steady thump lull her into a state of soft-focus semi-consciousness. The storm was a little quieter now, but every once in a while a low roll of thunder would rumble through the room, almost as if the world wanted to remind her that here, in his arms, was where she was safest.

Where she was happiest. Val was tracing idle patterns across his chest, and Nick caught her fingers in his hand and brought them to his lips. It was a sweet kiss, with so much tenderness behind it that her heart felt like it was turning inside out. She laced their fingers together and held their hands up, studying how they looked together in the warm, yellow light from his bedside lamp. Rain pounded against the windows in sheets as gusts of wind buffeted the trees outside, and Val nestled down even deeper into him. She was so warm and safe and happy that her brain couldn't quite process it all, and instead had just settled on feeling everything. Her cheeks ached from smiling, and when she glanced up at Nick, he was looking down at her pensively.

'Everything okay?' she asked, resting her chin on his chest.

Nick ran his fingers through her loose hair, catching on a tangle before smoothing through the ends. 'I really missed you,' he said, and she smiled softly.

'I missed you too,' she replied, looking into his eyes. 'Was that all?'

Nick shook his head. 'I have a confession to make. When I saw that picture – the first one – I wasn't just mad you didn't tell me. I think – I was a little jealous, too.'

Val raised an eyebrow. 'Of Caleb?'

'Not exactly. I knew how you felt about him, but I got scared. That maybe you'd figure out you didn't want me anymore, go back to Minneapolis and move on and I'd just be in Swede River, living the same quiet, small life I've been living, but you wouldn't be in it anymore.'

Val bit down on her lower lip. 'That's an awful lot of feelings from one blurry photo.'

Nick huffed out a short laugh. 'I didn't say it was rational. And I do tend to spiral.'

'So, you weren't really jealous of Caleb for kissing me, you were jealous of – the possibility of my future life?'

'Well, when you put it that way it sounds stupid,' Nick said with half a grin.

She giggled. 'I didn't mean to. I was just trying to get it straight.' She took a deep breath, but she seemed to have left that persistent fear of being vulnerable back in San Francisco. 'Does it help if I say I don't want a future without you in it?'

'It does, yeah,' he said, pulling her up and kissing her even as his smile threatened to split his face in two. He broke the kiss but barely moved away, just enough to make eye contact. 'I love you. I've loved you for – god, for so long.'

'I love you, too,' Val said, and it was shocking how easy it was to say to him. 'I just didn't think I was worth –'

Nick shook his head. 'No,' he said, his vehemence surprising her. 'Don't you dare doubt yourself. Not with me, not ever.' He took her chin in one hand, making her look at him. 'You understand?'

'I do,' she said quietly. The realization settled over her like a blanket – she *did*. It was hard fought, but she knew exactly where she stood with him, and always would. She opened her mouth to apologize to him one last time, but he pressed his finger to her lips. A tree branch from the oak tree outside scratched the window, and he cupped her cheek in his hand. 'No more apologies, okay?'

She lifted one eyebrow. 'What if I want you to apologize to me again?'

He chuckled. 'Then I'll do it.' His face grew serious, and she had to force herself to keep meeting his gaze, because the part of her that always wanted to run was rustling in her ribcage. 'I mean it, Valerie. I'll apologize to you every day for not trusting you more if that's what it takes to keep you.'

She made herself wrinkle her nose, because otherwise she'd start crying. And she, Valerie Nicola Costa, did not cry. 'Honestly, getting apologized to every day sounds boring.'

'How about every other day?' he suggested with a crooked grin.

She narrowed her eyes in thought. 'Twice a week,' she bargained.

'Twice a week, then,' he agreed, laughing until she surged up to kiss him quiet.

'Really though,' she said against his lips, struggling to keep her train of thought, 'you don't need to apologize either.'

'What if I want to?' he asked, settling a hand on the back of her neck, holding her in place. He kissed her softly and pulled back barely an inch. 'What if I want to spend the rest of my life making it up to you?'

Val pressed another kiss to his lips, hardly more than a peck. 'How about you spend the rest of your life making me happy?'

It was a flash of lightning that illuminated the room as bright as midday in summer, but it seemed like his smile was responsible. 'Deal.'

Val sat at the corner table farthest from the door, fingertips drumming nervously. Autumn had agreed to meet her to talk face to face, which was more than Val was owed, in her opinion. What's more, Autumn had asked her to meet in Swede River, and Val had a horrible feeling it was because she thought she might not be recognized there – which meant she was still dealing with the fallout.

Aside from with Nick, Val didn't have a lot of experience with apologies, or at least not with particularly sincere ones. She and Linds almost never fought, and her family preferred if she just stayed the permanent black sheep. But she felt utterly rotten about what she and Caleb had done to Autumn, someone who had done nothing but be supportive of her career at a time when no one else would.

Val threw a nervous look at the door and chewed on a hangnail. Livvy stepped out from behind the counter and wiped down a table three seats away. 'People aren't that mad at you, you know,' Livvy said quietly, not looking up from her work.

Val snorted. 'Thanks, kiddo, but I know an angry mob when I see one.'

She had been back in Swede River for three days but hadn't left the safe embrace of Nick's – their – house until today. Her walk to Pete's had involved the unsettling feeling of eyes on her back even though hardly anyone was outside. Curtains had twitched as she went past, and she had the distinct impression that she was once again back to being very close to Goody Smith claiming she saw Val at the Devil's Sacrament. Hell, there was a table of people Val didn't even know sitting on the other side of the café who had thrown her dirty looks just five minutes ago when she arrived.

'I just meant they're worried, that's all,' Livvy said, just as Pete came down from his apartment, Felix on his hip. 'Nick was, um –'

'He was a goddamn mess the whole time you were gone,' Pete supplied. 'Hey, Val,' he added, and swooped down and kissed her on the cheek. 'I'm sure Aaron says hey too, but he had to go into his office today.'

'Oh, uh, hi?' Val said, not able to hide her surprise at the warmth in his welcome. Felix clung to his papa tightly, peeking at her out of the corner of his eye. Out of a lack of anything better to do, Val waved to him. He waved back, so there was one more Swede Rivertonian who didn't loathe her, at least. 'How did everyone know I was back already?'

'Margie saw you standing out in the rain on his doorstep the other day. Like Cathy in *Wuthering Heights*, she said.'

'I think I read that for school,' Livvy cut in. 'Isn't she a ghost?'

Pete frowned. 'Not the whole time, I don't think? Anyway, Margie knew you weren't a ghost, she only said you were back.'

'And let me guess; the whole town knows I broke his heart and hates me for it, Margie included.'

'She's just pissed you left without saying goodbye to her,' Livvy said. 'If I give you a box of scones when you leave and you go straight to her place, she won't give a crap anymore.'

Val's heart lifted. 'That easily?'

'Margie always liked you,' Pete said. 'And she told me just a week ago that she wouldn't have been surprised if Nick did something to drive you away, because, and I quote, "men are rarely up to anything good, even ones with a face like an angel and an ass like the devil."'

Val chuckled. 'He didn't have anything to do with it. I'll make sure she knows that.' She lowered her voice and nodded surreptitiously to the Table of Anger. 'What about, you know, everyone else?'

'Just like before, if Margie forgives you, so will like, eighty percent of the town,' Pete replied. 'And the other twenty percent probably forgot who you were, or read his interview and understand, or just don't care. Believe it or not, we *do* have other drama in Swede River. Like the Schmidts and the Jacobsons calling a truce long enough to take prom photos of Carina and Ella.'

'Really?' Val said, just as the door jingled and Autumn walked in. Her stomach fell, and Pete dropped his hand to her shoulder. 'It'll be okay,' he said quietly. 'She wouldn't be here if she wasn't interested in hearing you out.'

Autumn tossed an inscrutable glance her way and went to the counter to order. Val chewed her lower lip the entire time she waited for her drink and walked across the café to take a seat. 'Cute place,' Autumn said stiffly. 'I remember thinking that – before.'

'It is, yeah,' Val replied, equally awkward.

Autumn took a sip of her coffee and darted her eyes around, looking anywhere but at Val. For a long moment, neither of them spoke. It was time for Val to take the bull by the horns. 'Look, I'm so sorry,' she said, and Autumn finally stopped looking out the window. 'Caleb and I were the absolute worst to you, and you deserved so much better from both of us.'

Autumn frowned and tilted her hand side to side, like she was a judge on a TV singing contest about to deliver a verdict. 'Not bad. Way better than Cal's apology, anyway.'

'I should have –'

'Yeah, you should have at least come clean around the time I started confiding in you,' Autumn said, and Val had never seen her like this. Cold and businesslike, without any of the easy laughter and smiles she was known for. 'But you didn't. At least you *are* sorry, unlike Cal.'

'He didn't apologize?' Val asked, surprised. Caleb was good at groveling when he needed to be, or else she wouldn't have taken him back so many times.

'Oh, he "apologized",' Autumn said with air quotes. 'It was just cowardly and self-serving, and he threw you under the bus like fifteen different times. Even said the whole thing was your idea, but when I asked why you would have bothered because, let's be real, it didn't seem like you, he didn't have a good answer. Everything was always someone else's fault. I knew that about him, but I thought – whatever, it doesn't matter. I thought I knew him, but I didn't, because apparently, he sucked. And like I said, at least you seem apologetic.'

Val let out a breath. 'I mean it,' she said emphatically. 'I will do anything to make it up to you. I'll be your photographer for a year for free, or if you'd rather never see me again, I'll do what I can to find someone who could take over for me. Anything you want, you name it, I'll do it.'

Autumn surveyed her for a long moment and took another sip of coffee. 'I'm not going to pretend like I wasn't mad at you too, but . . . I believe you. You're not totally forgiven, but it's a start.'

A start. Val could work with a start. 'I mean it. I'll work for you for free for a year if that's what it takes.' It was not really something she could afford to do, but whatever, Val owed her.

'There's no way anyone could afford to work for free for a year,' Autumn said, waving her hand. 'Don't be ridiculous.'

'Six months, then.'

Autumn cracked the tiniest of smiles. 'How about three weeks and we call it even.'

'Are you serious? Done,' Val said. She leaned forward, arms folded on the table. 'Thank you. I won't mess up this second chance.'

'Well, I don't have any other fiancés for you to have dated and lied about so I'm not terribly worried,' Autumn said wryly. 'And I know Caleb promised you extra money, but –'

'Oh my god, don't,' Val said. 'I wouldn't accept it, so don't bother.'

'I understand,' she replied. Autumn's brow furrowed suddenly. 'Wait, did you – Caleb said he agreed to hire you because you had a boyfriend, but you'd only been living with Nick for a little while at that point, right? And those rumors –' Her eyes got big, and she inhaled sharply. 'Oh my god, did you guys *fake date* and then actually fall for each other?'

The truth was the least she could do for Autumn, so Val sent a look around the café to make sure no one was listening, and then she gave the tiniest of nods.

'Oh my *god*,' Autumn squealed. 'That is basically fanfic. I love it. I promise I won't tell anyone but, oh my god, I can't. This is amazing.'

'I trust you,' Val said with a grin, and Autumn grinned back. The last weight that had been on her shoulders lifted, and at that moment the door opened again. Nick walked through and immediately caught her eye, smiling at her so broadly Val ached.

She bit her lower lip and smiled back because she was finally, *finally*, home.

Epilogue

'Mind if I steal him from you, Mary?' Val said, leaning her forearms on the circulation desk. Nick looked up from his computer, his eyes tired from the strain of compiling a research guide. The AP US History class at Swede River High had a major paper due soon on the Civil Rights Movement, and with budget cuts eliminating the school librarian several years ago, Nick was left to try and pick up the slack for any kids struggling to figure out research. He wasn't an academic librarian or a teacher by a long shot, but he could help them with the basics, at least.

Val smiled at him, and his heart did a somersault. Even after a year and change, he sometimes still woke up with her curled up next to him and couldn't believe his luck. She was working for Autumn still, and had added in working with Autumn's friend Reese, shooting their latest collection for their portfolio. Nick could never stomach a job where the next paycheck was never guaranteed, but Val was thriving. It was impressive, and he wondered if he would ever get over being blown away by her.

Mary took her glasses off and let them dangle on the chain

around her neck. 'He's been done with his shift for ten minutes, but you know how he gets,' she replied.

'I do,' Val said, grinning. 'Hey, nerd, you done yet?'

Nick snorted. 'Give me a few minutes to wrap this up.'

Val nodded and while he saved his document and started packing up, he could hear her chatting quietly with Mary about a TV show they both loved that involved people marrying total strangers their best friends picked out for them. It was a complete train wreck, but Val was rapt whenever it was on.

Nick was about to grab his sweater to leave when Henry approached with a large stack of books and his little brother, Teddy, in tow. Rather than interrupt Mary and Val, who were both cackling over something involving someone named Addysyn on the most recent episode, he pulled the stack closer to himself and grinned down at the boys. 'Did you have a good summer?'

'The best,' Henry chirped. 'Sucks that school is starting.'

Nick ran the barcodes under the scanner while Henry helped Teddy lift his stack of picture books up onto the counter. 'Watch anything good this summer?' he asked.

Just Us Boys had been the streaming hit of the summer, and the town of Swede River was working overtime to keep from asking him about it. About half the people he ran into seemed to be on the verge of exploding, and the other half were suddenly pretending they didn't own TVs.

Henry's eyes bugged out and he looked around for his mom, but Sarah was still over in the Mystery section. Nick leaned down, sliding the books back to the boys. 'It's okay, you can say it,' he whispered.

Henry's face lit up. 'But what about *Jakey*?' he practically yelled. Mary and Val looked over and snorted with laughter as Nick gave Henry and Teddy fist bumps and waved to Sarah.

He reached back for his sweater and Val shook her head before he could even ask the question. 'Way too warm for a sweater, you'll roast. It's perfect out,' she said, and Nick left it on the chair, said goodbye to Mary, and followed Val out the door.

Val tangled their fingers together before they were even on the second step. 'How was work?' she asked, bumping her shoulder against his.

'Long, but good,' he said. 'You?'

'Did a joint shoot with Autumn and Reese this afternoon,' she said, lifting her face to the sun and closing her eyes briefly. 'It was good, but apparently, Autumn ran into Caleb the other day.'

'How's that asshole doing?' They stopped at the crosswalk across from Pete's and waited for a pickup truck to pass.

'Not great, sounds like. Some of Autumn's fans were really, really pissed at him and, well, you know how stans are. The heat got too much for the real estate firm, so his mom had to let him go. He's working on his own now, and it's not going super well. Sounds like he's pretty bitter, but, well, eh. It's his fault, anyway.'

'He got fired by his mom? Even Candy wouldn't have done that.'

'Yeah, I was surprised too, but also? Kind of glad.'

'Just kind of?'

Val grinned up at him mischievously. 'Okay, fine, I'm ecstatic that he got completely screwed. It's what he deserves, and Autumn felt the same way. It was a good bonding moment for all of us.'

Nick held the door to Pete's Coffee open for her and then had to immediately catch Felix before he could dart outside. He was surprisingly quick, for a toddler, but Nick got him at the last second and deposited him back inside.

Aaron was working at a table near the window and sighed. 'Sorry about that. Buddy, you know you have to stay inside while Dad's working,' he admonished gently. 'Thanks. And hey, you two. How are things?'

'Couldn't be better, honestly,' Val replied. 'How's it going here?'

'Really missing Livvy,' Pete said from behind the counter. 'I'm going to have to train someone new, and I'm devastated.'

'Cheer up, Thanksgiving can't be that far away,' Val said.

'She said she won't be back until Winter Break, but then she'll be back for a whole month, at least. But still. That's so far away,' Pete whined, handing over Nick's tea and Val's glorified milkshake with a splash of coffee.

She held her drink out to Nick and he took a sip because those sugar bombs really were delicious, even if he didn't want to have them all the time. 'Are you guys coming to Game Night this week?' Aaron asked, hoisting Felix into his lap.

Val took her credit card back from Pete. 'We are, but Autumn wants to come too, if that's okay.'

Autumn had made the drives out to Swede River a handful of times and she and Aaron were becoming fast friends. She was also a huge Scrabble nerd, so she and Aaron were a match made in heaven.

'Obviously,' Aaron said. 'Can't wait.' They waved goodbye and walked back outside, Nick's hand finding Val's immediately.

They were still a block from home when they saw Margie out for her afternoon walk. She was moving a little better now that her knee replacement was healed, but still needed her cane from time to time. 'Afternoon, Marge,' Val said. 'How's things?'

She was one of the only people in Swede River allowed to call Margie 'Marge', and Nick couldn't even be annoyed that he wasn't. It was so nice to see Val like this, at ease with his people.

In fact, some of them probably liked her more than they liked him, and he couldn't be happier about it. Nick preferred to be in the background, not because he didn't think he deserved the spotlight, but because he just plain old didn't want it.

Margie shook her head sourly. 'Glenda said my decorations for Swedehearts are *tacky*, of all the ungrateful things.'

'Ungrateful?' Val asked.

'Her husband was going to leave her in, oh, what was it, 1992? And I was the one who stepped in and reminded him that she was the best he was going to do, so he stayed for another year. Like I said, ungrateful.'

Val widened her eyes at Nick in confusion. 'Just a year?'

Margie huffed grumpily, and Val fought a losing battle with a smile. 'Another year meant they had been married for twenty years, at which point the prenup said he had to pay her alimony, no matter what.' She fixed Nick with a dirty look, pointing at him emphatically. 'Men think they're slick, but you all are far too easy to trick.'

'No arguments here,' Nick said mildly, drinking from his tea and trying not to laugh. Margie knew exactly what she was doing; she liked having an audience to play to, and Nick found he rather enjoyed being her audience.

'I made Richard think it was *his* idea to stick around,' she continued. 'And then Glenda got to leave him *and* take his money.'

Val looked impressed. 'Shit, Marge. You're a genius.'

'Damn right I am,' Margie replied. 'And after all that, she says my decorations are tacky?' Margie clicked her tongue. 'Good thing no one listens to the *treasurer* of the Senior Center Planning Committee when it comes to design.'

'Good thing,' Val echoed. 'I'll come by Wednesday with your proofs, yeah?'

Val had taken a series of portraits of Margie a few weeks ago. She was in the early stages of planning a new exhibition, featuring pictures of people and places that made Swede River so unique. Margie's support would be key, and she had requested Val do her picture first, so she could decide.

Nick knew Margie would help Val get it off the ground, but he also knew she liked to be fawned over a little first.

Margie shook her head. 'Make it Thursday. I've got my poker game Wednesday.'

'Thursday it is,' Val said, and gave Margie an impulsive hug before they walked on. Nick saw the smile in Margie's eyes as they embraced, and he squeezed Val's hand as they turned up the walk to their house.

'It's still not fair how quickly Margie decided she liked you,' he complained. 'It took me for ever.'

'That's because she hates men,' Val explained. 'With good reason, honestly.'

Nick unlocked the front door and let her in first. Val toed her boots off and left them in the boot tray, which was maybe the clearest sign he'd ever had that she loved him.

Aside from all the other ones, of course. 'What's for dinner?' she asked.

It was lasagna, but he didn't care much about that right now. Nick dropped his bag in the general vicinity of the entryway and pulled Val into his arms, dipping his head down for a long, slow kiss.

'What was that for?' Val murmured as they broke apart, her arms still wrapped around his back.

'I love you,' he said softly and earnestly.

'I know,' she said with a crooked grin. 'And I love you, too. But is there a particular reason for this?'

There wasn't, not really. A glimmer of an idea was forming

in his head, one that involved a nice dinner and a ring, but now wasn't the time. Nick shook his head. 'Can't a man just want to tell his girlfriend he loves her?' he scolded, tucking her hair back behind her ear.

Val rose on her toes and kissed him back, and soon enough Nick forgot all about rings and questions and answers, because for the moment, he had everything he needed.

Acknowledgements

The first person I need to thank is Jess Dallow, for being willing to take a chance on a newbie writer who had no idea what she was doing. If it weren't for you seeing my potential, none of my books (including this one) would exist. You also helped create the relationship I have with Headline Eternal, and for that I am forever grateful.

As for the Headline Eternal team (Kate, Soraya, Sophie, Madeleine, and Jill), I sincerely appreciate all the hard work and thought you put into making this book the best it can be. Without you all, this book wouldn't have been nearly as good. And a special thanks to Kate and Sophie for the drinks we had that afternoon—I am very lucky to have found editors as wonderful as you.

Thank you to the readers, who have read my books and let me keep on writing them. You've made this book possible.

To my writer friends (Jeeno, Shep, Thea) and pocket friends (Erin, Brit, Chash): thanks for your ideas when I needed someone to offer a different solution, and for making me laugh when I needed it. Toni, thank you for always telling me I'm funny when I needed to hear it, and Linds, thank you for being such a steadfast and wonderful friend. To Hännah and Britt: I love you guys.

Kiana, thank you for being such a wonderful nanny for my kids. If it weren't for you, I wouldn't have been able to write this, and will be forever grateful for your hard work. The same goes for all my extended family members who pitched in when I needed a spare moment or to make a deadline.

Mom and Dad, thank you for always believing in me. Tdee Muay and Tdee Bee, thank you for being your silly, wonderful selves. Your creativity will never cease to amaze me.

And to my husband: thank you, and I love you.

Victoria and Owen *are bitter rivals.*
Nora and Luke *are friends online.*
*Who would believe these two couples have **anything** in common?*

**All's fair in love and law in this
irresistible enemies-to-lovers rom-com!**

Available now!

Logan Walsh doesn't do relationships.
Clare Thompson doesn't do casual.
What could possibly bring them ***together?***

**Two can play at this game in this smart,
sexy fake-dating rom-com!**

Available now!

HEADLINE ETERNAL

FIND YOUR HEART'S DESIRE...

VISIT OUR WEBSITE: www.headlineeternal.com
FIND US ON FACEBOOK: facebook.com/eternalromance
CONNECT WITH US ON X: @eternal_books
FOLLOW US ON INSTAGRAM: @headlineeternal
EMAIL US: eternalromance@headline.co.uk